D1080036

NIGEL WATTS

Nigel Watts spent two years in Japan where he wrote
a large part of THE LIFE GAME. He has travelled
widely throughout Asia and has spent time in the west
of Ireland. He is a trained teacher and a professionally
qualified shiatsu therapist. THE LIFE GAME is his
first novel, and won the 1989 Betty Trask Award. His
second novel, BILLY BAYSWATER, is also published
by Sceptre and his latest novel, WE ALL LIVE IN A
HOUSE CALLED INNOCENCE, is available in hard-
back from Hodder and Stoughton.

Nigel Watts

THE LIFE GAME

sceptre

With gratitude to my teachers

Brad Brown and Roy Whitten
Werner Erhard
Chogyam Trungpa
Alan Watts

'It is the business of philosophy . . . to make it possible for us to get a clear view of the state . . . that troubles us: the state of affairs *before* the contradiction is resolved. (And this does not mean that one is side-stepping the difficulty.)

'The fundamental fact here is that we lay down rules, a technique for a game, and that when we follow the rules, things do not turn out as we had assumed. That, we are therefore as it were entangled in our own rules.

'This entanglement in our rules is what we want to understand (i.e. get a clear view of).'

Ludwig Wittgenstein, *Philosophical Investigations*

'A guru is one who creates a package of nonsense, a package of illusions which successfully smashes the life-inhibiting illusions held by the seeker.'

Luke Rheinhart

ONE

Imagine this scene: a gunmetal sky lashed with rain. West of Ireland, mid-December. A young woman, hair plastered with the rain, runs stumbling towards a white-walled cottage. She stops to retrieve her shoe, sucked off by the boggy ground. She reaches the house and raps on the door. This is the heroine of our story. Her name is Kate.

'Come quickly. There's been an accident.'

The old man looked the woman up and down. For a moment she thought he was going to shut the door.

'What's happened?'

He made no sign of inviting her in and she edged under the eaves of the house to shelter from the stinging rain. Her astrakhan coat was sodden.

'I've run over a sheep and I think I've killed it.'

He stared at her for a moment and then turned back into the house to fetch his coat. He put a long carving knife in his pocket, and nodded for them to go.

They ran the fifty yards to the road and climbed over the low wall. The woman could taste salt water on the rain, but the bay was obscured by the thick mist. They hurried up the narrow lane, the rain running in rivulets down the cracked tarmac of the road.

They found her yellow sports car at a diagonal across the road. Its offside wing had demolished part of the granite wall, a tear in the roadside turf where she'd skidded. On the opposite verge was the sheep she'd hit: a rain-soaked bulk of matted hair. He ignored the car and crouched to look at the ewe. It was shivering, and when the old man touched it, it struggled to get to its feet. Its thin back legs were broken and bloody, a sliver of white bone sticking through the wound.

She was watching from a distance, hugging her coat to stay dry.

'Come over here,' he shouted.

She hesitated and then ran over to him.

'Hold it down.'

He saw her flinch, and pulled her down.

'Do it!'

She grasped the greasy wool round its neck, but the animal writhed out of her grip. Its bleat had turned into a frenzied bawl, its eyes glassy with terror. She had to kneel on its flank to keep it still.

'Now hold it!'

Water streamed down her face, into her eyes, and she grasped its shaggy coat. The animal bucked against her, using the last of its strength in a final effort. The old man took the knife out of his pocket and with a swift sideways motion slit the animal's throat.

The sheep coughed grotesquely, a gush of blood spurting from its neck. The woman felt it splash warm against her skin.

The animal shuddered, pumping its blood on to the shiny road. It gurgled, biting on the tongue which shot from its mouth; its eyes staring crazily in surprise. The woman ran to the wall and retched against it. Nothing came up, just the taste of bile, and she spat it out. Blood was on her hands and she crouched by the wayside and thrust them into a clump of wet grass.

Was he calling her? The rain was so heavy that it drowned all other sound. She could see the yellow of her car, and ran towards it and jumped in. She started the engine and threw it into reverse. The car screamed and juddered. The wheel arch had crumpled on the tyre. She pressed her foot down harder and the car, its front wheels locked, skewed across the wet surface of the road, slamming sideways against the wall.

She couldn't think. The rain thundered on the canvas sunroof, blocking out all thought. She leant forward and rested her forehead on the steering wheel. The door was opened and the old man reached in and switched off the ignition. She let him help her out of the car. She looked for the sheep, but he'd pulled it over the wall. The grass was black where it had lain, a slick of blood sliding across the road.

He led her through the kitchen to the front room. Taking her coat, he hung it from the high mantelpiece above the open fire. The neck and shoulders of her sweater were damp and her long hair hung in heavy wet lanks. She sat by the fire while he fetched a towel, easing her wet shoes off.

He was back in a minute and draped a shawl round her shoulders.

'Let's get yourself warm,' he said, handing her a bathtowel. 'We don't want you chilled.'

He banked up the fire with peat bricks and then sat in the chair opposite her, watching her as she rubbed her hair dry. She was about thirty-five. Her hair, still wet, would probably dry light: a tawny blonde. Hers was a finely shaped face: narrow, but with strong cheekbones. A man's nose, but a woman's full lips. Her skin was pale, blotchy with the cold.

'I'll get you some tea.'

He got up and left the room, closing the latched door carefully. Wrapping the towel round her head, she leant back into the armchair, exhausted. It was a disaster: two days in Ireland and she'd ended up in this mess.

She looked round the room. Low-ceilinged and almost dusk with the storm clouds outside, it had the peculiar odour of old houses: dust and damp, the smell of overripe apples and turf smoke.

'The rain's letting up a bit,' he said when he came back with the tea. 'I might just pop over and see James. His sheep, you see.'

He put a mug of tea and an unbuttered slice of bread on the table by her chair.

'My name's Michael, if you were wondering.' He smiled, showing his long teeth, yellowed with age and tobacco smoke.

She nodded. He was older than she'd first thought. Perhaps sixty, maybe more. He reminded her vaguely of someone she'd known: that square bull's head, the white stubble on his chin. In the middle of his face sat a large nose, like a potato. A vertical frown-line was etched deeply between his eyebrows. He was still smiling, but it was a stern face. She remembered the way he'd looked at her, frowning against the rain.

He slurped his tea, squinting against the steam. They were farmer's hands that gripped his mug: the nails split like wood shavings. She drummed her own nails, each as hard and glossy as a flea, against the wooden arm of the chair. Silence.

'Right. I'll be off, then,' he said at last. 'You rest a bit.'

The car. She suddenly remembered.

'I've got to get someone to see to the car. I don't suppose you've got a phone?' she said hopefully.

'James has. I'll give the garage a ring.'

She woke in the dark and it was a moment before she remembered where she was. A clatter came from the kitchen. He was back. The fire had nearly burned down – she'd been asleep a while.

She pulled herself from the chair and groped towards the door, barking her shin on a footstool.

He was busy at the table and looked up when she opened the door.

'Do you feel better now?'

She blinked in the light. 'You should've woken me,' she mumbled. She always slept heavily and woke badly, especially in the afternoon.

She stepped into the kitchen and squinted at her watch. Six thirty.

'What did the garage say?'

He didn't answer at first, concentrating instead on the rabbit he was skinning. A gift from the O'Neills. It had been trapped that afternoon and its fur was still wet from the rain.

'They said they'll pick you up tomorrow at nine.'

He had his long fingers under its skin and was peeling the fur from its body as if it was a glove he was taking off a shiny pink hand. She stared at the rabbit for a moment before she realised what it was, and then turned her eyes away.

'They can't come earlier? What am I supposed to do till tomorrow?'

She was awake now, her fingernails drumming the table.

She was stuck: the car immobilised, no help coming till the next day. The nearest town was eight miles – no bus, no way to get there.

She glanced around the kitchen; it was lit by gaslight, the corners of the room dimming into shadow. Something brushed her leg and she looked down. A tortoiseshell cat had smelled the meat and was rubbing itself against the table legs. She bent down and stroked it.

He ran his hands under the tap. 'I've lit the fire in the spare room. You're welcome to stay.'

She considered his offer, looking around the room. The walls were whitewashed stone, not even plastered; the floor, sweating black flagstone. A black-leaded Stanley range stood against one wall and in the corner was a pantry, and what looked like a meat safe. There was no choice, other than walking into town. She'd have to stay.

'Would it be an awful lot of trouble if I stayed?'

He dried his hands on a towel and turned. 'No trouble.'

Something in his offhand manner decided her. 'Thank you. I'll just get my bag from the car, then.'

She went back into the front room for her coat, and when she returned he handed her a paraffin lamp. 'You'd better take this. You don't want to go wandering off the path into the bog. And chuck Ludo out, will you.' He nodded at the cat. 'She's getting under my feet.'

The moon had risen low over the bay, a faint halo around its almost full disc. The air was crisp, the sky blown clear of cloud by the strong westerly wind.

She picked her way carefully along the path, the lamp casting a swaying circle of light around her. Somewhere in the darkness a sheep coughed. She climbed over the wall into the road and paused to look back at the house. Its whitewashed walls reflected the moonlight like milk; the lighted downstairs windows, two eyes.

When she got back with her suitcase, the old man showed her up to her room. It was small, dominated by a high old-fashioned bed, but a fire burned in the grate and it was warm. For some reason she looked under the bed and wasn't surprised to see rows of apples laid out on newspaper.

She unpacked a few things and changed into a long woollen dress, buttoned at the neck and sleeves. She brushed her hair and went downstairs.

He was waiting for her, sitting at the kitchen table.

'Now, that's a fine-looking frock. Sit yourself down and make an old man happy.'

She smiled at the compliment. This 'frock', as he called it, had cost her nearly two hundred pounds. She looked at him from the doorway. Seated under the yellow lamplight with his sleeves rolled up, he looked to Kate like a gambler at a card table with his pile of winnings. An opened bottle of wine and two crystal glasses were on the table.

'I thought I'd crack this open,' he said, filling the glasses. 'It's a while since I've had the pleasure of any company.'

He handed her a glass. 'Slante – your health.' He touched his glass against hers.

She drank and sat down. 'But I haven't even introduced myself yet,' she said suddenly. 'I'm called Kate – Katarina, if you want to be formal. My friends call me Kate.'

He rose and gave a mock heroic bow. 'Delighted and honoured, Kate Katarina. Michael O'Brien at your service.'

He was a good cook; the rabbit was perfect. Kate surprised herself at how hungry she was.

'So tell me something about yourself,' he said with his mouth full. 'You're not from these shores, I can tell that.'

'No, I'm from England – London. I came here on holiday.'

'Now let me see,' he said, moving to see her profile. 'Is there any Irish blood in you? I think not.'

'No – my father was Irish.'

'Was he now?'

'From Galway.'

'A local man, then.' He smiled. There was something unnerving about his look. His eyes seemed to be unmatched, so that she wasn't sure if he was looking straight in her eyes or at her hair.

After dinner she went into the front room while he cleared the table. She browsed through the bookcase: Kierkegaard, Abraham Maslow, Edwin Arnold's *The Light of Asia*; dusty but well-thumbed volumes squeezed together on the rickety bookshelf. She eased one out and stood with her back to the fire, flicking through the pages. It was quiet and cosy with the peat fire burning, the soft gaslight. She was glad she had stayed.

He came in a few minutes later. 'What's that you're looking at?'

She glanced at the spine. '*Philosophical Investigations.*'

She'd picked it at random, and hadn't been paying much attention to it. She realised she was a little drunk from his home-made wine.

'On a clear day you can see from here to the cottage in Killary where Wittgenstein wrote that . . . well,' he lowered himself into the rocking-chair, 'you could if the mountains weren't in the way.'

She put the book back and held her hands in front of the fire. Above the fireplace was an oil painting that had caught her eye earlier that afternoon. She looked closely at it.

'This is good,' she said, surprised. It was a portrait of a young woman, twenties or thirties, judging by the style. Its execution was impressively confident and exact: thick stripes of paint delineating the face in an almost impressionistic manner.

'My wife,' the old man said from his chair. 'She's dead now.'

Kate studied the face. Eyes downcast, perhaps shut, it was impossible to tell. The woman had an almost cherubic mouth, small and delicate. The artist had succeeded in capturing a remarkable face: a disconcerting mix of innocence and pain. Kate was reminded of a pietà.

'It's lovely, but you shouldn't hang it here,' she said, indicating the fire.

'Oh?'

'I'm a picture restorer. I've seen too many paintings damaged by heat and smoke.'

'A picture restorer? Perhaps you'd like to see some of the things I have.'

'You collect paintings?'

'Not exactly. I used to paint a bit myself.'

He went upstairs and returned a few minutes later with a portfolio of drawings and several dusty canvases. She leafed through the drawings in silence. The paper had yellowed and she asked him when he'd done them.

'Fifty odd years ago now,' he said, taking one from her and looking at it.

'Where?'

'Paris.'

She raised her eyebrows. She was impressed: the drawings were rubbish – pseudo-surrealistic doodlings. But Paris then; the mid-thirties.

'It must have been exciting.'

'It was, and some famous names were there.'

'Who did you meet?'

'Tanguy. Brancusi. That Andrew Breton. A lot more nobody would remember.'

She looked through the canvases. They had even less to recommend them than the drawings. He'd obviously been influenced by Duchamp, and several of them contained clearly recognisable references to paintings of his. One canvas, quite unlike the rest, was signed V.B. She looked at him enquiringly.

'Victor Brauner,' he said. 'Do you know him?'

'Yes.' Although not a major artist, his works were fetching increasingly handsome prices in London. Doubtless the old man knew nothing of its worth.

'How did you come by this?'

'He gave me that for a bet he lost on the horses. Though at the time I can tell you I'd rather have had the cash.' He shook his head at the memory. 'Sure the man was crackers. He used to drink whiskey from a baby's bottle. And fight: oddly enough we both lost an eye in the same year – '38 – he the left, me the right.'

Of course, she thought. That explained the lopsidedness in his glance. 'How did you lose your eye?' she asked.

'Remember the Buñel film? What was it called?'

'*Un Chien Andalou*?'

'That's the one.'

She looked at him, puzzled, and then laughed. She knew that the eye in the famous eyeball-slitting sequence was that of a bull.

'That's not true,' he said, pleased that she'd understood his joke. 'I lost it in an accident in Spain.'

She looked at the last canvas: a scrupulously precise painting of an eyeless man facing an open window through which could be seen a flower garden.

'What do you think?' he asked.

'A young Magritte fan, I'd say.'

'No – the title. What do you think of the title?'

She hadn't noticed it and looked at the painting again. Printed across the bottom in red: *Beauty is in the I of the beholder*.

'Hmmm . . . a clever schoolboy's joke.'

'True or false?'

'Beauty is subjective, yes, I think so.'

'So when you say that painting's good,' he said, nodding at the portrait of his wife above the fireplace, 'what do you mean?'

'I mean, I like it.'

'Is that all?'

They both looked at the painting.

'I mean there's a certain rightness of composition and colour.'

'Rightness? Is that subjective or objective?'

She smiled at the sudden inquisition. 'There's generally a consensus of agreement.'

He stretched his legs in front of him and laced his fingers over his stomach. 'So if everyone in the world disagrees with you, does that make you wrong?'

She laughed. 'Unfortunately in the world of art it usually does.'

They lapsed into silence, both staring into the fire. She suddenly had the feeling of being abroad. She hadn't felt it up till now, but looking round the room, at the old mahogany floor polished by generations of feet, the Victorian prints, the heavy antique furniture, everything seemed so foreign. It was only Ireland, hardly five hundred miles from London, but it was all so different. Or was it just him? She looked over at the old man – he appeared to be nodding off. There was something about him, something she couldn't fathom. He seemed safe enough, but his strange intense questioning; the way he looked at her – there was a depth to him, something that frightened her a little.

She was tired, and soon excused herself and went up to her room. He'd just nodded from his chair, and said nothing. The house was quiet, her room strange in the flickering candlelight. She undressed quickly, leaving her underwear on. The sheets looked clean enough and she found that he'd put a stone hot-water bottle in her bed, but the heavy flock mattress still felt damp.

Sleep was a long time coming, the night black and cold.

TWO

She was glad to be getting away in the morning. The cold bedroom had given her a headache, and she'd slept badly. She couldn't wash: the only water was in the kitchen, and she wasn't going to use the washstand in her room.

She jammed her feet into her shoes. She was looking forward to getting to Dublin, finding a hotel and having a hot bath. She was a townie: it was stupid to come this far into the countryside.

She offered him some money for the sheep, but it was covered by insurance, so she thanked him and left. How much was a sheep worth anyway? She turned at the road and waved back to him, a small figure framed by the blue doorway.

The damage to the car wasn't as bad as she'd feared. One wing was crumpled, and the paintwork was scratched down the side, but the door and front bumper were untouched. Somebody had reassembled the drystone wall she'd knocked down, and the sheep had gone. The only evidence of the accident was the incongruous sports car with its sad dent.

She could see the bay now: flat and grey, dotted with little clumps of islands like floating vegetation. The road – a lane really – was pitted with scabs of tarmac, a brow of grass growing along its middle. It wasn't surprising she'd crashed – she'd been driving much too fast.

The early-morning frost had gilded the tough grass a silver-green, and her breath steamed like a horse's. Weird countryside, she reflected. Barren and deserted, moss-covered granite outcrops sticking up from the frozen soil like abstract sculpture. His was the only house in sight – the only inhabited one. She could see the shell of the farmhouse tucked into the bottom of the valley. Only a few of us left, he'd said, small farmers scraping a living out of the reluctant land.

She wondered why anybody would choose to live here in the first place. Exposed to the Atlantic on one side, hedged in by mountains on the other, there was hardly enough flat land to build a house. Below her, to her right, the land dropped away into a valley of scrub through which a swollen river coursed down to the sea.

The breakdown truck ambled into sight nearly an hour later. West of Ireland time, she muttered to herself when the two men tut-tutted over the damaged wing. And they hadn't even apologised for keeping her waiting.

She stayed in the car while they made their inspection, and then the older one of the two tapped on the window. She rolled it down.

'We'll just get it hooked up and tow it into town. There's nothing we can do here.'

He opened the door for her, and she swung both her legs out like a film star, aware of their eyes on her.

'Come on, Dave,' the older one said, nudging his partner into life. 'Give us a hand with this chain.'

They drove back to Westport, the woman wedged between the two men in the front seat of the cab.

'So you stayed with Michael O'Brien, did you?' the older man shouted above the racket of the engine. 'What did you make of him?'

She couldn't be bothered to answer – the noise and shaking was bringing her headache back, and she just shrugged in reply.

The driver glanced at her. 'Huh! I know what you mean. Known Michael all me life, I have, and still I can't make him out. His missus – she was an odd one – died not so long ago, so he's on his tod now. Comes into town once a month or so, sometimes sees the O'Neills. That's their place over there.' He pointed to a cottage in the distance.

He lit a cigarette, guiding the steering wheel with his elbows. 'Yerman has upset a few people in his time, so he has.' He snorted with laughter. 'But you managed to get away in one piece, I'm glad to say.'

The wing was too badly damaged to hammer out – it would have to be replaced. She asked if they could do it, and the mechanic hummed and hawed and then went to the office to see if a new wing could be sent. Kate spotted a smeared washbasin in the corner of the garage. She ran her fingers under the hot water, and flicked them dry.

'You're in luck. They can get one here in a couple of days.'

'Good,' she said, without looking at the mechanic. 'I'm going to Dublin. I'll phone in a day or two.'

She tossed him the car keys and he caught them.

'How do I get to the station?' she asked, tugging her case from the back seat. He didn't say anything, and she turned to look at him.

'Walk.'

She sighed. God save us from bolshie mechanics. 'Yes. Where?'

He gave her brief instructions and she picked up her case. She paused in the entrance of the garage. The mechanic watched her standing silhouetted against the light. Tall and slim; gold hair catching the winter sun. How could such a good-looking class of woman be such a stuck-up cow? He wiped his hands on his overalls and turned away.

She called to him, 'Are there any buses to . . . wherever it was we came from?'

'You're wanting to go back?'

'I've forgotten something. Shit! Only my antique rings. A thousand pounds' worth of gold and stone and I leave them on the dressing-table!'

'No buses Louisburgh way,' he told her. 'Not enough people to warrant one. How about hitch-hiking?'

'Where can I get a taxi?'

'By the post office.'

She left her suitcase in the office, saying she'd collect it later. Halfway down the main street someone called out to her. She looked up in surprise and saw three men sitting on a bench at the edge of the green. She clicked her tongue in annoyance and continued walking.

'Kate Katarina!'

It was the old man. She turned and squinted at them. Sure enough, there he was, sitting with two other men. She crossed over to them. 'So we meet again.'

'Indeed we do, and a lovely surprise it is too,' he said, looking lopsidedly at her from under his French beret.

'I was just on my way back to you. Did you bring my jewellery?'

'Jewellery?'

'Yes, I left my rings in the bedroom. Didn't you find them?'

He considered it for a moment. 'I can't say I did. Now, is that a problem? You can come back and fetch them, if you like, or I can send them to you.'

'I'd rather come and collect them.'

He nodded. 'But I'm forgetting myself,' he said suddenly. 'Let me introduce my two friends here – Patrick senior and his son Patrick junior.'

She glanced at the men and nodded almost imperceptibly. She was about to ask when they could go back to the cottage when the two men stood up and extended a hand. She absently shook the older man's hand.

'Patrick senior here is a hundred and twenty years old,' Michael said. 'This is his son. How old are you, Patrick junior?'

Kate shook hands with the younger man. He grinned and bobbed his head. His hair had been cropped short at the back and sides, but the top was disproportionately long, so that his hair flopped in front of his eyes. He continued to shake her hand enthusiastically.

'How old are you, Patrick?' Michael repeated.

The man opened his mouth to speak, but to Kate's horror, instead of words came inarticulate sounds.

'Fir . . . fir . . . fir—'

His head was ducking up and down, a thread of dribble descending from his lips on to his shirt front as he struggled to complete the word.

'Fir . . . fir . . . fir . . . tee . . . five.'

She tried to pull her hand away, but his grip tightened and he continued to shake it, grinning into her face.

'All right now, let the lady have her hand back, Paddy,'
his father said.

He abruptly released her hand and sat down on the bench.

'Patrick junior is a fine man,' Michael said. 'He can't speak
so well, and he's not so clever, but he's a gentle, honest man
and a good son to his father.'

She knew she was being watched, but she couldn't stop herself from wiping her hand on her coat. She flicked a look at the
idiot and tried a conciliatory smile. The man beamed back.

'So anyhow, what about the car? Can the garage do the
job?'

The old man filled his pipe as she explained the situation.

'Now, I tell you what,' he said when she had finished. 'Seeing
as how you'll be going back to fetch your things, why don't you
stay the day or two? You're more than welcome.'

'Well, I don't know,' she hesitated. 'I said I'd be in Dublin
tomorrow. I've got a bit of business to see to.'

He shrugged. 'Just a thought.' He sucked on his pipe. 'Oh
– and I found some more drawings. I'll show you them if
you're interested.'

'That'd be nice,' she lied.

'You probably know Giacometti.'

Her eyebrows went up. 'Alberto or Giovanni?' Either would
be valuable, but if he had some of the son's work, then he
could be sitting on a gold-mine.

'The son – that's Alberto, isn't it?'

She tried to hide the excitement in her voice. 'How many
have you got?'

'Two finished drawings and a page of sketches.'

She took a deep breath before she answered. Even if they
were no good, they'd be worth thousands. 'Yes, I'd like to see
them.' She paused. 'And perhaps you were right – maybe it's
best if I stay in Westport rather than go all the way to Dublin
just for a few days. Could I take you up on your offer?'

'You're welcome, but I thought you said you needed to
be in Dublin.'

He'd caught her off guard and for a second she was at a loss
for what to say. 'It's not so important. I can make a phone call

and put it off till the car's fixed. But you must let me pay.'

He shook his head. 'The money's all right.'

'No, no – I insist.'

'Well, you could do a spot of work for me, then. There's a painting that needs a patch – that'd be payment enough.'

There was a phone box by the bench, and she went in to make the call. Inside, she rummaged in her purse for a coin. My God – three sheets of Giacomettis! She lifted the receiver and began to dial. Turning her head, she looked at the men and then stopped dialling. She held the receiver to her mouth for a minute and pretended to talk, and then replaced it and returned the coin to her purse.

A friend of his was going to give them a lift back to the cottage, but first the old man needed to do some shopping. He asked her what he should get so that she could repair the painting and she wrote a few things down. They arranged to meet in front of the monument at three o'clock and then said goodbye.

Kate spent the rest of the morning in the bookshop, dipping into books at random, and then found a pub to have lunch in. She buried herself in the corner with a new book and a glass of wine, enjoying the quiet comfort of the pub. When the two Patricks came in half an hour later she pretended not to notice. The spastic son saw her, though, and called across the room.

'He . . . he . . . he . . . llo . . . hello . . . Kay . . . Kay . . . Kate.'

She reluctantly looked up from her book and pantomimed surprise and joy at seeing the two men, and sighed with relief when they sat down at the bar.

She'd had enough by two thirty, and was just thinking about fetching her luggage and waiting for the old man, when he came in. He looked around and saw her in the corner.

'Ah, Kate, there you are. I was told I'd find you in here.' He dumped a box of groceries on a stool and tossed his cap on top of it.

The barman appeared and squinted into the corner. 'Is that yourself, Michael? How are you keeping? What'll you have to drink?'

The old man left Kate at the table while he chatted with the barman. She tried to read, but her attention had gone. She flicked through another book, and then snapped it shut and looked at the two men.

The old man had his back to her, leaning on the bar talking to the barman. She studied the back of his head, the deep lines at the base of his neck, the patched elbows of his jacket. A white strip of long underwear showed between his shirt and his trousers.

Kate lit a cigarette and finished her wine. What the hell am I doing here? she thought. I should never have left London.

She went over to them. 'I'll get my suitcase from the garage. I'll see you at the monument in – ' She looked at her watch. It had stopped. She glanced at the clock above the bar, ' – twenty minutes.'

THREE

They were dropped on the road in front of the house. Kate looked at the building in the approaching dusk as if for the first time. Not the simple thatched cottages of postcards, but nevertheless quite picturesque in its own way: whitewashed stone walls, a slate roof, the front door painted a childish blue. It was more substantial than she'd first thought. At this distance she could just make out the shape of two outhouses with corrugated iron roofs – a shoulder-high heap of peat bricks against one of them. At the back of the house was a stretch of cultivated land, now mostly fallow. Beside the outside toilet was a hawthorn tree, twisted like a witch.

There was no gate and they had to climb the low wall to get on to his land.

'To keep the sheep out,' he said in answer to her question.

She tapped him on the sleeve and pointed. As if to purposely contradict his words, there – knee-deep in the boggy ground – was a sheep. It turned its black face and stared at the man and the woman, its jaw going methodically. Suddenly it darted into life and scrambled over the wall.

The old man laughed and walked to the house along the path which skirted the marsh. Inside, she helped him unload the 'messages', as he called them: flour, tinned meat and fish, Brussel sprouts, pipe tobacco and coffee.

He showed her round in the remaining light. To her surprise, one of the outhouses turned out to be a potter's studio and kiln. On racks against one wall stood a collection of rust-red unfired pots and bowls, and on a table some glazed and patterned finished things. She picked up a long-necked jug and turned it over in her hands.

'A potter! I didn't know!' She turned to him, but he'd left.

She stepped out into the cold and looked around for the old man, just catching sight of him turning the corner of the house. She stared after him, puzzled.

The other outhouse was divided into two parts by a wooden partition, one side containing a row of chicken coops. The birds were roosting and stared unblinkingly back at the woman. She could see the pale glow of an egg and wondered if she should take it in for the old man, but she left it.

The second compartment was a pen of some sort; a gate fastened by a latch to the wall. Peering into the darkness, she thought at first it was unoccupied, but then she saw that it housed a cream-coloured goat sitting on a pile of straw. It stood up when it saw the woman and moved towards her.

She patted its bony head. Like the sheep, she thought. Those eyes, horizontal irises – like a devil's. The old man had a glass eye, which was it? She couldn't remember.

'What's your name, then?' The goat held its head up for her to scratch its neck. She found herself unlatching the gate and sliding into the byre. That smell – dung and compost – it was almost intoxicating. Such a change from London. The goat and the woman observed each other without moving, and then it stepped towards her. She stroked one of its ears and allowed the goat to nuzzle her sleeve. It began to nip at the wool of her jacket.

'Don't do that.'

She yelped and raised her hand to her mouth – she'd been bitten. The goat was butting her, softly but powerfully pushing her backwards against the wall. Panicked, she pushed its head aside and darted out of the open gate, slamming it behind her.

She ran out of the outhouse and looked at her hand, but it was too dark to see if blood had been drawn. Leaning against the wall she breathed the cold air deeply, her eyes shut. Its strength was amazing, like a coiled steel spring. Locked up there in the dark – all that hidden power.

She shivered and rubbed the bitten hand. The sky was purplish with dusk and she could smell snow in the air. She turned up the collar of her jacket and walked back to the house.

After dinner he showed her the Giacomettis. They were obviously early works, not the popular reduced figures of the forties and fifties. Kate placed them some time before 1937. Pencil portraits, not masterpieces, but recognisably Giacometti, and signed as well. She asked him if he'd thought of selling them – she knew a dealer in London who'd probably be interested. As she'd guessed, he had no idea of their worth and when he asked her opinion, she halved the amount they'd probably fetch.

'That much?' he said, surprised. 'I don't suppose you'd be, you know, interested in . . . '

'Well, I could see if he was interested.'

'You'd get a cut, of course. It's just that they've been lying around for years, doing nothing except gather dust. I might as well get rid of them.'

She slid them carefully into the folder, and put it on her lap. At that price, she could think of buying them herself. She resolved to look through the rest of his collection.

She asked to see the painting he wanted repairing. To her surprise he indicated the portrait of his wife hanging above the fireplace. He lifted it down and showed her a tear in the top left corner. She held it under the light. Strange, she hadn't noticed it the day before when she'd first seen the painting. She looked at the L-shaped tear carefully. Something sharp had gone through the canvas.

December 12th
It was a butcher's knife. I found it in the kitchen drawer. I'd never seen it before – she must have brought it with her. The black wooden handle fitted well into my palm. The blade scared me. Steel, tiny cross-hatched lines where it had been sharpened. It was too sharp – too pointed. It was an instrument to stab and slash flesh. It wasn't as though I was blind with rage. I was cool as ice and God forgive me, I knew exactly what I was doing.

'This'll be easy enough to mend. The paint hasn't lifted.' She handed him back the painting. 'It'll need a bit of retouching, but you won't notice it.'

She passed a trembling hand over her eyes.

'I've a strip of canvas you can use for a patch,' the old man said, hanging the painting back on the wall. He turned to look at her. 'Are you all right?'

She was white, her face suddenly waxy. 'Just tired.'

He guided her to the chair by the fire, making her sit while he fetched a cup of tea. He brought it on a tray and set it on a small table beside her.

'Feeling better?' he asked, checking her eyes.

She nodded. 'It was nothing.'

He poured out the tea and gave her a cup. They sat in silence for a few minutes.

'Something else I found with the drawings was this,' he said abruptly. He picked up what looked like a brass snorkler's mask with a screen attached to the front. 'A Victorian stereoscope. God only knows where it came from.'

It was the first time she'd seen one, though she knew the principle of how it worked: a couple of photographs and mirrors – it gave the impression of three-dimensionality when you looked into it. Her grandfather had had something like it, which she used to play with as a child.

She held it up to the light and peered into it. It showed the cluttered interior of a Victorian parlour; a man sitting at the table with his back to his nagging wife. There was a caption under the photograph, presumably comic, but it had been made illegible by the damp. She could understand the Victorian craze for stereoscopes: the scene looked as tangible as if it was in front of her.

'It's uncanny how real it looks.'

'I wouldn't know,' he said, slurping his tea.

She looked over the top at him. 'Why not?'

He closed one eye and pointed at the other with a finger. Of course, she remembered. He had a glass eye – he'd only see a flat photograph.

He handed her another set of pictures. She slid out the first and replaced them. She recognised it as soon as she saw it; Michelangelo's *Virgin and Christ*.

'I call this one the Immaculate Misconception.'

She laughed and peered into the stereoscope. 'Why Misconception?'

'Well, although it may look like it, Kate, the Holy Mother is not actually in front of you at the moment.'

She put the thing down on the tray. Was he laughing at her? He was certainly enjoying himself; his legs stretched in front of him, cradling his mug of tea in his hands.

'The thing is,' he continued, 'what we know as the world is only a view.'

'What do you mean?'

' "As a Man is, so he sees. As the eye is formed, such are its Powers." '

She looked at him questioningly.

'William Blake. We see the same thing in different ways. You have two good eyes and a brain, so when you look in this yoke,' he nodded at the stereoscope, 'you see a solid world. The question is – is that world real or is it an illusion?'

'It's an optical illusion – the mind is being tricked into seeing something that's not true. It looks like a solid object, but it's just two flat photographs.'

'And if you tell yourself it's two flat photographs, can you see it as such? Or do you always see it as solid?'

She picked up the stereoscope and looked into it again. She shook her head. 'Seeing is not always believing, apparently.'

'So which is the more important? The seeing or the believing?'

She paused to think about it. 'It depends,' she said at last. 'If I want to touch the image, I won't be able to – so belief would be more important. But if I just want to enjoy it, then the seeing – even if it's an illusion – is more important. It's a toy, after all. If you destroy the illusion then you miss the whole point. That's what so much of art is, after all.'

He finished his tea and stared into the bottom of the cup. 'And what's the difference between illusions and delusion?' He looked up and held her gaze.

She was suddenly aware of how quiet it was. No sounds from outside, not even the wind. Just the crackling of the dry peat as it burned.

Illusion and delusion? What the hell was he talking about? *Ludere*, that's right – to play. *Deludere*, to play false.

She shrugged. 'Delusions are dangerous – they get us into trouble.'

He nodded as if satisfied with her answer, but said nothing more. He closed his eyes and rocked back and forth, the chair creaking with the movement. She waited for him to say more, but the pendulum action of the chair decreased until it stopped. He'd fallen asleep.

She got up quietly and went through to the kitchen. So what was all that cross-questioning about? Perhaps he was just lonely, needing another mind to sharpen his wits on.

The cat was yowling outside the back door and she let it in. She poked her head round the door, looking out on to the moonlit moor. Who would want to live here? She bolted the door.

He seemed harmless enough. A little weird, but that was understandable. She'd stay a couple of days, wait for the car to be fixed. He might even have some more paintings.

She lit a candle, and shielding the flame with one hand went up to her room.

FOUR

There's always that peculiar shock when you look out of your window in the morning to see an unexpected snowfall. For a fraction of a second you stare, as dumbfounded as if you'd woken to find yourself in some alien landscape. When Kate tugged open the curtains the next day she took a sharp intake of breath. Yesterday this was as dull and dead as winter: the moor, the tumbledown walls, the hump-backed mountains; now it was a startling white Christmas card. As white as Norway, she thought, leaning on the windowsill, her breath fogging the pane. Flake white, not the yellow slush of London snow, but like Oslo: thick and sudden and clean.

She dressed and went downstairs. He'd gone out – she could see his footsteps in the snow leading from the kitchen door.

It seemed like an age since she'd seen snow. She stood outside the door, her head back, catching the flakes in her open mouth. Years, ten years. She knew it wasn't true – it had snowed in London the year before, but this sharp, clean cold was like something from her childhood. Tobogganing snow. Snowman snow.

She hopped to keep warm in the outside toilet, struggling to get her jeans down. This was the worst bit – this primitive toilet. It was clean enough, white-tiled and fresh-smelling, but as cold as a fridge.

The snow decided her. There was nothing to do other than keep warm and dry. She'd spend the day smoking cigarettes and leafing through books. He'd come back soon probably. He couldn't have gone far in this weather, but it was nice to be alone for a while, unbothered. She brought a couple of books down from her room and settled herself at the table.

It was two or three hours before he came back. She was at the sink and saw him through the window as he climbed the wall into the garden. She smiled at the sight. Muffled with hat and scarves, he waddled towards the house, black against white, like a figure from a Breughel snowscape.

She was glad of his company and they chatted while he made a cup of tea. He'd been out since daybreak helping James, his neighbour, check on the sheep, making sure none had fallen into drifts. Snow this heavy was unusual in these parts – there was a good three inches already fallen, drifts a couple of feet deep in places.

After lunch she started on the painting. She heated up a mixture of beeswax, resin and turps in an old saucepan on the range, while he brought the painting into the kitchen and laid it on the table.

She worked quickly and neatly, brushing the waxy paste on to the back of the canvas while he sat at the table, watching her, his chin cupped in his hands.

'Are you happy with your job?'

'Most of the time.' She coated the patch of canvas he'd given her and laid it in place on the painting. 'Sometimes it can be a bit dull, though.'

'And your life? Are you happy with that?'

She frowned and went over to the range. 'I don't know anyone who is. Totally, I mean.'

She felt the flatiron that had been heating on the range.

'I am.'

She turned to look at him. Yes, she could believe that. There was something unruffled and satisfied about him. She brought the iron back to the table and carefully pressed the patch on the back of the painting.

'Well, you're one of the lucky few then.'

'One of the few perhaps,' he replied, 'but there's no luck in that.'

She turned the canvas over and inspected the mend. An easy job – just a bit of retouching and that'd be it. She showed him.

'Now, that's a fine job you've done.'

'If you can find those oils you mentioned, I'll retouch it tomorrow. It's too dark to do it now.'

She went up to her room to get her diary. She'd kept a diary since the age of sixteen. Paul had thought she was neurotic about it, but it was her touchstone, the most constant companion she'd had throughout her life. He'd never understood why she scribbled in her closely guarded journal every day or so. Her friends were lucky if they got a letter from her once a year.

She flicked the pages of the exercise book. June, she'd started this one. When things had started to go wrong. She frowned at the doodles – it didn't take a psychologist to see they weren't the work of a happy woman. Boxes within boxes, grids, nets – there was no organic shape in her scribbles. They were a tossed bag of cogs and springs and mechanical junk. The margins of June and July were crammed. August, September, October, November – four, nearly five months now.

She opened the diary to a clean page. She stared at it for a moment, and then went to the window. The day's snow had further rubbed out the features of the landscape until now it looked as smooth and blank as a sand dune. Only the low wall marking the line of the lane and the occasional tree, edged with snow, stood out against the white. Even the sky, gently greying with dusk, was unmarked. A blank canopy hanging over this moonscape.

She could feel it; physically feel the touch of her depression. In her mouth and her throat and her stomach. She scowled and went back to her diary, flicking through the pages until she came across a photograph. She tossed the diary on to the bed and held the picture to catch the last of the light.

It was the only photo she had of him – a blurred snapshot taken that day they'd spent in Brighton. His hair was long then, flopping over one eye, black and silky as a Red Indian's. He'd often been mistaken for a foreigner – it was the hair and dark complexion that did it. Kate was his negative: hair just as silky, but white to his black. Her skin pale, his easily tanned.

She slid the picture back into the diary and then hoisted her suitcase on to the bed, undoing the clasp. She pushed the

clothes aside and took out a bundle of identical red exercise
books, tied together with string. She slipped the string off and
scattered the books across the bed – how many years, four?
Four years of her life here. She spread them across the counterpane, looking for last summer's – eighteen months ago. She
found the one she was looking for and turned to May 24th.

*Interesting day. Went to the Munch exhibition at the Royal
Academy. Pretty lousy exhibition, badly arranged, but this guy
kept following me, talking in this ridiculous way about Munch
and the European angst. It was an obvious pick-up. He looked
a bit of a jerk, but I didn't mind it really – it was quite
flattering really.*

    *Did I like the paintings, he asked. It was obvious from the row
he was making that he didn't. I wasn't sure, but I said I did just
to annoy him. In that case you must be Norwegian, he said. Only
a Norwegian would like Munch. It was an amazing fluke – he had
no way of knowing, and when I told him I was half-Norwegian, he
nodded and tried to look cool. What a jerk! There was something
interesting about him though, and he wasn't bad-looking, so I
accepted his offer of coffee and we went over the road to that coffee
shop with the prints. I said it was my turn to be inspired, and
told him he was a painter – probably misunderstood, underrated,
but soon to be discovered. I'd hit it on the nose obviously, and it
was his turn to be impressed. I didn't tell him he had oil paint all
over one cuff. I told him I knew everything about him. I gave him
my telephone number – I sort of hope he gets in touch, I could do
with some livening up.*

She tossed the exercise book into the open suitcase and went
to the window. It was nearly dusk. The snow glowed blue-white
in the dying light. She drew the curtains and went down to
the kitchen.

    He insisted she sat down after dinner, and left the washing-up
to him, so she went into the front room, browsing through his
collection of old 78 records. He came through after a while,
smiled at her and sat down without saying a word. She watched
him as she stood by the fire.

This was what she needed: the unhurried routine of his quiet lifestyle, the countryside hush. She was more comfortable with him now. There was a solidity, a realness about him that she welcomed. And she welcomed his attentiveness; it was a long time since anybody had looked after her so well. She sat down and studied him as he filled his pipe. There was something about the way he moved that was pleasing to watch: a sort of ease and exactness. He took his time, teasing the tobacco out with his long fingers and tamping it into the bowl. Slow and exact, he retrieved every stray strand. He *was* happy, like he said. Contented.

He struck a match and sucked the flame into the pipe, illuminating his face with each draw of his breath. His eyes were squinted against the smoke, his lips pursed around the pipe-stem, deepening the two vertical lines which creased his cheeks. He still hadn't shaved – the stubble almost a beard now.

He took the pipe from between his teeth and studied it. 'You need to decide if you're going to leave while you've the chance. Another day like today and we'll be snowed in.'

He sat back in the rocking-chair and put his feet on the stool. He was right. It hadn't occurred to her, but another couple of inches of snow and the lane would be impassable. She tried to remember if she'd heard any cars that day – perhaps they were cut off already.

'What shall you do?'

She shook her head. 'I haven't thought about it.'

'What do you want?'

She looked up at him. The gaslamps were turned down low; the light from the fire flickering over his face. 'What do you mean?'

'What do you want from me?'

'Nothing,' she said, surprised.

'You're perfectly satisfied?'

The smoke from the pipe hung in blue layers above the rocking-chair. She twisted her ring round her finger, aware that he was watching her. What was he talking about?

'Are you happy?' he said after a moment.

She folded her hands in her lap. 'Yes, I think so.' She levelled her eyes at him. His eyebrows were raised questioningly.

'As much as I could hope for,' she added defensively.

His expression didn't change; his forehead wrinkled into a chevron of frown-lines. He was calling her bluff, waiting for her to speak first.

'Well?' she said at last.

'When are you going to tell me the truth?'

'I *am* telling you the truth.'

She twisted her ring again and again round her finger, the diamond catching the light at every revolution.

'I'm not trying to get at you, Kate. You look like a person in pain to me.'

She looked at the ring, her eyes stinging with sudden tears. 'I don't know what to do,' she said after a while.

'Live your life as if your life depended on it.'

'Meaning?'

'Stop running away.'

For a moment she thought he must have read her diaries. But no – it was obvious. And he didn't mean it like that anyway.

'What do *you* think I should do?'

He got up and crumbled a peat brick into the fire, and sat down again. 'I think you should ask yourself how important your life is.'

'What are you trying to say?'

He held her gaze until she became uncomfortable and looked away. 'What are you willing to do to save your life from –' He gestured vaguely.

'What *can* I do?'

'Stay.'

'Why?'

'I'm here to help you.'

She studied his face, craggy in the shadows, trying to read his intention. 'Help me?'

'Anything and everything can help you. Whether or not it does is a choice that only you can make.'

'How can I use this–' she indicated the room '–to help me?'

'Stay and find out.'

It was simple, obvious, and part of her responded to it. There was no reason why she shouldn't stay. God knows she was in no hurry to get back to London.

'If I stay until the worst of the snow's over, will you let me pay for food?'

'Yes, in fact I insist. But I won't take your money from you. You can pay me by your willingness to help yourself – nothing else.'

She thought for a second. 'Can I tell you tomorrow?'

'Make your choice now.'

She got up and crouched by the fire, holding her hands out to the heat. Yes. She swivelled round to face him.

'Thank you. I'd like to stay.'

FIVE

It was still dark when he shook her awake the next morning. He was standing over her, a lighted candle in his hand.

She started, pulling the bedclothes around her. 'What's wrong?'

'We need an early start. Get yourself dressed and come down.' He put the candle on the bedside table and left the room, his footsteps clattering down the stairs.

Kate groped for her watch but then remembered it had stopped. It was early – six or seven, she guessed.

She snuggled back into the warmth of her bed. An early start? Her eyes wanted to shut, and she had to blink to keep them open. A draught had caught the flame and the room seemed to expand and contract in the candlelight.

She stared at the ceiling, watching the shadows as they moved. What had she agreed to last night? To stay in this spooky place with an old man she didn't know – a complete stranger?

'I know, I know,' she told herself, swinging her legs out of bed. 'I'm crazy.'

She wrestled into her jeans, struggling with the zip. She'd forgotten what it was like to be this cold. Choosing her thickest jumper, she pulled it over her head. She was feeling a mess – a bath would be good, but no chance of that. She poured some water from the jug into the basin and splashed her face, gasping at the coldness. She dabbed her face dry with a flannel, checking herself in her hand-mirror. Picking up the candle, she felt her way downstairs.

The kitchen was only a little warmer than her bedroom, and she pressed her hands against the dull warmth of the range. Her face was yellow in the gaslight, hung over with lack of sleep.

'Porridge?' he asked.

She shook her head. 'A cup of coffee would be nice, though.'

'Help yourself.'

He went to the window and peered out. 'So, Kate,' he said, looking into the darkness. 'How serious are you?'

She spooned some coffee into a mug. 'About what?'

He chuckled, still with his back to her. 'Change.'

'Change?'

He turned to face her. 'Shite into gold. Like the old alchemists.'

He pulled up a chair and sat down at the table. He seemed much older now, the gaslight carving his face into pits and ravines. 'It can be done,' he said. 'I mean, you can change your life around. It all depends on how willing you are.'

She sat opposite him, her eyes flickering to his face and then back to her coffee.

'Can I trust you?'

His expression didn't change. Stupid question.

'You didn't answer my question. How serious *are* you?'

She tapped a cigarette out of her packet and he watched her as she lit it. 'I'm serious.'

'Serious enough to give me your word to a couple of things?'

She sipped her coffee. 'Like what?'

'Following instructions.'

'Instructions?'

'You do what I tell you.'

She put her cup down precisely, taking her time with her reply. 'How can I agree to that? What if you tell me to . . . ?' She shrugged, looking vaguely round the room.

'If you don't want to do what I ask, then you go. That's the point. You only stay if you want.'

She waited to hear more before she decided.

'I notice you read a lot.'

She shrugged.

'I want you not to – at least until I say so.'

'Why?'

'And no booze or pills. Aspirin included.'

'But what if I get a headache? Do you want me to grin and bear it?'

A smile flicked across his face. 'The grin is optional.'

'But why?'

'That's the deal. Take it or leave it.'

She glanced over his shoulder through the window: still dark. What the hell am I doing here? It's ridiculous!

'How long for?'

'Let's say three days?'

She shook her head. What the hell. 'Okay.'

He got up. 'That's not enough. Your word is a valuable thing. I don't want it given lightly.'

He pulled a broom out from a tangle of things in the corner and dropped it with a clatter between the table and the range.

'When you give your word to something, you're taking a stand. A stand which says: This is me. This is what my life is to be about.'

He stood by the broom-handle, legs apart, hands on hips – a picture of solidity. 'Would you come here?'

She hesitated and then stood and faced him, the broom lying between them.

'Are you willing to bring some changes into your life?'

'Yes. I told you.'

'Are you willing to stick to our agreement?'

'Yes,' she said, puzzled.

'This,' he said, tapping a flagstone with his foot, 'is the land of doing something about your life. Step out and commit yourself to it.'

She looked down at the broom and then up at him. 'What are you doing?'

He was half-hidden in shadow and she couldn't see his face clearly. 'Making a scene.'

She stared at the broom-handle. Ridiculous – her heart was thumping as though he'd asked her to step off a cliff. Her hands were clenched into fists at her sides. For a moment she thought she wouldn't be able to move.

'Well?'

She lifted one foot and held it poised over the broom-handle and then gingerly lowered it on the other side. The second foot followed.

'Good.' He bent to pick up the broom. 'Now, let's get to work.'

He pulled her coat off the back of the door and held it open for her. She let him help her into it.

'Do you have boots? No? Well, you can use these. Stuff some paper in them if they're too big.' He tossed her a pair of green wellingtons.

She ran her fingers through her hair, dazed. 'What do you want me to do?'

He nodded at the boots. 'Put them on and I'll show you.'

He opened the door, letting in a flurry of powdery snow. She slipped the boots on and followed him. There was only a hint of dawn: a greyness diffusing the black along the rim of the horizon.

He stood in the pool of light from the door and gestured instructions to her. 'I want you to clear the snow round the house.'

He crunched through the snow to the back; she following in his footsteps: Wenceslas and his servant.

'Down here to the jacks.' He pointed to the outside toilet. 'Along here to the sheds, and then the path to the road.'

Snowflakes dropped through the windless air, settling for a moment on his head and shoulders before they melted. The moon was low and behind him, and though she couldn't see his expression, his tone was unmistakable. This was not a request. It was an order.

He turned as soon as she took the shovel from him and went back to the house. She stared at his retreating figure. What the hell was he up to now? What had shovelling snow got to do with anything?

She began by the front steps. The wind off the bay stung her face like cold water, but it felt good. Good to be up so early, scrunching this snow underfoot. She couldn't remember the last time she'd stretched her muscles out of doors, breathed anything other than London air.

She tried various ways of working: fast, slow, scraping, shovelling. She set herself tasks: to clear the path to the privy before she could count to a thousand, to reach the corner of the house before the crow on the chimney flew away.

There was no clear point when night ended and day began. Dawn was a creeping increase of illumination until black became grey and the snow reflected back in Kate's face. The day brought with it no colour, only tones: a monochrome of grey and white, splashes of black like Indian ink. An occasional crow flew across the landscape.

He must have been watching her, because as soon as she reached the outhouse, he came out. She'd been going for about an hour, and was resting against the peat stack having a cigarette.

The wind had dropped and it had stopped snowing, but it felt colder to her now, and she cupped the cigarette in her hands as she watched him approach. She sensed trouble when he kept stopping to kick at the packed snow on the path.

'You can do better than this,' he called.

He came up to her, so close the steam from their breaths met. 'You've hardly scraped the top.'

She looked past him at the path. 'It's good enough, surely.'

'Do it again, Kate. And properly this time.'

He turned before she had a chance to protest, and walked back to the house. Damn! She flicked her cigarette butt into the snow, watching him until he turned the corner of the house. She plucked at her sodden mittens, flexing her fingers, and then picked up the spade, leaning it into the ground.

What was he up to? What was all this bullshit about giving your word, and then being told to dig this snow? She looked back at the house: white against white. Use me, he had said. Use me? She started to scrape at the ground, picking up as much earth as snow.

She was frightened of him – *that* was the truth. That uncompromising look he had; that mocking see-what-you've-got-yourself-into expression.

She stamped her feet, slapped her arms against her sides. Careful, Kate – you don't know a thing about him.

She reached the house half an hour later. A mug of coffee was waiting for her in the kitchen.

'So, Kate? How's things?'

She turned her back on him and warmed her smarting fingers over the range. 'I'm tired.'

She heard him scrape a chair back to sit down. There was a moment's silence.

'You can be starting on the front after your drink.'

She closed her eyes. 'You didn't say anything about all this work.'

Turning, she saw him shrug. He doesn't give a damn, she realised. He's sitting happy with his unpaid servant.

'You don't really want it done, do you?'

He considered it for a moment, his eyes fixed on the ceiling.

'No. I *do* want it done.'

'Well, will you help me?'

Again he looked at the ceiling. 'I will not.'

'But why should I do it on my own?' She heard the whine in her voice and checked herself. 'I could do with some help.'

She saw the expression on his face and sat down. There was no point in arguing – he was immovable.

He was watching her, and she hurried her coffee. As soon as she'd finished, he stood up and opened the door.

He showed her what he wanted doing from the doorway. The path was buried under snow and he sketched its course to the lane.

He pointed out the marshy ground – an area of uneven snow, tufts of grass showing through – and warned her not to get too close to it.

She hesitated on the threshold. A white uncut Christmas cake, not a mark between the door and the lane. A lot of work there – and for what? They weren't going anywhere.

He was just behind her, edging her off the step.

'What are you doing?'

She nearly fell. The door slammed and she spun round. The blue door looked blankly back at her – as blank as the old man's face.

Her hand was on the latch, but something held her back. Just go back in, she urged herself, tell him to stuff it. She squeezed the door-handle until her hand hurt. Damn, damn, damn!

'I don't want your interfering!' She sat on the doorstep, her legs drawn up to her chest. Bastard!

She stared ahead at the expanse of white. If only there was some colour; something, anything to break the monotony. But just this wasteland; this frozen nothing.

Low cloud topped the mountains in the distance, their seaward flanks striped grey and white where the wind had blown the snow away. Which was Croagh Patrick, the holy mountain? she wondered. This was the land of doing something about your life, he'd said. This holy wasteland.

There was nothing: no sound, no movement. The land had been drowned in snowy silence. Frozen in time. Waiting for her to make the first move. The land of doing something about your life. The seat of her trousers was wet and she pulled herself to her feet.

It would take for ever to do what he said – the path meandered in a crescent to the lane. If she cut straight across, she could save herself half the work.

'Okay, you old bugger. You can have a straight path or no path.'

She picked up the spade and began scraping the snow from the path, left and right, parting the white layer down to the frozen black grass.

It took her nearly an hour to get to the lane. She scooped the snow off the top of the wall and sat down. She peeled her mittens off and studied her hands. Red and puffy; two large blisters had formed like pads on each hand. She blew on them to ease the pain.

The old man heard her stamping the snow from her boots on the front step and opened the door. He looked at the path and then at Kate.

'What's this?'

'Your path, oh master.'

'No,' he said quietly. 'This is *your* path. The one I want goes round there.' He drew a curved line in the air with his finger.

She didn't bother turning to look – she knew where it should go. She brushed past him into the kitchen.

'If you want it done, do it yourself.' She strode over to the range and pressed her thighs against it. The door clicked shut.

'I've had enough,' she said to the washing hanging above the range.

'I thought you said you were serious.'

She turned. 'I did.'

'And now?'

'I didn't know you were going to treat me like this.'

'So, does this mean our arrangement is at an end?'

She stared at her boots, refusing to meet his eyes.

'If that's the case, then you'd better be off,' he said, 'because I don't want you here.'

'I want to stay, but—'

'But nothing, Kate. It's very simple. If you want to stay, you play by the rules.'

'And if I don't?' she said, stung. 'You throw me out in the snow?'

He shrugged. He would – she knew it.

'Let me warm myself first.'

She'd been outside fifteen minutes when there was a knock on the door. He must have been expecting it, because the door opened immediately. She was on the doorstep, snow clinging in patches from her sleeves and knees. He motioned her into the kitchen.

'I fell in the marsh.'

'So I see.'

'My trousers are soaking . . . ' She waited, arms held stiffly from her body.

'Get yourself changed then.'

'You don't care, do you!'

'I'll not be blackmailed by you.'

'What?'

He spoke in an exaggerated Irish brogue. 'Ah, poor little crature's got herself all wet. Well, she can't work if she's all wet now, can she?' He looked her up and down as though she was a horse he was thinking of buying, and then shook his head. 'I'll not pay. You go and change and then get back to work, or – ' he jerked his head at the door ' – leave.'

'I don't believe it! You cruel—' She wrenched the woollen hat off her head and threw it on the table.

'So, what's it to be then?' he said calmly.

She stared at him and then turned and rushed upstairs.

SIX

It was already getting dark. From where Kate sat at the window, the snow-laden trees beyond the lane looked like shrouded giants approaching the house through the gloom. Giants: had she dreamed about them last night? Threatening figures looming over her, vaguely malevolent. She'd slept badly for the last couple of nights – disturbed, restless sleep. Something was working inside her – some gnawing acid. She could feel it now, pricking behind her eyelids, a bitter taste in her mouth. Giants; watching, waiting. She dropped her gaze to the two paths she'd dug. They diverged at a distance from the house, forming a huge, unexpected Y-shape.

'Y,' she murmured. She smiled at the irony. 'Why indeed?'

Kate tugged the linen curtains shut and fell on to the bed. The old man had lit the fire in her room, and now, with the last of the day shut out, the room flickered with orange firelight. She twisted on the heavy flock mattress so that she could face the fire. The final pieces of the kindling were flaring up, giving way to the duller glow of the peat bricks as they caught. She didn't move, her body bent at an angle, the firelight diminishing until only her silhouette was visible. It was anger that had driven her back out into the snow. She'd attacked it as if it was the old man himself, scattering the snow from the path in a frenzy until she'd exhausted herself. Nothing would stop her finishing though, and she'd ignored the burning pain between her shoulder blades, her arms getting heavier and heavier. She'd finish it: if she did nothing else, she'd finish this bloody path.

The old man was in the front room when she came through, and she managed to get up to her room without being seen. He'd filled two jugs as well as lighting the fire, but she ignored the hot water: she'd ask for nothing from him. She understood him now: he was a spiteful old man, crazy perhaps.

She pushed herself up off the bed. She'd face him now. It was too late to get away tonight, but she'd tell him now, while her resolve was hot, and leave first thing in the morning. The firelight caught the brass doorknob, making it glow gold in the almost dark room. Its cool bulb fitted into her palm, and she paused. It's what I want, isn't it? To leave? She turned the knob and groped her way down the the dark stairs.

He was in the front room. She tapped on the door and pushed it open. The room smelled sweet: turf smoke and pipe tobacco.

'Come in and sit yourself down,' he said without turning to look at her. The cat was on his lap, the old man's legs stretched out to the fire.

She eased herself into the armchair. The work had taken its toll on her: her back muscles were tight, her hands raw and smarting.

'I've finished the front,' she said after a moment.

The old man looked over at her. He nodded thoughtfully and returned his attention to the cat.

'Don't I get *anything* from you?' she said.

He thought about it, but didn't reply.

'Look at the state of my hands!' She thrust them in front of her, palms facing him. 'Look!'

He turned towards her, but instead of looking at her outstretched hands, he stared straight into her eyes.

'Say something,' she snapped.

'Such as?'

'Some thanks? I worked my guts out for you today.'

'Tell me about it.'

'I've had a bloody awful day!'

'And?'

'It's all your fault.'

'It's all my fault,' he said to the cat. 'Did you hear that? I suppose she means the bit about falling in the bog and getting wet. Or is it her hands?'

She'd regretted saying it almost as soon as the words had left her mouth, but it was out now and she stood her ground, her face red. 'You know what I mean.'

'I know *exactly* what you mean. You mean I'm the cause of all your misery and if I'd just say sorry, then you'd feel a lot better.' He pushed the cat off his lap. 'Sorry, Kate, I'm not playing.'

'*I'm* not playing. I'm bloody serious.'

'I know you're serious. Deadly serious. And it's a deadly game you're playing. The stake is your life.'

'What are you on about?' she said irritably. 'What game?'

'You tell me. What sort of game would you call all this falling in the bog and digging the wrong path and then blaming me for everything?'

'It's not like that.'

He ignored her protestation. 'And the first rule? That is, apart from being right all the time? Not letting anyone know you're even playing a game.'

She clicked her tongue against the roof of her mouth. 'I don't have to take this from you.'

'Of course you don't.'

'You said you could *help* me.'

'And?'

'It just looks like you're using me. I mean – what are you trying to do?' She pursed her lips for a moment, a steel door shut tight. 'Look – I'm not going to carry on with this. You've got me here under false pretences.'

'You agreed to stay for three days.'

'I know.'

'And you'll give your word away just like that?'

'Don't try and blackmail me with that. I can do what I want.'

'That's the whole point,' he said quietly. 'It's *your* life, Kate.'

She glowered at the fire.

'So, we're through then?' the old man said after a moment. 'It's back to your old ways?'

'Meaning?'

'You know your ways better than I do.'

She stiffened with sudden anger. 'Don't patronise me.'

'And *that's* one of them. Nobody is going to get the better of you – least of all a man.'

She leant forward and savagely jabbed at the fire with the steel poker, opening up an orange-red core at its centre.

'The recipe for an unsatisfying life is simple,' he said, watching her. 'Find something that doesn't serve you, and then do it again and again.'

She let the poker fall into the grate with a clatter, startling the cat. She leant back into the shadows of her armchair, pressing the watery blisters on her palms.

'So, do you want me to go?' she asked.

'I want you to stay.'

'But why?' *That* was the question. 'Why are you so concerned about me? You don't even know me.'

'What's it to be? Go or stay?'

'*Can* you help me?'

'If you're willing to put in the work.'

'And is it all going to be like this?'

'That's up to you – it's your training. If it's a fight you're wanting, then that's what you'll have.'

'And you want me to agree to do whatever you say, is that it?'

'I want you to start taking responsibility for yourself and stop pushing it on to me,' he said sharply.

She flinched. He was angry – genuinely angry. She'd pushed him too far and her face flushed, smarting from his rebuke. They sat in silence, watching the wreaths of turf smoke slipping up the chimney. She glanced over at the old man. What to do?

She opened her mouth to speak, and he held up his hand. 'If that's a sentence starting with "but" I advise you to close your mouth again,' he said without looking at her. 'It's a yes or a no, Kate. One or the other.'

She nodded slowly. 'All right. I'll stay.'

SEVEN

It seemed always to be dark. Even the sky seemed dark, as though it was a thin white sheet stretched over the landscape: a sheet which would fall away at dusk to reveal the blackness once more.

And it was dark when he woke her the next morning. Pitch-black. Not the orange half-light of London streets, but a profound darkness – a fairy-tale dark as though the sun had sunk, finally, and would never rise again, not for months.

She was free to go or stay, she knew that. She chose to stay, remake her world, stick it out for another forty-eight hours.

It had snowed in the night, another powdery two inches, and when she came down in the morning he asked her to clear the paths again. She'd been expecting it, and agreed with no further protest. Her hands were still sensitive: the blisters had burst, revealing moist pink patches, and after breakfast he rummaged in a drawer for sticking-plaster. He bandaged her hands and she was surprised how gentle his touch was, how soft his fingers were: not the farmer's hands she'd expected.

He was taking more care of her: he'd warmed her coat and scarf by the range, and handed her a thick pair of darned socks. She hesitated a moment and then pulled them on over the socks she was already wearing. She needed all the warmth she could get.

Dawn saw her in the back yard again, scraping away at the snow. She worked slowly and methodically: there was no hurry. Her hands were hurting, even through the plasters and gloves, and she had difficulty handling the spade.

The snow was like a thick white blanket thrown over the land, muffling everything; not only sound, but movements too. No birds, she realised. Strange, she could see their trails – arrow prints trodden into the snow – but no signs of their authors. The trees were empty, the sky an uninterrupted white. She turned a full circle. No sign of any life; the only movement the streamer of smoke being pulled from the chimney.

What about the sheep? she suddenly thought. Where had they gone? Surely they couldn't stay out in weather like this? There must be five inches of snow.

The accident came back to her. The pathetic, stupid sheep, its eyes glazed in panic. The warm blood splashing over her skin. She shuddered and involuntarily wiped her hand on her sleeve.

June 1st
I think I'm in lust. I met Paul again today. It surprised me – I'd given up on him after a week had gone by without hearing from him, but he phoned me and invited me to his studio-cum-flat on the Hammersmith Road. He showed me his work – great messy, de Kooning type things. His prices were high, he said – had to be, just to pay for the paint, and I can believe it.

I should've expected it: the chilled wine and cold chicken and the mattress prominently displayed under the huge windows. It was fairly civilised at first – talking paintings and prices. Halfway through the wine he gave up the pretence. 'Let's fuck,' he said. Jesus – what a Bohemian cliché! I turned him down – it was just too gauche – and we ended up going for a drink. He invited me back and coffee turned to brandy and we ended up in bed. He came too soon – over-excited little boy, but it was fun.

She paused to stamp some life back into her frozen feet. Nearly finished the back. She dropped the spade for a moment and shrugged her shoulders. It seemed so long ago, that summer – years, not the eighteen months it actually was. But, God – it was hot that summer! He never opened his studio windows, no matter how stifling it got. He hated noise when he painted – he'd rather suffocate.

It was light he loved. Light and heat. He painted with his shirt off, squinting against the smoke from the fag in the corner of his mouth like a young Picasso.

What a summer! What a beautiful, gorgeous summer! There was so much sun that year, and his lovely body browned like a piece of toast.

It came to her: an image of watching him paint, one Saturday, lying on the bed, a stripe of shadow from the window moving across the floor as the afternoon slipped by, drowsing in the heat and smoke and the sleepy sound of traffic.

She stooped to pick up the spade, and started work again.

She was back in the kitchen by nine.

'I've finished the back,' she told him, struggling out of her coat.

'Good. Sit yourself down and I'll get some coffee.'

He was quite chatty, asking her how she was getting on, if she was wrapped up enough. Something had changed his manner towards her; he was being less offhand than yesterday, more as he'd been when they'd first met.

He put a mug of coffee in front of her and sat down.

'Thanks.' She warmed her hands over it. 'It's cold out there.'

His eyes scanned her face as though he was reading something written on her skin. 'When you're through with your drink I want you to do the front.'

She closed her eyes. 'Is it really necessary?'

'No.'

'Then why do it?'

'Because I'm asking you to.'

She stared at the mug. 'What are you up to?'

'What are *you* up to?' He raised his eyebrows. 'That's the question to ask.'

There was a yowl from outside the kitchen door and the old man got up to open the door to let the cat in.

'It shouldn't take you too long to finish up.'

She heard the door click shut and turned round to speak to him, but he'd gone out. She looked down at the cat, watching her from the doormat.

'Don't ask me,' she shrugged. 'I don't know either.'

It was getting colder; spits of snow on the wind. She worked, head bent, hurrying to get the job done.

What's he up to? She scraped at the snow as though she might find the answer somewhere below its surface. There's got to be some reason behind all this. Is this some sort of trial, a test? But what for? Maybe it does have some point, she thought. Maybe the road will be open soon. Maybe it's obvious and I'm just too stupid to see it.

June 17th

We go from strength to strength. Our first row yesterday – well, not row, but he did lose his temper. I'd gone out with Julie and Marie after work, while he'd been struggling over this giant purple painting. He's been at it all week, painting this ugly oval thing and it just gets bigger and fatter every day like a huge ripe plum. I was a bit pissed when I got back to his place, and I made the mistake of asking how his plum was getting on. He looked at me blankly, so I pointed at the canvas, expecting a laugh. That's the last time I'll laugh at his paintings – he freaked! He threw his brush at me – a two-inch decorator's brush covered with bright orange paint. Of course I had to have my new white blouse on – an orange streak all down one arm. He apologised almost immediately, and started dabbing it off with white spirit, but he was just making a balls-up of it, adding purple to the orange, so I told him not to bother and I took it off. He looked so guilty and sorry – I think I fell in love with him there and then. He kissed me, and said he was sorry, and then started tugging off the rest of my clothes, hanging them on the mannikin he keeps. He's crazy – he dressed that dummy with the clothes he was taking off me – hanging my knickers over its head like a ski mask. And then – good job I was drunk, I'd never have done it otherwise – he took the canvas off the easel and dropped it on the floor and then pulled me down until we were both lying on it, like it was a multicoloured double bed. It was still wet, greasy with oil paint. What a turn-on – I was pissed, that was part of it, but it was just so erotic making love, slithering around on that painting – outrageous! We were as embarrassed as hell when we

*finished – it was stupid really, I'm still covered with the bloody
paint. He showed me my bottom in the mirror – a crazy whirl of
purple and orange. I went back to his studio today and saw the
canvas hanging up. He said he'd invented a new style. Fuck art
he called it – the movement of the future.*

The spade slipped from her grasp, and she left it where it lay in
the snow. Any more of this and I'll seize up. She turned to look
back at the house, unexpectedly picturesque against the white
backdrop. Solid and worn; there was something of the old man
in it. The upper windows with their heavy sills were like his
eyes, the snow on the roof like his white hair.

He was waiting when she came back in; his arms folded on the
table as he was when she left him. She didn't bother taking her
boots off, but walked straight up to him.

'All right. I give in.' She pulled her gloves off and dropped
them on the table. 'Tell me – what's the use of digging a path
to a road no one's going to use?'

He looked surprised. 'None, obviously.'

'Then why not dig in the opposite direction?'

'Why not, indeed?'

She blew on her fingers. 'And if I did that you'd have made
me do it again – right?'

'Of course.'

She tapped on the table. 'Now *you're* playing games with
me.'

He thought about it for a moment, but didn't answer.

'There *is* some point to all this work – yes?' She spoke to
him as if he was a foreigner, and she wasn't sure he was going
to understand her.

'That depends on you.'

She shrugged off her coat and pulled up a chair. 'Look,' she
said, sitting opposite him. 'I don't want some metaphysical
final solution. I just want to know your reasons behind what
you're doing.'

'You asked me for help.' He held her gaze, his eyes as blue
and crooked as a Siamese cat's.

'But why digging?'

'Why not?'

'But what's the point?'

He nodded at the window. 'The story of your life lies out there.'

She obviously didn't understand.

'It's not snow out there,' he continued. 'It's a mirror.'

She flicked her eyes skyward to signal her contempt and cupped her hands over her ears, massaging the cold out of them. She saw his lips move and she stopped.

'What did you say?'

'I said why look in a mirror except to see yourself.'

'Let's get this right,' she sighed. 'You think the way I handle a spade is a fair indication of the way I handle my life, is that it?'

'It doesn't matter what I think.' He raised a finger and slowly lowered it in an arc until it almost touched her nose. 'Just notice how you're dealing with this whole business.'

She pushed herself to her feet. 'I'm going to lie down.'

A fire was glowing in the grate in her room, and she squatted in front of it, poking it into life with a wedge of turf. What did he mean, notice? She stared into the fire, her face tingling with the sudden heat. Notice what? The way I've been dealing with this whole business? Just the way I always have done – no surprise in that.

She frowned and climbed on to the bed. She knew herself well enough, so what the hell was there to notice?

Without getting up she slid the suitcase from under her bed and took out a book. She flicked through the pages until she found her place, and then stared at the page for a moment before dropping it on the floor. No concentration.

She shrugged her shoulders to ease the tension; moving her head from side to side on the pillow. Damn him! Patronising old bore!

She heaved herself up and went to the washstand and sat down, scanning the objects on the small dressing-table. Picking up her nail varnish, she shook the scarlet bottle carefully and unscrewed the cap. She held her hands out in front of her. The nails were anaemic-looking, like boiled almonds. She couldn't remember the last time she'd been without nail varnish.

She began expertly stroking on the paint, fanning each finger out when it had been done. When the left hand was finished, she waved it and then tested the paint – dry.

'Poor hand!' she whispered, touching the sticking-plaster on her palm. She held it in front of her and studied it. It was like someone else's hand. Not hers – she'd never seen it before. She turned both hands over – one with scarlet nails, one with white, as though the left hand had been dipped in blood. Were these *really* her hands?

She picked up the mirror and held it in front of her. Dreadful! She brought it closer, scrutinising her lips and eyes, and then held it at arm's length to get her whole face in. Suddenly her skin prickled. This was the face of a stranger.

Half-fascinated, half-horrified, she studied the face as though it was a photograph of someone else, vaguely familiar. She compressed her lips and watched the face in the mirror do likewise. She widened her eyes and then squinted them into slits. It was hard to believe this was the face she'd been carrying around with her. Those hazel eyes, too close together; the over-large nose. Whose were they?

She stared until there were just two eyes looking back at her, flicking from left to right, right to left. Two hazel eyes, pupils like black holes, set in a swirling, dissolving skull.

There was a tap on the door and she broke away. She put the mirror face down on the dressing-table and rubbed her eyes.

'What is it?'

'Lunch is on the table.'

She pushed the stool back and stood up, knocking the open bottle of nail varnish over.

'Damn!' She scooped the bottle up and dabbed at the splash of red with a paper tissue. She carried the tissue between finger and thumb, like a bloody handkerchief, and dropped it in the fire.

EIGHT

Lunch was a glum affair. He refused to eat and talk at the same time, and whenever she tried to start a conversation he'd either grunt a couple of words or ignore her completely. The quiet was getting to her. She hadn't realised how much she depended on noise: chatter, traffic, the radio. It was oppressive, this silence: every sound of their eating, grotesquely magnified. She pushed her plate away and stood up.

'I'm going into the front room for a cigarette. Sorry I couldn't eat the—' She stopped. He wasn't listening to her. She turned and left.

It was chilly in the front room, even though a fire was smouldering in the grate. A nice smell though, she thought, almost like stale cigar smoke. Homely.

She pressed her nose against the window-pane watching the snowflakes zig-zag down through the windless air. They'd be snowed in if this continued. Snowed in: it would be disastrous, stuck here, unable to get away, but she didn't want to think about it. She could stay warm here, stay out of the old man's way. She blew a mushroom cloud of smoke against the glass. If only there was something to do, something to fill this gaping void of silence.

She couldn't read – it wouldn't be worth the fight that would ensue. He said he hadn't got a radio. Sensory deprivation – was that it? Was he trying to send her crazy? She drummed her fingernails against the window. How the hell did he live out here all on his own, cut off from the rest of the world? She hadn't read a paper, heard the news, seen another person since she'd been here. She didn't even know what day it was.

She spent ten minutes poking at the fire and then went up to her room. She'd tidy herself up, finish her make-up. Maybe he'd heat some water for her to wash her hair and do her laundry.

The only mirror in the house was the hand-mirror she'd brought with her: too annoyingly small to make up with. She had to pass his room to get to hers, and she paused outside it. He'd gone out, messing around in his studio probably; there might be a mirror in his room. She pushed open his door and slid in.

It was larger than her room, though it shared the same chimney-breast. A single bed, neatly made; two pillows; a gaudy Sacred Heart tacked to the wall (Are you Catholic, she'd asked him. Very, he'd replied); beside the candle on his bedside table was a framed photograph of a woman. Kate picked it up and held it to the light: brown and fuzzy, obviously taken a long time ago. Pretty, the woman: dark eyes staring from under a broad-brimmed hat straight into the camera. Might be the same woman in the painting downstairs, impossible to tell for sure.

No mirror, as she'd expected. She put the picture back and quietly left the room.

She emptied the contents of her make-up bag on to the dressing-table. A single bed – he must have slept alone, his wife in this room. He hadn't said what her name was. She looked at herself in the mirror and selected a blunt pencil of blue eyeliner. No. She dropped it on the table and picked up another. Something different – black for a change.

She took her time making up, mixing her colours as carefully as she did when restoring a painting. She held the mirror at arm's length to assess her work and grimaced at her reflection – too much, overdone it with the kohl.

'Like a bloody prostitute,' she said aloud.

No, not a prostitute – where had she seen that look? The too-red lips, the startling eye make-up? She remembered – the transvestites in Thailand. Over-painted, pretty young men: a travesty of femininity.

She watched herself in the mirror. Why do I bother? Anyone who looked could see under the paint: the pinched lips, bags under the eyes. God, I can be stupid! She smeared her lips with the back of her hand, a streak of pink scarring the skin, and then scooped a fingerful of vanishing cream. She spread it over her eyes and lips, scraping it off roughly with a tissue. She looked across the dressing-table, pasty-faced from the cream, and had a sudden urge to sweep it all away: the bottles and lipsticks and pencils, all the goddamned men-pleasing junk.

He'd refilled her water jug and she poured its contents into the washbasin. The soap wouldn't lather in the cold water and she had to smear the greasy white stuff over her face and lather it by rubbing with a flannel. She scrubbed at her skin, cursing when soap got in her eye. She groped for the water jug and cupped a palmful of clean water in her hand to bathe it. The stinging made her dizzy and irritable, and she carelessly rinsed the rest of the soap off and threw herself down on the bed.

She grabbed a hank of unwashed hair and tugged till her scalp tingled. 'What's happening to me?' she whispered.

She fumbled under the bed for her diary, found a pencil and began writing furiously.

December 17th?
I knew Paul had other girlfriends when I met him. I didn't ask him to change. I thought he would be different in time, I thought when he knew how special we were, he'd change – and it was something special at the beginning. I just knew we were right for each other. I wasn't jealous – we were so powerful, nothing could come between us.

Is it always the way – this stupid craving right at the beginning? And then downhill all the way? We couldn't stay away from each other at first – God, it was wonderful! I loved him. He'd phone me at work, leave silly messages on the answering machine; pick me up at lunch and get me half drunk so I couldn't do a thing all afternoon. I'd rush to his studio at five and he'd be waiting for me, too horny to paint, a huge grin on his beautiful brown face, and we'd make love standing against a wall, on the kitchen table, the floor. When he bent between my legs to eat me I wanted to push his head inside me – his head and shoulders and whole body. I wanted to swallow him up. I wanted him inside me like a drug.

She suddenly flung the exercise book away from her in a flutter of pages. 'Fuck him!' She kneaded her eyesockets with her knuckles and sat up. There was a clatter from downstairs – he'd dropped a saucepan. She thought for a moment and then sprang from the bed and hurried downstairs.

He was peeling vegetables at the sink.

'Why won't you talk to me?' she said to his back. 'I've got to do something or I'll go round the bend.'

He spoke over his shoulder. 'Go through to the front room. I'll join you in a minute.'

She did as he said. Her entrance woke the cat, Ludo, which jumped down from its peat bed beside the fire. Kate idly watched it as it cleaned itself. Paws first, then behind each ear, finally it threw itself on its side to lick its flank, the hair flattening into damp stripes under its rough tongue. It stopped as suddenly as it had begun and sat up, ready to take stock of the world. Its head swivelled, scanning the room; its eyes flickering over the woman, the empty rocking-chair, the Victorian print on the wall. Its gaze returned to her, and after a moment's consideration, the cat stalked towards her, tail held stiff and proud as a standard. It halted in front of Kate and levelled its eyes at her. She had followed its approach, and when it looked up, their eyes – one pair amber, one pair hazel – locked together.

For some seconds the cat and the woman stared at each other as if each expected the other to speak. Then Kate, as the cat had earlier, surveyed the room. She was getting to know it; not that she felt at home, but it was taking on a familiarity that surprised her when she considered how long she'd been here – just four or five days.

She glanced down. The cat was still staring at her as if waiting for something. Kate looked at it closely. Was it her imagination, or was that a smile playing on its bearded lower jaw? It looked like it was smiling at her. Staring and smiling. She shifted in her chair, but the cat's gaze didn't falter. It was unsettling: those lazy unremitting eyes, the hint of a smile; in human terms that look could only be interpreted as critical. That face on a child would be called insolence.

She flicked a hand at it as if brushing away a bothersome fly, but the cat only lowered its lids into a defiant blink and resumed its staring. She hissed at it, sounding surprisingly like a cat herself, but it continued unruffled. By leaning forward in her chair, she could reach it with an outstretched leg, and just as she kicked it, almost knocking it off balance, the door opened and the old man came in. The cat escaped like an arrow through the open door and he turned to watch it go. He glanced at her and then sat in his chair and pulled out his pipe.

She said nothing, but got up and browsed through the bookshelf, embarrassed that he should have caught her. He was filling his pipe, and not going to speak till he had finished. The silence was oppressive, so she forced herself to speak.

'Why won't you let me read?' she said with her back to him.

'I'm not stopping you reading.'

She slid a book out and turned round. 'So it's okay if I do, then?'

He glanced up at her, his eyes heavy with contempt. 'Grow up, Kate.'

He struck a match and lit his pipe, puffing great belches of smoke into the air. She sat down, the book in her lap, watching the smoke disperse into a blue halo above his head.

'Well?' he said at last.

She'd prepared what she was going to say, and it came out without any thought.

'What are you doing to me?'

He shot a spurt of smoke out from the corner of his mouth. 'I'm doing nothing to you.'

She clicked her tongue in annoyance. 'Of course you are!'

'I'm just telling you what to do. It's yourself making things happen.'

'Very clever!' she said sarcastically. 'So tell me – why the ridiculous tasks? Why your pig-headedness?'

'Stick to "what" not "why", or we'll never finish this conversation,' he said between teeth clamped on his pipe.

She drew in a deep breath and exhaled each word in the outbreath. 'What . . . are . . . you . . . '

He interrupted her. 'Keep me out of this. The problem is yours, not mine.'

She let out the last of her breath in a sigh. They watched each other for a moment.

'What's happening to me?'

'You tell me.'

'But I don't know. That's why I'm asking you.'

'How can I know what's going on inside you? I'm not God.'

'But you can explain. You're supposed to be the teacher, remember.'

'Where did you get that idea?' he said, surprised. 'Not from me.'

'But—'

'You're doing everything you can to disown this, aren't you? It's your life, Kate. Your responsibility and nobody else's.'

He pointed the pipe-stem at her. 'Tell me. What's happening to you now? In your body?'

'I've got a headache.'

'Where?'

She drew a line across her forehead. 'Here.'

'What else?'

'I'm a bit cold.'

'That's a concept. What's happening in your body?'

'A wobbly feeling here—' She patted her thighs and stomach.

'Anything else?'

She shook her head.

'What thoughts do you have?'

'I'm wondering what you're doing.'

'Emotions?'

She was blank and then a frown passed over her face. 'I'm sad,' she said, surprised.

He nodded, sucking on his pipe. 'You've answered your question.'

'But I still don't know what you're—' She caught herself and paused.

'Congratulations, Kate,' he said drily. 'You're starting to notice.'

She scowled. 'I think you're the most arrogant man I've ever met.'

He tapped his pipe out on the hearth and blew into the bowl. Conversation over.

'Aren't you interested at all in what my feelings are?'

He stood up. 'That was a thought, not a feeling, and no – ' He put his pipe on the mantel and turned to go. 'I don't give a damn what you think.'

NINE

She woke with a cry, a stabbing pain in her chest. She was winded and inhaled with a rattling gasp, fighting her way out of the nightmare. Fumbling for the matches, she managed to light the candle.

It had been awful, a suffocating dream. She lay back on the pillow, breathing heavily, calming her pounding heart. Her face was wet, from tears or sweat she couldn't tell, and she wiped the sheet across her forehead. The dream – what was it? – trapped inside a rubber membrane, a giant balloon. She could see through it, see a man and a woman – her sister? – frantic, trying to break through the membrane with a spade. Every time they struck at the rubber, she felt a sharp pain in her middle. And this panic of suffocating, arms and legs pinned, mouth gagged so no sound came out. Kate shivered into the blankets, pulling them up to her neck, her eyes fixed on the candle. In the dream, she was going to die – she knew it. They were trying to save her, but it was impossible – they couldn't break through this impenetrable membrane. And this is how she would exit her life: screaming, floundering in panic. She wormed an arm from under the bedclothes and traced the white line of a scar on her left wrist, shining like a thread of silk in the candlelight. She winced at the memory.

Feeling in the dark for her shoes, she swung her legs out of bed and slipped them on. She struggled into the flannel dressing-gown he'd lent her, and taking the candle, went downstairs. She hesitated when she saw the light coming from under the kitchen door, but holding the candle away from her puffy face, swung it open and stepped in. The old man was sitting at the kitchen table, and looked up at her, surprised. She mumbled good morning and quickly stepped out into the snow, the candle guttering and blowing out almost immediately.

She hurried through the cold to the privy, snow finding its way into her shoes. She didn't bother to relight the candle but sat on the cold seat in the dark. She suddenly realised she'd had enough. She couldn't take any more. She sat on the toilet, her mind a blank. She knew she had to face him; that when she went back into the kitchen he'd be waiting for her. He wasn't going to let her go – not ever. There was no escape. There was nowhere to go except forward into the hands of her nemesis.

Her skin was purple with the cold when she came back into the kitchen. She waited by the door for him to speak, the green of the dressing-gown she clutched to herself livid in the gaslight.

The setting moon allowed her enough light to see all she needed, and she made some sort of progress, scraping away the night's snowfall from the back path. The paths were shallow trenches now, the untrodden snow six inches deep.

She had no idea what the time was: there was no clock in the house and her watch had stopped days ago. Until now she'd guessed the time – sunrise at eight, sunset at four – but she didn't know how long she'd slept for, and there was still no sign of dawn.

It must have been an hour later when he called her in. Breakfast was ready for her: suety porridge, which she barely touched, and a steaming mug of tea. He'd sugared it, even though he knew she never took the stuff, but she drank it anyway. He watched her in silence and when she had finished, opened the door for her.

A blackness had overcome her: a mechanicalness that paid no heed to the aches and the numbing cold and the pointlessness. There was nothing left inside her: she'd been sucked dry. She went back without a word.

Dawn surprised her. Suddenly it was light and she could see what she was doing. She straightened up, dizzy and confused. How long have I been working for? She was in the front; half of it done already. How did I get here? She couldn't remember doing the work.

A sudden crack! and she jumped as if somebody had slapped her. She spun round to look back at the house, thirty yards away. Again, crack! clear, almost preternaturally loud in the dawn stillness. She flinched at the sound. It was the old man chopping kindling beside the outhouse. As loud as a pistol shot, it came again and again, urgent and violent, like the sound of one person beating another.

She found herself running, stumbling through the snow, desperate to put distance between herself and the sound. Each shot was like the crack of a whip above her head: she, like a panicked horse, high-stepping blindly into the snowfield. The snow was calf-deep and she tripped and fell several times but then – thank God – it stopped; the sound of the last blow hanging in the air.

She turned, panting, to look back. She was a hundred yards, maybe more, from the house; she could just see him pottering around in the back yard. He disappeared round the corner of the house: he hadn't seen her.

She bent over to regain her breath, her eyes fixed on the house. She wouldn't go back. That was it.

She followed the line of the half-buried wall to the lane, occasionally slipping up to her knees in the untrodden snow.

At the road she paused to look back again. The house seemed so insignificant now: a toy she could pick up with one hand and crush. She'd left; escaped. As easy as that.

The snow on the road was deeper, drifting to the height of the wall: she'd have to walk on the wall until it got shallower. She climbed up on it and looked around at the surrounding countryside. It was flat: its features rubbed out by the snow. The great hump-backed mountains lay across the horizon like beached whales, the ground between her and them as featureless as the sky. Croagh Patrick, she recognised – just go in the opposite direction and she'd find Westport. There could be no turning back.

She hurried for the first couple of miles, hardly daring to believe she'd actually got away. It was difficult walking, though once she reached the main road the going was easier: it was sheltered by trees for much of the way, the snow only three or four inches deep.

She tired quickly and after an hour or so became clumsy, wandering off the road into deeper snow, stumbling into drifts.

There was no sign of anyone: the road was completely impassable, its surface marked only by birds and unidentifiable animal tracks. She passed the occasional farmhouse or holiday cottage, but she saw nobody; just the smug line of smoke rising from their chimneys.

It took her nearly three hours to get to Westport. The snow had been lighter in the valley the town nestled in, and there was some traffic on the roads. Most of the shops were open and people were to be seen making their way carefully through the slushy streets. Kate went into the first grocery store she saw and warmed herself over the paraffin stove while the young girl who seemed to be in charge of the shop stared at her sullenly. Kate needed cigarettes; she was hungry too. She was just surveying the well-stocked shelves of the shop when she realised. No money! She patted her trousers and felt inside her coat pockets. Nothing: a cigarette lighter, a business card and a crumpled paper tissue. Damn! She turned and left the shop without offering any explanation to the girl.

Outside, she looked up and down the street. Which way was the garage? As long as the car's ready, she told herself, I can get away. Get some money sent from England and leave this goddamned country.

The garage was locked, the metal shutters of the repair shop padlocked. Shit! She hammered on the shutters in her frustration. What do I do now?

'There's nobody here,' a woman's voice called from above her.

Kate stepped back and looked up. A middle-aged woman was leaning out of the upstairs window.

'Frank couldn't get in today on account of the snow.'

'Is my car ready?' Kate called back. 'The yellow MG?'

'Now, I wouldn't know about that. Even if it was, you wouldn't be able to get at it. There's no keys here.'

The woman smiled apologetically and shut the window, twitching the lace curtains back into place. Kate's eyes pricked with the start of tears. This is ridiculous – I can't even get a cup of coffee.

She wandered aimlessly for a few minutes, and then stopped someone and asked where the railway station was. It was worth trying, even without any money.

The tiny station was deserted, and Kate thought that all the services had been cancelled, but a blackboard informed her there would be one departure that day, at midday, going to Dublin.

She looked at the clock above the ticket office. Twenty minutes. There was a waiting room on the other side of the track and she stepped off the platform and crossed over. I've got no choice, she told herself. If I can get to Dublin I can borrow some money from Jayne's mum, phone the bank. Fuck it! She didn't care what happened as long as she could get away. First get on the train, and then worry about paying for the ticket.

It was bitter now. She'd stumbled through the snow like a sleepwalker, oblivious to the cold, but once inside the waiting room she realised how cold she was. She stamped her feet and slapped her arms against her sides as though she was performing some arcane folk dance, reading aloud the graffiti scratched on the walls. *Sharon loves J.D. Hunger strike for freedom. Everybody's a junkie.*

Cold, cold, cold. She looked out of the window. Can't be long now. She saw two figures across the track: a man and a porter. She stood still and squinted at them, and then with a jolt realised who it was. Impossible! She stepped back from the window. It's him – he's followed me!

She leant against the wall in the corner, her heart pounding. What shall I do? She closed her eyes to think, but her mind was blank. What shall I do? She cast around the waiting room – there wasn't even anywhere to hide.

She could have walked out of there. She could have confronted the old man, demanded to be left alone; called the police if necessary. She'd committed no crime – in fact, it was she who was the injured party. Then why was she feeling so guilty, expecting a heavy masculine hand on her shoulder at any moment – the old man, the porter, the police?

She slid down the wall until she was sitting on the floor.

'Just let me get away from him,' she whispered. 'Please God.'

The train came soon, and she hadn't been discovered. She slipped out of the waiting room into the nearest carriage and found an empty compartment. She scanned the platform for the old man, but she couldn't see him.

The train was delayed so long she thought of hiding in the toilet, but eventually it pulled out of the station. She sat back in her seat, hoping against hope that she'd finally given him the slip.

He found her within five minutes. Kate gasped when she saw his face through the corridor window, and by the time he'd slid open the door, she was on her feet. She pushed past him and hurried down the corridor. She hesitated when she saw the inspector coming in the opposite direction, and then dodged into the nearest compartment. The old man was not in a hurry – he'd caught her now, and he paused to let the ticket inspector in before entering himself.

There were three others in the compartment: a nun and a middle-aged couple. The old man said hello, ignoring Kate, and took the seat opposite her. She couldn't look at him and fixed her eyes on his wellington boots while the conductor clipped the tickets.

She didn't know what to do. She could have pretended to have lost her ticket, but not with the old man watching.

Her view of his boots was blocked as the conductor moved in front of her.

'Ticket please, miss.'

She looked up at his expectant face, then leant to one side to see the old man. He stared back at her blankly.

Nothing else for it – I'll have to admit it.

'I haven't got a ticket.'

The inspector didn't have time to register what she'd said: the old man had tapped him on the elbow. He held out two tickets.

'For me and the young lady.'

She watched in disbelief as he punched the tickets. He's playing with me!

'You bastard!' All eyes turned to her, but for once she didn't care. 'You bloody . . . bastard!'

There was a stunned silence and then Kate burst into tears. The inspector thrust the tickets back at the old man and left hurriedly. The nun looked accusingly at the old man and laid a hand on Kate's shoulder.

'Don't!' he snapped.

The nun's hand jerked away from Kate as if scalded.

'Just leave the girl alone, please,' he added in a conciliatory tone. 'She's my daughter and she's just heard some terrible news.'

'Oh the poor creature,' the wife said, hoping to invite herself into the unexpected drama.

They all looked at the weeping woman. She'd closed her eyes and was crying almost noiselessly, tears squeezing between the lids and running down her cheeks to the corners of her mouth.

'A death, was it?' the wife couldn't help asking the old man.

'I expect so,' he muttered, not taking his eyes off Kate.

Her tears stopped, but she stayed with her eyes shut. She was exhausted: it was all she could do to smear her tears and wipe her nose with the back of her hand. A flood of fatigue had swept over her as she cried: the accumulated exhaustion not only of the past few days, but, so it seemed, the past few years of her life.

That was it: nothing to do with the recent drama she'd been through. That was just another crisis in a long series. It was the awful weariness of day-to-day living, the being weighed down with the baggage of the past, and the limitless future that stretched ahead of her. It was a mess – a horribly complicated tangle.

She kept her eyes closed. Open, she would have to face this Gordian knot, unpick the tangle of her life. She rocked with the motion of the train, suddenly drowsy. Sleep, that was the answer. Sleep and never wake up.

When they saw she'd finished, her co-passengers turned their attention from her to each other, and the conversation which she'd obviously interrupted, resumed. Kate paid no attention to it, but she was comforted by the soft drone of voices and gradually, with the warmth and motion of the carriage and the lulling sound of their talk, she drifted into a half-sleep.

A hand touched her knee and she opened her eyes. The old man was leaning across and shaking her.

'This is as far as we go,' he said, standing up. Without questioning, she rose too and followed him into the corridor.

They were approaching a station, and he slid down the window, letting in a blast of icy air. She was still half-asleep when they got off, and she found herself on the platform of Claremorris station, shivering in the cold.

They waited on the platform until the train pulled out. Kate watched it go. It would be in Dublin by the afternoon.

'Are you coming home, Kate?'

She turned in the direction of the receding train, waiting until she couldn't hear it any more, and then looked at him, a question in her eyes.

Home? She looked at his old stained overcoat, tied around the middle with twine. Home? Was that it?

She knew that if she said no, he would, there and then, let her go. She knew now that she had no obligation to return – it was her life and hers to do with as she pleased.

She lifted her eyes to his and gave an almost imperceptible nod. No thoughts, no consideration – she didn't know where the answer came from, but it was yes.

He took her by the elbow and steered her through the wicket to the ticket office. They were lucky: there was a return train in just over an hour. She watched him as he paid for the tickets. She hadn't seen it before, but talking to the man in the ticket office, she noticed how mobile his face was: as supple as a leather glove. And what she'd taken for scowl-lines were laugh-lines: she didn't hear what the other man said, but it made him laugh, softening his face.

Why return with him? She didn't know. It was an impulse, an instinct that made her follow him. A gamble, she knew, to put her trust in him. But with him there was at least a possibility of the future being different. Without him the future was certain. Good or bad, she would take this leap in the dark, and if she landed in the Devil's quarter, God help her.

TEN

It was already dark when he woke her. She'd collapsed, fully clothed on the bed, when they got back and he'd left her to sleep throughout the afternoon.

They'd arrived back in Westport by two thirty. Her resolve had grown with each passing mile and she'd been almost glad to be back in familiar surroundings. James, the old man's neighbour, had met them at the station in his tractor, and they'd returned to the cottage clinging on to the back of the cab. She was here now, back in the same room as if none of it had ever happened.

He'd drawn her a bath, and told her to get down to it quick before the water got cold. She thanked him and collected her washbag and went down to the kitchen.

The bath, an ancient tin affair, sat in front of the range like a mythical aquatic beast, exhaling clouds of steam. On the range two saucepans of water were heating: refills for the bath. The lamps were low, dimming the whitewashed stone of the walls into warm cream marshmallows.

He left her to it and she quickly undressed, dropping her clothes carelessly on to the floor. She paused, naked, before she stepped into the bath: a peculiar luxury, this bathing among the chairs and table and saucepans. The water was almost too hot, and she gingerly lowered herself until she was kneeling and then sitting in the bath. It was just long enough for her to stretch her legs out. The bath was corroded and old, its edges sharp, but it didn't matter. She closed her eyes in pleasure. Ridiculous, she smiled; primitive – but God, it felt good.

Oh, Paul. She frowned to keep from crying. I've never loved anyone as much as I loved you. You were everything I ever wanted. A year – a whole year, and we were so good together. And then four months of agony – off, on, off, on. I know I was being possessive, but we were so good. I didn't mind you going off with her, but why didn't you come back? I would have forgiven you if you'd just let me share you. Why wouldn't you let me into your life? We were still good together – I would have shared you. You knew I couldn't live without you.

She shook her head like a dog coming out of water. 'Forget him,' she whispered.

She scooped palmfuls of water and splashed it over her shoulders and breasts, flinching from the heat, and then bent forward and dipped her hair in the water. Using the jug he'd left for her, she poured water over her head, shivering as it coursed down her neck. She shampooed her hair and then stood up to soap her body with the foam.

'Forget him,' she said loudly. She looked down at her body as she washed herself: she'd lost weight. Her life of the last four months had gnawed into her flesh; anorexic angles at her elbows, hips. She knew the body well, didn't respect it. Knees were wrong, boobs too small. She soaped her armpits, her crotch, glancing over at the kitchen window to make sure the tea-towel curtain was still in place.

She missed it, the beauty; the occasional highlight of a brass ornament, a Delft plate, the shading of her limbs into a delicate chiaroscuro. Her skin was eggshell in the lamplight and when she bent to wash her legs, bending from the hips like a dancer, her wet hair hung like a sheaf of corn. Rembrandt would have painted her like that.

There was a knock at the inner door, and she dropped like a stone into the water.

'Do you want to be rinsed off yet?' he called through the door.

She hesitated. The water was thick with lather, and she hadn't rinsed her hair. She glanced up at the saucepans of water on the range, out of reach.

'Can I come in?'

What was he up to now? She suddenly realised: naked in a kitchen bath, miles from anywhere. She slid down under the foam, her knees rising from the bath like mountains being born. 'What for?'

'Give you a helping hand,' he shouted through the door. 'You need to rinse off in the yard.'

Rinse off in the yard? In this weather? She stared at the door, willing it not to open. 'I can manage, thanks.'

She heard his footsteps recede and then stood up and stepped out of the bath to lift the pans off the range. She put them both by the bath, hoisting one above her head. It was heavy, and she spilled most of it over the flags. It was barely tepid, and she gasped at the sudden cold. She poured the second pan over herself and darted, shivering, for the towels.

They had been warmed by the range, and as she wrapped herself in them, she remembered how her father used to bath her and her sister, being rubbed to a glowing pink and then wrapped together in the one towel. Peas in a pod, he used to say. She smiled. A lifetime ago.

She mopped up the puddles on the floor and washed her underclothes in the bathwater. It felt good to be so clean; pleasantly tired. She wrung her clothes out and hung them over the range, a scuffle of wet footprints, black on the flagstones. The old man came in and helped her drag the bath into the yard and tip the water away.

'Be sure to salt the steps in the morning,' he said. 'This is going to be ice.'

He'd brought her dressing-gown downstairs, and when his back was turned, she slipped into it, draping a towel over her head. Her arms were aching, and she winced once or twice as she rubbed her hair dry.

He noticed. 'I can ease some of that pain if you want.' He held his arms out, fingers spread like a goalkeeper's.

She hesitated. 'No, thank you.'

'What are you afraid of?'

She looked at him from under the towel. It was a straight question – not a challenge, not a taunt. Yes – what *am* I afraid of? She relaxed. 'Thank you, I'd like that.'

She sat at the table and tied the towel round her head while he stood behind her. Putting one arm round her neck so that it supported her head, he began to knead the muscles at the base of her neck. 'Relax.'

His touch was seductive, and she closed her eyes. It was strong, nearly too painful, but good – he'd done this before. She felt her muscles opening to him and slowly leant forward until her turbaned head rested on the table.

He was massaging her shoulders, squeezing the bare flesh between powerful fingers, easing the aches away. He worked down her back, through the towelling dressing-gown.

She wanted more but he placed a flat hand against her back. 'Sit up.'

Much gentler now, he massaged the base of her neck, her temple and the bridge of her nose. His hands were strong, warm against her skin. Her skin stretched like rubber beneath his fingers. She let out a little moan of pleasure. His voice came from behind her.

'Such a lovely innocent girl. What happened to you, Kate?'

The towel had fallen from her head and he was massaging her scalp. Below the impassive surface of her face flickered a sign of having registered his question, but she made no reply.

Very gently he began to massage her eyeballs, pressing into their sockets with his fingertips.

'What brought you to this state? What happened to that little girl?'

'No more,' she suddenly said, and his fingers left her as if they'd never been there. He draped the towel around her shoulders and sat down opposite her.

She observed him calmly for a moment before she spoke.

It was the same story. She, too, had been innocent and flawed once. The world had been her oyster and she its pearl and everything had been well. Once.

And, of course, with time she saw there was sickness and pain in the world. She saw that pain came from people and the mistakes they made and she vowed she was going to be different. She wasn't going to make the same mistakes.

But it had started. Not overnight, but with the passing years there came a creeping, insidious cynicism. Ideals were mocked, suspicion was learnt and it all began to go wrong, until she found herself, one of the people she despised.

And now? Now she was thirty-four and her life was looking as though it was a failure. Alone, with a life to live: she had set her course and it was headlong into chaos.

She paused in her narration and pulled the towel closer around her. She spoke slowly, tiredly.

'I lied to you. I'm not really here on holiday. I'm . . . well, I had to leave England in a hurry, and I don't suppose I've got a job to go back to.'

She couldn't meet his eyes. 'I said my father was Irish – that's not true either. Nor . . . ' she sighed, 'I feel so stupid but my name's not Katarina. God knows why I told you that. It's just plain Kathrine.'

She rested her head in her hands. 'I'm sorry.'

'Thank you for telling me.' He gently pulled her hands away from her face. 'What is it you want from life, Kate?'

'I don't know. I don't even know what I think.'

He turned in his chair and took a pencil and some paper out of the dresser drawer. He put them in front of her.

'You have five minutes,' he said. 'Write down what you want. Any order, anything, no matter how far-fetched you think it is.'

She picked up the pencil, studied it for a moment, and then began to write. When she paused he told her to add to the list, until after five minutes she'd filled one side of the paper.

He asked her to read the list aloud.

She frowned at the paper and reluctantly started reading.

'Someone to love, marry and have children with. Satisfaction. I want to like myself. I want other people to like me. I want to be more confident, stronger, more assertive, clear-headed. I want more real friends. To be more accepting, less critical. To be myself. More committed. Less changeable.'

He smiled when she had finished. 'Not bad for someone who doesn't know what she wants.'

She laid the paper on the table. 'So what?'

'So now you know that at least you're not dead – there's still some life in yourself.'

He got up and went to the door. 'Oh, and any or all of those things can come true.' He winked at her and then walked out.

She looked blankly after him, and then carefully folded the paper and put it on the table.

So this is nearly a week's work, she thought, flicking the corner of the sheet. A shopping list of the things I want.

She looked up at the door. He'd changed: friendlier, more familiar, as though he was preparing to let her into a secret.

There *was* something – not just this piece of paper. She couldn't pin it down, but it was a feeling. A feeling that, after all these years, she was finally taking herself in hand. She was right in sensing something momentous in what they were engaged in. They were working at ground level, building or destroying – she wasn't sure yet – the very basis of her existence.

This was something big. Something that, now she thought about it, her life seemed to have been inexorably heading towards: the showdown.

ELEVEN

Another day. One more ticked off, torn out and discarded like a page from a calendar. One day away from the beginning, one day closer to the end.

He allowed her to stay in bed, dozing with the blankets over her head until a persistent headache forced her to get up. She struggled into her clothes under the blankets and reluctantly hauled herself out of bed. It was getting colder: the aching, deep cold of a Scandinavian winter. She poked at the ashes in the grate, but the fire was dead, a little puff of ash rising like smoke when she riddled it.

She pulled aside the curtains and looked out. Wouldn't it ever stop snowing? The landscape was losing all its features: walls indistinct ridges; trees half-buried, ridiculously stumpy on short trunks, their boughs heavy with apparent plum blossom.

It seemed as if a vast advancing glacier had swallowed up the house; it only remained for it to entirely cover the building and they would be deep frozen for an entire ice age. Like mammoths, Kate thought wryly. She went downstairs to get some water for washing.

There was little to do that day other than talk. He no longer wanted her to dig the path, and after she'd lugged in a basket of peat bricks, he asked her to sit down at the kitchen table.

She waited for him to speak first; the headache was still nagging her, and she felt restless: suffocated by the thought of all that snow.

'Tell me about yourself, Kate.'

It surprised her: he'd shown little interest in her past up till now. She flicked her cigarette pack with her nails. She wanted to talk, but about anything except herself.

'Do I have to?'

'You're a big girl now, Kathrine.' Her head jerked up at the use of her childhood name, but he pretended not to notice. 'You don't *have* to do anything.'

She thought about it for a moment. 'Where shall I start?'

'At the beginning?'

She narrated the story of her life dispassionately: a well-rehearsed curriculum vitae. Born in Paris; she told him how as a young girl she'd moved from European capital to European capital with a sister, mother and minor diplomat father. How, when her mother had died, she and Mary, her sister, were looked after by a moustachioed Spanish nanny called Carmen. She told him about how lonely she was at boarding school in Kent; how she had tried to run away to see the grandparents she didn't know. A brief spell in a London squat – a poor little rich girl slumming it up as a flower child – and then off to a finishing school in Geneva. Back to Paris where she found and married a blond, blue-eyed gym instructor who, it turned out after two years of abuse and beatings, was gay. She divorced him, Jacques, and went to England. Art college for four years, and then the National Gallery as a picture restorer. Six years it would be, next spring.

'And that's just about it.'

The whole story had taken less than five minutes, and the old man had observed her as detachedly as if it was a television programme he was watching.

She waited for him to say something.

'Tell me more about your mother,' he said at last.

She stiffened. 'Don't try and psychoanalyse me – it doesn't work. Yes – ' she said to his raised eyebrow ' – I've spent my time on the couch, wasting my father's money on some Freudian, neo-Reichian, Jungian bullshitter—' She was angry now. 'And it doesn't work.'

He nodded slowly, showing no emotion at her sudden outburst. 'So, tell me about your mother.'

She frowned. 'It's not a pretty story,' she warned.

He waited for her to begin.

She took a cigarette out of the pack and lit it.

'I don't know if she was an alcoholic, I was too young when she died.' She crushed the burnt end of the match on the tabletop. 'I know she was unhappy, married to the wrong man.'

She stalled and the old man prompted her. 'How did she die?'

'She had a brain tumour,' she said matter-of-factly.

'And it killed her?'

'She committed suicide.'

He nodded, and she continued.

'I felt guilty for years about it – I thought I'd killed her, you see. She was a bitch – she hated my father and I adored him. He was this handsome stranger to me, appearing every month or so loaded with gifts and limitless patience. She didn't have anything with him – she'd married above herself, and resented our relationship like hell.' She inhaled the smoke deeply. 'Of course I got the brunt of all her neurotic Norwegian jealousy. She was a lousy mother, and I hated her. She used to spend days in bed when Papa was away, leaving me and Mary – six and four we were when she died – to fend for ourselves.'

The old man reached behind him and took an ashtray off the dresser. He pushed it across the table to her.

'She used to drink when she was depressed,' she continued, 'and this time she sent me out to buy a bottle of brandy. Courvoisier. She overdosed on pills, but I wasn't to know that – I thought I'd killed the bloody woman. I mean, there was the bottle of brandy, the vomit on the floor – I knew she got ill when she drank the stuff – and her in bed, dead. I didn't get to grips with that until . . . ' She didn't bother finishing the sentence.

'Psychoanalysis?'

'Okay. It helped a bit.' She flicked some ash off the end of her cigarette. 'Anyway – that's it. End of story.'

'If you didn't kill your mother, then what's the truth of it?'

'She was a bad mother, she loved me the best she could. I was jealous because I couldn't marry my father – you know, all the Freudian stuff.'

'So, why are you here?'

'What do you mean?' she said, squinting against the smoke.

'What are you running away from?'

'Why have I got to be running away?'

'What was it you said? I had to leave England in a hurry?'

She played with the ash in the ashtray, deciding whether to tell him or not. She stubbed the half-smoked cigarette out. 'Okay. I'll tell you. I had this lover – Paul. He was a painter.' She picked at a piece of fluff on her sleeve. Her eyes flicked up at him and then down to the table.

'He was good – as a painter, I mean. At least that's what the critics said. Modern art's not my field. I don't really know . . . ' She trailed off.

She took out another cigarette. 'He loved his painting, more than anything else in the world. He'd get so excited when one was going well, and so depressed when it wasn't.' She smiled at the memory.

'He was an impossible show-off at his exhibitions – he'd nearly always get drunk and when he sold a painting we'd go and celebrate. They were horribly expensive – he only had to sell a handful a year to get by. So it would be champagne, an expensive meal.' Unaware of what she was doing, she started unravelling the paper of the cigarette, spilling crumbs of tobacco on the table.

'He was generous – ridiculously so. He'd spend a hundred pounds on a couple of grammes of coke and then just give it away.'

She smiled at the old man. 'Cocaine,' she explained. Her eyes slid down his body to the table.

'He *was* kind. He *was*.'

She scooped the tobacco up and dumped it in the ashtray. Her nostrils flared as she tried to keep her tears back. 'I hate myself.'

There was a pause.

'What happened?' he asked gently.

She looked straight into the old man's face, her vision blurred with tears. 'He cheated on me. He *cheated* on me!'

She fumbled for a tissue. 'He was seeing someone else. For months. Behind my back!' She appealed to the old man, shaking her head in disbelief.

She tore the paper tissue. 'Bastard! So I hit him where it hurts.' She clenched the tears back. 'I destroyed all his paintings. I went to his studio – took a knife and slashed every painting of his I could find.'

She shaded her eyes with her hand. 'Everything.'

He said nothing, and she looked between her fingers at him. 'Give it up, Kate.'

'What?'

'Holding on to all that anger and resentment.'

'Why the bloody hell should I? He did it to hurt me! She was a tart!'

'Give it up – it's stinking up the kitchen.'

'Get off my back!'

His face remained blank. 'Going to carry it around for the rest of your life, are you?'

'That's *my* business if I do.'

'Paul's too. He has the proof of that on his studio floor.'

She jerked her head aside as if she'd been slapped.

'What do you want to do now?' he asked.

'I want to scream my fucking head off!'

He got up and went to the door and opened it. He breathed in the cold air and then turned to her. 'James lives a couple of miles away and he's the closest.' He indicated the doorway. 'It's all yours. Scream for all you're worth, Kate.'

'You're not serious?'

'I mean it. If you're going to start living your life free of your past, you'd better start learning to scream when your body tells you to.'

She was nervous now, her anger gone. 'I couldn't,' she smiled.

He gave the slightest jerk of his head, a whole sentence of contempt in that gesture.

'I couldn't,' she repeated.

'How old are you now?'

'Thirty-f—'

'You know what I mean.'

'Six?'

'So, what's it to be, Kate? A little girl or a woman?'

She pushed herself to her feet, finding herself standing next to him in the doorway. The snow was unmarked, bright to her eyes. 'I don't want you to listen.'

'I'll be in the front room,' he said. 'Give it at least ten minutes. All you've got, Kate. All that anger about your mother, about Paul.'

It was difficult to start. She felt naked, exposed in all that whiteness. Several times she had her hand on the latch to go back in, but something made her stay outside. She wasn't going to live with it any more. It was too painful. It had to go.

Her first attempt petered out in seconds, weak-voiced, pathetic. Then something snapped. She began shouting, her throat open, shouting at the sky. Then she screamed. It frightened her and she stopped herself, but again the anger welled.

'Fucking bastarrrrrrd!'

Who? She didn't know. Everybody. Everybody who had hurt her, deserted her. Again and again and again, she screamed the same words. She began thrashing at the snow, kicking wildly. She fell, wrestling with her anger, snarling, barking. Her energy was amazing, animal. Every time she thought her anger had burned out, there was more, and she began again, screaming as though she was vomiting an unending stream of puke, spewing demons that had lived inside her for years. She screamed until her voice was hoarse, and the rage had gone. She lay on her back in the snow, exhausted, staring blindly at the blank sky.

TWELVE

She balled up an old newspaper, stuffing it into the grate, and laid a little wigwam of kindling over it. She tried several times to light it, but the paper had been screwed too tight and it wouldn't burn. She stabbed at it with the fire tongs and then tried again. The paper caught this time. Her hands were shaking as she watched the orange flames flicking around the wood.

It had scared Kate, the rage that had possessed her. It was like madness, to be that out of control. For those minutes she had been insane, actually insane, capable of doing anything: murder, anything.

She pushed a piece of kindling into the centre of the fire, the flames licking her finger for a second. It was hitting her now, the shock. She crouched by the grate, shaking. It had been hideous, a nightmare, a screaming nightmare, but something had happened, a release of something. She felt so real, so alive.

She kicked off her shoes and fell on to the bed. She was still shivering, and tugged the counterpane round her. Now what? The old man had suggested lunch, but she'd turned it down. She'd felt exhausted and nauseous when she came back into the kitchen, and went straight to her room. But there was more to come – there had to be. He hadn't said anything when she saw him, but this wasn't it: she wasn't through to the other side yet.

Suddenly an image came to her. A hot day, she about five years old, running out into the garden crying. Something to do with a tricycle and her mother. She groped for more detail. That's it – her mother had given it away to a neighbour, and she hadn't even asked me. The tricycle Papa gave me.

What was the girl's name? Little sneak – she'd told Miss
Barnett how I used to peel chewing gum off the streets and
eat it. Anna, that's it.

As though a door had been unlocked, sudden flashes of her
past came to her. Faces, people she hadn't seen for years: Rosi,
her school friend; the owner of the newsagent's near her flat
in London; the neighbour's daughter who wore a neck brace.
It was all there, like an unedited home movie of the random
moments of her life: the significant and the trivial given equal
time, all recorded in the minutest detail.

She remembered carving the name of her first boyfriend,
Pieter, into the soft wood of her desk at school. She remembered falling and grazing her knee on her way to a birthday
party. Learning the word 'fragile'. How she used to say
'die–nasty' for dynasty.

Where had all this useless information been stored? Normally
she couldn't even remember her own telephone number, but
here, suddenly, was her friend Lisbeth's address: Antwerp-
sesteenweg 2192, St Amandsberg 9110, Gent.

She got up and went to the fire, trying to shut off the
uncontrollable playback of memories. It was scary, this instant
perfect recall. She squatted by the grate: the paper had burned
to a black ball, leaving a jumble of scorched kindling. She poked
at it, but there was no flame. Sod it – she stood up and went
to the window. A tune came into her head – Peggy Lee singing
Golden Earrings, harmonies, string section and all.

She huffed against the window, fogging the pane. So cold.
Could it possibly get any colder?

Nothing moved outside. No birds. No sound. This is what the
end of the world would be like, Kate decided. Blank, empty,
silent. Not even the rising smoke of destruction, not even the
echoes of cries. Just nothing.

It was hard to believe that life was continuing as normal in
other places; that people still peopled the planet, that there was
still activity in the world.

She imagined the sea freezing. Thousands of miles of ice joining the continents, the entire world. An ice ball. How long would
it take to walk from here to London? What's Paul doing now?

What would happen if the snow never thawed? How would they survive? She remembered the story she'd read about an air crash in the Andes; the survivors living for months on the flesh of the dead passengers. Who would go first? She or the old man? Would he eat her if she died first? Could she bring herself to eat him if the worst came to the worst? How much meat would there be on him? Not much – and tough and dry probably, like beef jerky – ugh! Where would she start? Perhaps on the calves, then arms, thighs, belly. What wouldn't she eat? Buttocks? Perhaps. Head? No way – that would have to be buried in the snow. Feet and hands would be good in a stew. Penis? She laughed aloud. How would you eat penis? Fried, sliced and skewered on a stick like a kebab. Perhaps in a sausage roll. But of course – there are the chickens and goat. They'd last a while. And the cat too. That would go last. But it would have to be shared with the old man so it wouldn't last so long.

She rubbed her eyes with her knuckles and looked out at the garden. Its boundary was completely hidden and she tried to remember where it lay. Somewhere under that snow was frozen earth and frozen plants. How could they live through this? Did there used to be a flower-bed along the path? Or was it along the wall?

December 14th
I got the summons today – a court appearance set for the 20th. The copper said they wanted to get it out of the way quick, make way for the Christmas rush. It was the same policeman that came round to arrest me. I thought it was nice they sent the same one – it's more personal. He was quite pleasant about it – a bit embarrassed if anything – he couldn't have been much more than 20. The whole thing has been quite civilised really – they had to take me to the police station, arrest me and all that stuff, but it was quite nicely done. Paul had to be there though, to make a statement and say that he wanted to prosecute me. He was livid – a couple of coppers stood ready to pounce on him – he did *look dangerous.*

'God, it's cold!'

Her toes were leaden, and she stamped her feet to get the blood circulating. How was it that amputees felt sensation in limbs they didn't have? What was it called? Ghost pain?

Stomach's tight, what is it – period? What's the date? 19th, 20th? About time. Damn!

Period. Full stop. Fool stop. Fool's cap. Why was that? Why call paper fool's cap, not as she used to think, full scap? Scap – strange word. Of course, strange, she smiled, I invented it. Coxcomb – that's the word. Like Capsicum. Catacomb. Where do words come from? People just making them up. Oh God, stop thinking.

She spun round. Had someone just come into the room? No. She watched the door: it was as real as if he was standing there: the old man, his green corduroy trousers, threadbare and shapeless. That square peasant's head and lopsided look. She could smell him. She'd never been able to pin it down – it was a mix of pipe tobacco and something else; some mysterious old-man smell like aniseed or liquorice or something.

She turned back to the window, returning the blankness of the snow with her stare. She was here, now. This pressure, this suffocating closeness of objects, two-dimensional. She suddenly felt sick. Dizzy. She steadied herself against the sill.

She gazed at her ghostly reflection in the window-pane. She started shaking again; she couldn't stop it, her teeth chattering. 'Stop, please.'

Then it began: the feeling she used to dread as a child. Sometimes on the verge of sleep she would feel unaccountably huge; her body ten feet tall, her arms and legs like logs; the distance between objects, vast gulfs. A giant in a giant's world. She closed her eyes.

I've got to make a move – do something. Get some air.

She groped her way out of the room like a drunk. The old man met her at the bottom of the stairs.

'How are you doing, Kate?'

She stared blankly at him, swaying.

'Come and sit down.'

'No. I've got to go out.' Her voice was still hoarse from the shouting. He followed her to the kitchen door, watching her. She stepped carefully, precisely, as though she was afraid that if she fell over she would shatter like glass.

The path was now a knee-high trench. She paused to listen, but the air was still and no sound reached her. She crunched through the snow, amazed at the sensation through her boots. The cold air stung her cheeks, making her skin tingle, like tiny electric shocks. Finding herself at the outhouse, she looked in at the goat. It looked surprisingly cosy on its straw bed and the chickens were quiet – roosting, their feathers ruffled up as though they were wearing coats and scarves. Kate laughed at them, drunk.

She peed, sitting on her hands to cushion herself against the cold toilet seat, stood up and tugged the string to flush the toilet. Nothing happened. She tugged harder and it snapped. She looked at the length of string in her hand, confused.

He was in the garden, waiting for her, and guided her back to the house. He took the string from her and ushered her to a chair and sat her down.

'What's happening?'

She was frightened now. 'I don't know. I feel really weird. Spaced out.'

'You're doing fine, Kate.' He sat opposite her, watching her closely. 'You're safe.'

'I'm scared,' she whispered hoarsely.

'I know.'

She looked into his face, suddenly desperate. 'It *hurts*.'

'I know.'

Her face was haggard, taut with grief. She glanced at the range and started to get up, but he held her sleeve. 'Let's press this a bit further.' He nodded encouragingly, and she relaxed in her chair.

He waited, the only sound in the kitchen the subdued bubbling of the pot on the stove.

'All those paintings,' she said at last. 'It would have destroyed him.' She delicately pressed the tip of her little finger into the corner of her eye, stemming the tear that formed.

'Just let it go, Kate.'

A sob escaped her, tears springing to her eyes. She abruptly pushed herself to her feet, scraping her chair noisily on the floor. She strode to the stove, peering into the pot. 'So, what's for lunch?'

'Just let it go,' he repeated gently.

For a second she made no sound, her back to him, and then she began to cry.

'I'm sorry, Paul. Oh God, I'm sorry, sorry, sorry.'

She cried childishly, distraughtly, her hands hanging limply by her sides. The old man stood up and held her from behind and she sagged into his arms. She could hold it back no longer and she wept, abandoning herself to the surge of grief; weeping for the pain and the confusion and the sorrow.

THIRTEEN

'Katie?'

She lowered her pen and looked up. Gabrielle was standing in the doorway, drying her hands on a tea-towel. 'Shall you be wanting a cup of tea?'

Kate smiled up at her. 'Thanks, but easy on the sugar, please. I could almost stand a spoon in it last time.'

'But you need the energy, my dear – you're so thin.'

The old woman went back into the kitchen and Kate closed her diary. She tired easily after her illness. This was only her second day out of bed, and she still couldn't stand for very long.

She sat back in the chair, thinking about the old man's sister. Gabrielle had arrived somewhere in the middle of Kate's illness; had just turned up one day and taken over from the old man. At first, in her feverish state, Kate had thought she was a nurse come to look after her. Physically, she seemed to be quite unlike her brother: small-boned and fragile-looking; their accents were quite different too: he sounded almost English compared to her Cork lilt. But now Kate was getting to know her, she could see some similarities: there was a likeness about the brows, the same precise movements. She said she was older than her brother, though her age was impossible to tell. Probably older than she looked: Kate noticed a slight tremor in her hands when she returned with the tea tray.

Kate put the diary on the table beside her. 'Where's Michael?'

She felt strange saying his name: it still didn't come naturally. His sister called him 'Mihool' – when Kate first heard it she wondered who she was talking about.

Gabrielle poured out the tea. 'Gone to Westport he has – to see about your car. You went on about it so much when you were ill, and you made him promise to go and see it as soon as he could.' She smiled, nudging the teacup across the tray to Kate. 'You really did go on.'

'I don't remember anything about that.'

'Well, you're bound to forget – you were so ill. Our hearts were scalded for you, so they were.'

Kate was only just beginning to realise how ill she'd been. Christmas and the New Year had passed unnoticed – it was the third week of January now, over a month since she'd left England. She vaguely remembered the doctor coming somewhere in the middle of it; having no idea what was causing her temperature, but prescribing pills anyway. The old man had thrown them away as soon as the doctor had left. Gabrielle had mentioned something about being 'purged' by illness – pills would only get in the way.

Kate sipped her tea, wincing at its sweetness.

'I'm afraid you haven't had much of a holiday here,' the old man's sister said. 'Michéal said that before I came you –' She smiled shyly. 'Well, you were a little troubled.'

Her face wrinkled in concern. 'I hope he wasn't too hard on you – yerman can be a bit too strong at times. I'm sorry if he upset you.' She leant over and touched Kate on the knee. Kate had the impression Gabrielle was keeping her brother away from her: she'd seen little of him in the last four weeks: he'd occasionally come and sat with her, keeping her company as she lay in bed, but they'd hardly spoken since the day she fell ill.

'Michéal is a good man, but he doesn't know when to call a stop. He may look like a tyrant, but he's soft as butter really. He always was – he was the dreamer in the family, the one with the ideals. Our dad said he had both feet planted firmly in the air, and horizons in his eyes.'

They both laughed.

'Tell me about him, Gabrielle.'

'Well,' the older woman began, 'he was the youngest. Women never stopped having children in those days – ten, fifteen wasn't unusual. We were seven, nine really, but two little ones died before they reached a birthday. Seven children and Mam and Dad – nine of us packed into this little house. The two eldest boys in one bed, us four girls in another and Michéal in a cot. And we thought nothing of it – can you believe it?

'Then the Great War came. Our dad hated the English – a real Republican he was, and when the two boys went off to fight with the Brits he swore he'd never forgive them. And the poor man lived to regret that, because they never came back. Both of them killed in France, they were.'

She gazed out of the window for a moment. 'Then the next year Mam died in the flu epidemic, leaving us a ship without a rudder. So us four girls took over – looking after the farm and the old fella. I must have been eight or so, and do you think I ever went to school? In between cutting the peat and shearing the sheep I did – one day a week if I was lucky.

'We lived in this house, the six of us, until our dad died. That was in 1923 – the poor stupid man. He'd avoided mass slaughter in Europe and then blew himself up in his own back yard making bombs for the cause.'

'The cause?'

'The IRA. Oh yes, quite a hero, and some fine speeches were made at his wake for all the good it did us children. They paid for the funeral and made sure we never went without, but they couldn't replace the father we lost.'

She paused, lost in thought. 'It hit Michéal bad – first one parent, then the other. He grew up strange – slow to learn, moody, a little wild. Anyway, by that time Brenda, the oldest, had gone off and got wed, so it was up to Kathleen to take over. She found a man and married him and brought him back here. And that's where Michéal stayed till he was eighteen or so.'

Kate was interested in finding out more about the old man, but oddly, his sister seemed to know little of what he'd done after he had left the cottage. She knew he had studied for a while in Galway, and then gone to England. He had stayed for a few years in Paris with what Gabrielle called the 'painting set', and then went to Spain. The next time she saw him was in 1939. She hardly recognised him when they met, not only because of the years he'd aged, and his emaciated, haunted look, but because half of his face was swathed in bandages. He'd been wounded in the eye, fighting for the Republicans in the Spanish Civil War.

'That was Micheál all over – forever fighting other people's battles.

'So,' she continued, 'he came back here and Kathleen looked after him till he was well. She moved out not long after – it was Micheál's home by rights – he was the only son left alive, and Kathleen needed a bigger place for her family.'

She put down her forgotten cup of tea. 'It was a sore time for Micheál, the war years – stuck out here trying to manage the farm on his own. And then Ann came along and made things . . . well, she was hardly a settling influence.'

She saw Kate's enquiring look. 'He didn't tell you about her – about his wife? No, I don't suppose he did.' She looked at the door as though expecting him to walk in. 'She was hardly a conventional woman, was Ann. She ruled this place, *and* yerman's heart. I never really knew what he saw in the woman, but—' She glanced up at the portrait of his wife above the fireplace.

'Instead of settling the man down, marriage stirred him up something awful. He took to the drink and the farm started to fall to pieces. He left her – Ann – more than once. 1943 it was, and then my husband goes and gets drowned in the bay. There I was, thirty-three years of age – five children, no husband and no money. So, God bless him, Micheál took us all in. Truth be told, yerman needed to surround himself with women – especially women who would mother him. After all, he'd grown up with four of us sisters. And Ann wasn't exactly . . . Well,' she brushed the thought away. 'He saw himself as the great patriarch. He always felt at home in a big family, and with my Edward gone he had one ready-made. So, though it meant living like sardines in a can, I brought my lot here.'

'Didn't they ever have children?'

Gabrielle looked up again at the painting of Ann. She was about to say something, but checked herself. 'No, they never had any, and a great shame it was too.'

Kate watched her as she smoothed her apron thoughtfully. She had the same hands as her brother: long fingers; knuckles just a little arthritic.

'Michéal was never one for too much domesticity, though. He had the O'Briens' passion – hobble him for too long and he'd start to kick. In the early days he'd disappear for days on end – gone to Dublin on the batter. And back he'd come, shame-faced and laden with presents. And we weren't exactly living on the pig's back, even though he'd got himself a job writing on the paper. No, we were poor – eight mouths to feed and not enough to put in them. I remember him weeping with shame – weeping like a baby because there wasn't enough food for the little ones. Then he'd throw himself into his work, and we wouldn't see him for weeks. Constancy and temperance were not yerman's strong points!'

The daylight was beginning to fail, but neither wanted to break the narrative by pausing to light the lamps, and so they continued to sit, the approaching dusk filling the room.

'He didn't want me to leave, but in '53 or '54, Flann, my eldest, got himself a job in Cork, and the farm was getting too much for me and Ann, so we sold the stock and I went off to live in Cork with the two youngest. It was a relief to Michéal, I think, when that responsibility was gone and he went wild for a time – drinking and travelling all over, until he lost his job. Then –' she laughed to herself, 'he got it into his head that it was a potter he wanted to be. A potter! Ann was a saint, I'll give her that – she stuck with him, somehow managing to feed the both of them, taking in sewing and the like.'

'But why didn't she leave him?'

Gabrielle was surprised. 'Divorce him? Is that your answer when things don't go your way – throw everything in? Anyway – she loved him.'

'But he was so irresponsible!'

'He was that. And kind, clever and honest. Funny and wild, too. I know it doesn't agree with your modern views, but then the woman's job was to support the man – to be his rock.'

She paused and looked towards the window, her eyes glistening in the last of the daylight. 'Michéal has not been like other men. Brother of mine though he is, he's altogether a remarkable man.' The voice coming from the shadows had become lyrical and powerful as she chose her words carefully.

'Let me tell you. Micheál founded a newspaper union and wrote for the papers what he thought and divil the difference. He stood for the Dáil. Had famous – yes, *famous* friends. He sang like an angel and drank like a demon. Swore and fought against corruption and evil wherever he found it. He loved my children like his own, educating them himself. He loved his wife and never raised a hand to her, which is more than many a husband can say. He was a *man* – at least in my book.' The voice was agitated, almost irritable, and she paused before she spoke again. 'An old-world man perhaps, but the greatest man I've ever known.'

They sat in the darkness, each thinking their separate thoughts: Gabrielle of her dead husband, Kate of her father and sister.

'I'll be getting on and making supper,' Gabrielle said briskly, getting up. She lit the lamps before she went, and Kate thought she noticed the glimmer of unshed tears in her eyes.

FOURTEEN

Michael came home later that evening when Kate was already asleep. He'd driven the car back from Westport, cross-country by the look of it, and had left it in front of the house slowly sinking up to its hubcaps in the marsh. Gabrielle accused him later of having been drinking, but Michael blamed his unfamiliarity with the car, not the drop or two he'd taken in town.

He spent the next morning with sacking and planking, coaxing the car out of its soggy trap on to dry land. Kate stayed in bed for as long as she could bear, listening with mounting concern to the whine of the tortured engine and the whizz of the spinning wheels. The noise finally drove her out of bed, and she was just in time to see the triumphant emergence of the car from the muddy grip of the marsh. As soon as its tyres bit on substance, the yellow sports car leapt angrily towards the house, and was only pulled up a few feet short of entering the kitchen by the window.

In possession of her car again Kate decided, if the old man would drive, to go into Westport to make some phone calls. She'd been fretting about getting in touch with her father and Mary, her sister, to let them know where she was, and to ask a friend to look after her flat in north London. The cats were all right: she'd left them at Mary's before she left, and they'd be looked after till she got back, but she'd left in a hurry, and the electricity and gas were still connected. And – she remembered with a sudden surge of blood to her face – she hadn't cancelled the milk! She'd been away over a month. She imagined thirty bottles of milk clustering around her door as though asking to be let in. Surely the milkman would have stopped delivering after a day or two?

The fuss and tangle of a complicated life – she'd almost forgotten what it was like to be free of the ball of string that knotted itself around her ankles. Sod it – don't go into town, she told herself. Let the food rot in the fridge, let burglars steal the telly – all the plants would be dead by now, anyway.

This was as much what she was escaping from as the whole ghastly Paul affair: the dirty washing in the laundry basket, the dripping tap that needed a washer, the damp patch coming through the hall ceiling.

Was any of it worth it? she wondered. The scramble for a mortgage, a good job, a good lover – the desperate race to get, get, get. She looked out of the window and watched Michael and his sister washing down the car. Such a simple life they led: uncluttered, basic, sane. That was the word – sane. There was something in both of them: a sense of purpose – or rather a not-questioning. Taking life as it came. They had taken on this world and it was a perfect fit.

And the glittering prizes? Are they worth the struggle? Have they any meaning? Not here, not for these two. How much simpler it would be, to be old, she thought.

Michael and Gabrielle moved out of sight and she heard the kitchen door open and them come in.

They were a quaint couple, Kate thought. Obviously brother and sister; their relationship had that unmistakable familiarity, unlike husband and wife: an understanding of having come from the same womb. Even though both were white-haired, it was easy to see the youth in each: the maternal older sister; the awkward, proud brother. Gabrielle treated him with a sort of offhand respect, though in conversation together she was the dominant one. Michael was boyish and good-humoured in her company, but almost wary of her sharp tongue, and usually the first to acquiesce in any minor disputes. Their love for each other was touching and obvious.

She decided to go to town – it had to be done. Then come back and stay until she had the strength to go back and face the music. Not yet, not yet, she told herself. But soon.

The following weeks saw Kate back to full health. By mid-February her weight had returned to near-normal, and apart from her slightly pallid complexion, there were no signs that she'd recently been so ill.

Gabrielle stayed with them throughout this time, taking over much of the household duties and joining them on their daily walks. With each passing day the distance Kate could walk increased from a shaky hundred yards being supported by Michael, to fifeen minutes round the house with a walking-stick, to – after a month – a four-mile round trip to the O'Neills' and back.

As spring slowly heaved itself out of the fallow winter land, so Kate's strength and resolve grew. She felt as if she'd passed from some dark place through the gateways of her illness: passed into a world of infinite possibility. The future was no longer inevitable – nothing was inevitable. She couldn't look at her life beyond leaving here: the prospect of facing Paul, dealing with the police, was still too huge and frightening, but she had a sense that, whatever had gone before, the future was as yet untouched.

FIFTEEN

She pushed the letter across the kitchen table to him.

'I knew he wouldn't forgive me.'

The old man reached behind him for his reading-glasses and read through the letter quickly. 'May you rot in hell?'

'He gets religious when he's angry.' She took the letter back and looked at it sadly. 'He'll never forgive me.'

'The point in writing wasn't to unburden him, but to unburden yourself. All we can hope is that he doesn't carry that poison around for too long.'

'So, what do I do now? Go to the police? I jumped bail, don't forget.'

She gazed out of the window, squinting her eyes against the light. It was the second week of March; green and wet and chilly. Gabrielle had left two weeks earlier and with her departure, so, too, went Kate's privileged status of invalid.

'What do you think they'll do to me?'

'Probably less than you're doing to yourself – unless the English police are still using torture.'

She frowned. 'I can't go back. I'm terrified!'

'Can't or won't?'

They'd been busy since the old man's sister had left, and Kate had welcomed the activity – anything to take her mind off the future. They'd spring-cleaned: swept, dusted and aired all the rooms, scrubbed every floor, whitewashed the kitchen walls and mucked out the animals.

Throughout all this, no mention was made of her return to England. She didn't want to break the spell of silence that filled their days, and he seemed happy to have her there. But then he had suggested she write to Paul – and this was the result; a half-page of angry scrawl. She looked closely at the page. The paper had scuffed in places where he'd dug the pen nib in.

He'd never forgive her, and she couldn't blame him. He was right – it was as though she'd committed murder. Not a clean crime; not justifiable homicide. No – it was perverted, obscene: a child murder, a sex killing.

He was violent, and that scared her, but she'd try to see him if she thought there was any chance of him understanding why she had done it. But he wouldn't – she knew that. He had tried and convicted her in her absence, and her punishment was a life sentence of hate. She had hurt him too deeply for the crime to be expiated by anything else. His punishment was going to be in never forgiving her.

If he wouldn't absolve her, then the police would have to. She'd have to go back and face them; somehow get the courage to take that step.

Michael had spent a lot of time in his studio during the last couple of weeks, glazing and firing stuff for the St Patrick's Day fair in Galway city. I'll think about going after that, she told herself – some time next week.

Kate hated fairs, but she agreed to drive him there and give him a hand with his pots. They packed the pottery in a tea chest and jammed it in the back seat of the MG. The sunroof had to be let down to fit it in and they drove the forty or so miles to Galway, the wind catching at their clothes.

The Galway fair came in two parts: business and entertainment. The centre of town was given over to a cattle and sheep market. Their destination, the funfair, was on the outskirts. It was a public holiday and the streets were crowded with people and animals. The pedestrians ignored the traffic which tried to thread its way through them – this was their day: the people's day. It was a time for the farmers of the outlying villages and crofts to renew bonds, catch up on gossip, and do some hard bargaining and serious drinking. The farmers, red-faced and dog-eared men, arrived early with their livestock: sheep crammed into the back of Land-Rovers, cattle trucks packed with lowing, frightened cows. By nine o'clock the town was already reeking from the pools of curry-coloured cowshit that covered the streets and pavements.

Michael and Kate stopped the car to look at the goings-on. Barely past breakfast-time and the pubs were as packed as on a Saturday night; lines of Guinness queuing up on the counter; men, shoulder-to-shoulder, gulping down pints – cementing a deal, considering an offer, giving advice.

It was a leisurely affair, this buying and selling. No deal was hastily done, not like the big cattle markets with their rattling auctioneers. This was personal, measured. Time was the thing: time was free, and the prospective buyer could afford to spend it, wearing down his opponent and the price with affected disinterest. They would pull back the lips of donkeys to look at their teeth, tut knowingly, nimbly step aside to avoid a kicking horse, feel flanks of cows with an expert touch, pat hides, pull tails and ears, argue, walk away, return, and eventually exchange money. It hadn't changed for years: it was a tradition as ancient and earthy as the Gaelic some of them spoke.

They drove to the fairground and parked the car. Nothing much was happening yet. It looked desolate and dismal; the fairground rides like architectural skeletons against the lowering sky. They carried the tea chest to the huge marquee and found their stall.

Michael introduced Oliver, an agitated young man with a pasty face and weak moustache who was in charge of the stall Michael was going to share with several other local artists. It was already half-full and Oliver was in a mild panic: there wasn't enough space, he had no spare change, nowhere to keep the takings. The old man listened patiently, and with a few quiet suggestions put him at his ease. Kate watched them as she unpacked the pots. He looked the picture of gentleness: the indulgent grandfather, no hint of the severity he'd shown her. True, he *had* lightened up since her illness, but there was still something – a steeliness under his soft exterior. She was more at ease with him, enjoying his company now. But she was still a little wary – she couldn't forget how he'd been before.

Kate would have been happy to have stayed with Oliver and helped – it was peaceful inside the marquee, with its smell of freshly trodden grass and the light mellow through the canvas. But this was a funfair, Michael said, and fun is what they'd come for.

He was like a child. She couldn't believe it: he wanted to try everything. The coconut shy, tossing hoops over bottles of whiskey, the bran tub. He had a go on the rifle range, threw darts at cards and shoved pennies on a table. She trailed after him, declining a go at every stand they came to. It was starting to get more crowded, and the clang and clamour of the rides was beginning to annoy her.

She was about to suggest she went back to the car when he tugged her sleeve and pointed skywards. The Ferris wheel.

'Come on,' he urged her. 'You can't come to a fair and not have a go on the Big Wheel.'

'Oh yes I can. You're not getting me on that thing – look how high it is!' Just looking up at it made her dizzy.

He considered it for a moment. 'It's supposed to be high.'

'But I'm afraid of heights.' More accurately, she was afraid of what she might do in high places. Once on the roof of her Paris apartment she had had an irrational urge to jump off, and since then she'd felt panic every time she was in a high and exposed place.

He didn't budge when she moved off, and she turned to look at him.

'So what, you're afraid?' he asked.

She walked back to him. 'I don't enjoy being scared.'

'I'm not asking you to enjoy it. I'm asking you to have a go on it.'

She recognised the tone in his voice. This was the old Michael, the Michael she'd first met. She hesitated before she answered.

'Why do something I'm afraid of?'

A young boy with an ice-cream forced between them, and she took the chance to turn away, but he took her arm and walked her to the side of a stall where it was quieter. He looked up to the top of the Ferris wheel and then at Kate.

'Indeed. Why do things we're afraid of? It makes sense, does it not?'

Why his sudden interest in getting her on the thing? This was leading up to something – she could sense it.

'But there again,' he continued, 'who wants to live sensibly?'

'Look. I don't want to go on it. I'm scared to death of heights.'

He looked around as if he hadn't heard her. 'True or false?' The question seemed to be directed at a dog which was nuzzling an empty chip bag. He turned to her. 'Does it really matter *what* you feel? I mean – do you see the world taking much notice of your feelings?'

She looked at him. What was it Paul used to say? Go tell it to the stars.

'No, of course it doesn't matter. But I still don't want to go on it.'

' "Wanting to" is a feeling as well.'

She opened her hands in a question.

'We're not just talking about this yoke here,' he said, nodding at the Ferris wheel.

'What then?'

He looked blankly back at her.

'You mean Paul – going back to England?'

'That, and everything else in your life.'

The merry-go-round started up and she had to shout to be heard above the raucous music.

'What are you trying to say?'

'You don't have to do what your feelings tell you.'

'Okay, well, thanks for the lesson.' She frowned at the racket and moved away. He followed her.

'You haven't had it yet. That's where you'll do the learning.' He pointed to the top of the Ferris wheel. She stopped and looked at him. Was he serious? There was a playful look in his eyes, but his mouth was unsmiling.

'And if I don't want the lesson?'

He shrugged.

The panic started when the metal bar was hooked into place across them. Kate was sure she'd slip through the gap, or that she'd lift the bar and throw herself out. Such a little between herself and death. She began gabbling nervously and he held a finger to his lips to silence her. 'Just breathe.'

Without warning they were jerked backwards into the air, the ground beneath them falling away at an alarming rate. In two seconds they were ten feet off the ground, swinging up into space. Kate screwed up her eyes and gripped the bar in front of them as though it was only her willpower keeping them from plummeting to their deaths. Twenty feet, thirty feet – she could feel the chasm opening up beneath her.

She heard his voice close to her ear. 'Don't fight the fear, Kate. Just let it be.'

She found herself shaking, her fingers frozen to the bar.

'Open your eyes and look down,' he said.

As she did so, she felt as though a cord had been pulled through her body, being drawn up from her feet, through her abdomen and out through her mouth, turning her inside out. She realised that the scream she heard was her own; torn from her body. She shuddered as if she was coming: waves of contractions rippling through her.

As they reached the highest point of the arc, she looked down between her feet.

'Don't forget to breathe.'

She gulped down some air. She felt light, her fingers tingling, her senses sharp as a bird's. It wasn't fear any more, but exhilaration. It was like flying.

'You can see so much from up here,' she gasped.

She didn't see his smile. 'The whole world,' he said quietly.

Her legs buckled when she got off and she had to lean on his arm as they walked away.

She turned to look up at the Ferris wheel. 'That,' she said, her face split in two with a smile, 'was amazing!'

As if in acknowledgment, the sun came out briefly from behind the clouds, lighting her hair into a sudden gold. She looked around the fairground as if she had just arrived.

'Come on.' It was her turn now. 'I want to go on something else.'

Something had happened halfway up on that ride. It was as though a weight had been physically lifted off her. Of course she could go back to England. She could be afraid *and* go back. She saw for the first time how much she had allowed fear to govern her. Fear of what? Some unchallenged nightmare, the bottom line: I won't survive. Somehow, by some diabolic alchemy, she had believed, her very being would be swallowed up. If she faced the fear, she would shrivel like a sweet wrapper in an incinerator. But she had survived, plainly, just as everybody else had survived. The question was, at what price? The price of a life worth living?

She threw herself into the enjoyment of the rest of the afternoon. They rode together on the merry-go-round: she on a zebra, him, gleefully, on a sheep. She bought some candyfloss, hated it and gave it to a little girl; tried her luck on the tombola and won a tiny synthetic teddy bear; wrote a message on a gas-filled balloon: there's nothing to be afraid of. She let it go, craning her neck to watch it diminish into a silver speck against the steel-grey sky.

SIXTEEN

'It's yourself!'

He was thrilled, taking her arm with one hand and her bag with the other and steering her into the kitchen.

She shrugged off her jacket and hung it on the back of the door. She smiled at him. He was getting younger every time she saw him. He was wearing a new sap green shirt and he looked spruce and healthy. He was fresh-shaved as well, his jaw shiny and soapy-smelling. She'd hesitated from kissing him when he opened the door but now she leant across the table, kissing him on both cheeks, Continental-style.

Five weeks, she'd been away. She'd had her doubts about coming back to Ireland, but here, in his kitchen, she knew she'd done the right thing. It all seemed to be welcoming her: the familiar black-leaded range, the string of onions hanging in the corner, the wellingtons she'd forgotten.

'You look nice. Expecting company?'

'Well, I was expecting this young lady for tea, but—' He glanced at an imaginary watch on his wrist. 'Seeing as how she's late I think we'll start without her.'

He put the kettle on and watched her as she bent to stroke the cat. 'It's grand to have you back.'

'Thank you.' She was pleased. Touched. 'I'm glad I came.'

Glad but apprehensive: a lot had happened in the last month. She'd dismantled the rest of her London life so quickly it had frightened her. But the England trip had been a success. She hadn't seen Paul, though she'd written to tell him she was back, but the court business had gone well. The trial was a swift, bureaucratic affair. She'd expected wigs and gowns and wooden gavels, but it was an embarrassingly ugly formality.

Criminal damage, the charge. The statement she'd made after her arrest was read out. I don't know how many paintings I slashed, perhaps four or five, the magistrate droned. She'd tried to look serious, but it was too unreal for that. Her private life, her past actions, spilled open in public like this; having this dreary middle-aged man read her own words. I was aware I was breaking bail. He'd paused at that, looking over the top of the paper at her; disapproving. Paul had had the paintings – five of them, it turned out – valued at £5700; over-priced in Kate's eyes, but it was out of her control. She'd half expected to see Paul there, but she'd scanned the place as soon as she'd walked in and he wasn't to be seen.

She was taken into a shiny basement room, photographed, fingerprinted and processed on to the street, a barely legible carbon copy of the outcome in her handbag. Just under six and a half thousand pounds: fine, damages and costs.

She'd put her flat on the market, completing the sale within the month. Her furniture had gone into storage and Mary, her sister, had taken most of the rest of the stuff. Eight years of building up and it had been scattered in just a few weeks. It was a relief, and it scared her.

Michael had made it clear she could come back to the cottage at any time. At first she hadn't even considered it, but as she sought to regain her place in London, and failed, so she found herself thinking more and more about Ireland, about that quiet, cold countryside. She'd returned to London like someone waking from a dream, marvelling that she'd once been part of this anthill. Some of her friends had invited themselves round when they heard she was back, and they spent a dull, gossipy evening together. Nothing had changed. Suzy and Brad had finally split up, Sara had broken her leg skiing, David and Linda were still sniping at each other. It was as though she had stepped out of time – a Rip van Winkle in reverse – ageing ten years in the time it took her friends to drink a cup of coffee.

She looked over at Michael, busy with the tea. The land of doing something about your life? She didn't know about that, but the futility of recasting the thread of her own life was plain.

There was little there: no job, no flat. Her time in London became a wait.

A couple more weeks saw the loose ends tied, and she was ready to return. She packed one suitcase, told nobody except her sister, and sailed one night from Fishguard, watching the lights of the mainland twinkle into obscurity.

Michael plonked the teapot down in front of her and she smiled up at him. He never liked talking and doing, and he wasn't ready for her yet. He rinsed the mugs under the cold tap, and she watched his back. Now she was here, she had no doubt. She'd run to him, and he'd opened his arms. She'd packaged and sealed her past, and here she was in an Irish kitchen, on the threshold of her future. She remembered the time when he had made her step over that broom-handle, committing herself to change. She remembered exactly – it lay across those two flagstones there. One step, and how far had it taken her? How much further?

He sat down opposite her and poured out the tea, and she told him her news. He nodded, the same old Michael. He was interested and he wasn't. He cared and he didn't give a damn.

'Stay for as long as you like.'

She looked doubtfully into his crooked blue eyes. He frowned in response, and she knew he was making fun of her. Everything was going to be all right. She smiled as if it was a present for him.

'Thank you.'

He'd been busy. He'd just fired a recent batch of pottery and the next morning she discovered he'd painted the inside of the privy door. It had always been clean, but the paint on the door had been cracked and lifted through countless severe winters. He'd rubbed it down, and in its place he'd painted what looked like a farmyard scene. Kate studied it as she sat on the toilet: there were two figures, a man and a woman, and several animals: a horse, a cow, two goats and what she took to be chickens. An orange sun and a white crescent moon hung in a starkly blue sky, and under this was a green and yellow patchwork: presumably fields. He hadn't tried to give it perspective: the animals were tiny compared to the people, and the figures seemed to float off the ground – the man and the woman standing at an impossible angle, as though they were flying. Around every object, including the flowers and clouds that made up the border of the painting, was a red aura, so that each thing seemed to inhabit a separate universe of its own. Looking closer, Kate noticed that what she'd taken for cracks in the paint was in fact a complicated network of thin lines connecting each figure, binding each object to the others. She studied it, puzzled. It was like a painting of a myth, but there was something about it she couldn't grasp, some hidden significance.

It was as though she'd never been away. Within twenty-four hours she'd settled back in – her tights hanging above the range to dry, a couple of her books in the bookshelf, the cat sleeping at the foot of the bed.

It rained just about every day for the rest of April, keeping them indoors for much of the time. Kate welcomed it, though: it was cosy in the cottage watching the unending rain lashing the windows; and she enjoyed his company. He never asked her what her future plans were, and she was grateful for that. She'd got a few thousand pounds left from the sale of the flat – there was no hurry to begin working. She didn't know what she wanted to do, and until she knew, she'd be happy to stay with him.

The winter was like a dream to her now. It was hard to believe what she'd been through: the fighting and struggle and that long illness. She hadn't told anybody about Michael. Mary had quizzed her about who she'd been staying with, but she'd given little away. She wanted to keep it secret, untouched by the rest of her life.

The days were long. They were both getting up at dawn, and by nine the chores had just about been done. He did most of the cooking, and left the animals up to Kate. The cat had disappeared one day, but there was still the goat and the chickens. She enjoyed collecting the eggs. She learnt their secret hiding-places: behind the cartwheel, under the spare straw. She felt a bit mean taking their eggs, but Michael explained they wouldn't hatch anyway: there was no cock.

After supper they usually sat together for a while to talk
or listen to music. He'd dug out an old wind-up phonograph
and a stack of opera 78s. She knew nothing about opera,
and he introduced her to his favourites: Caruso, Gigli, John
McCormack. He surprised Kate with his singing voice: an
unexpectedly rich baritone. Sometimes he sang folk songs to
her, some in Gaelic.

They'd taken to painting together: something Kate hadn't
done since art school. He was a clumsy draughtsman, but
inspired. He'd spend half an hour studying a flower, and then
paint it in thirty seconds. She never asked him about the
Giacomettis – they were probably under his bed, gathering
dust, just as they had been for the last fifty years.

It was an unexpectedly fine day, the sky clear of clouds, the
sun promising to be hot. Perfect weather for a picnic. He
suggested they go to the river, do some painting and maybe
have a swim.

It took them an hour or so to reach the river. They walked
along its bank until they found a place by the bend in the river,
a broad bank of yellowish mud like a platform, sheltered by a
screen of hazel scrub. They spread the blanket on the grass and
rested their feet, listening to the water. The river was about
ten feet across, deep and fast-flowing; swaying weed breaking
the surface here and there.

They painted for most of the morning. Michael was fascinated
by the light playing on the water, and used up sheet after sheet.
Kate tried a portrait of him, but when he asked to see it, she
laughed and tore it up.

The sun was hot by midday. The light dappled their bodies
through the canopy of overhead branches. The sky was as blue
as the sea; so blue Kate wanted to dive into it. She was happier
than she could ever remember: the easy silence, the warmth.
It was perfect.

She lay face-down on the blanket and watched him as he
moved about barefoot on the river-bank. He'd rolled his
trousers up and taken his shirt off, and her eyes wandered
over his body. He had a broad chest, a V of curly white hair

tapering to his stomach. Thick strong arms; it was the body of a much younger man. He turned and smiled at her. His hands were covered with mud up to the wrists.

'Have you not discovered mud yet?' he called.

She decided to have a swim. No costume, she'd have to swim in bra and pants. He was busy on the bank and she undressed behind his back. Her skin was white from the winter: this was the first sun she'd had this year. She slipped into the river, gasping at its coldness, and paddled out to the middle, her body blue-white through the water.

It was too cold to stay in for more than a few minutes. The bank was slippery and there were no handholds so he hauled her out, holding on to a branch with one hand. A long piece of river weed had caught around her neck, trailing between her breasts to her belly like a string of emeralds. She crouched in a patch of sunlight and squeezed the water from her hair.

He had made a large puddle on the bank and was scraping mud into it, working it with his fingers until it was soft and pliable like clay. She watched him and then stood up and stretched, enjoying the warmth of the sun on her bare skin. She slid her foot through the mud.

'Did I tell you I studied ballet till I got too tall?'

He sat back on his haunches and looked up at her. She had a dancer's body: long legs, lithe and firm. She didn't realise it, but her pubic hair showed through the lace of her pale blue knickers; the outline of her nipples clearly visible. She'd surprised herself, normally she was shy of showing her body. She took a few steps, skidding slightly in the mud, and he applauded. She tried a pirouette, but she slipped sideways, nearly toppling into the river.

He was on his feet and beside her in a second, but she was all right.

'That was very nearly Swan Lake,' he said, and went back to what he'd been doing.

The mustard-coloured mud had splashed on to her arms and legs like flecks of yellow ochre. She swung her legs round, dangling her feet in the river. The strand of river weed had gone astray and she bent forward and plucked a handful from the

water. She wound a length of it around her neck, trailing its cold
wetness over her shoulders and breasts. She gathered the rest
into a handful and buried her face in it, inhaling its green tang.

Michael was still playing around in the mud; making something. Absent-mindedly she scooped a handful of wet mud from
under her and squeezed it in her fist, enjoying its greasiness as
it oozed through her fingers and trickled down her wrist to her
elbow. She opened her hand: tacky, almost edible – like peanut
butter, she thought. She stared at her palm and then smeared
it on her belly.

She squeezed the water from the weed and circled her hand
on the bank, making more mud, and then scooped a handful
and began smoothing it over her thigh, from the knee to the
hip. She added more with slow self-absorbed strokes; the
kneecap, the inside of her thigh, encasing the whole upper
leg in the yellow paste. It dried quickly, like a face pack, and
she propped herself up with her arms behind her and watched
it change colour, becoming lighter yellow on the outside and
rapidly drying towards the centre, slightly puckering the skin.

She suddenly realised he was watching her. Their eyes met
for an instant, and then she looked away. She slid, one lithe
movement like a seal, into the river, seeking the cover of
water. He'd been watching her. She stood midstream, her
back to him, the water up to her shoulders. She washed the
clay from her body, the water clouding round her. She turned
her head, watching him out of the corner of her eye. He was
pottering around on the bank again. Had he been watching her,
or had he just glanced over when she happened to look up?

She tried to get out by herself, but had to call him over in
the end. She searched his face when he pulled her out, but the
look had gone. There *had* been a look. Not just friends: it was
a man's look. Naked.

She changed behind a bush, shimmying into her cotton
dress. She'd brought no spare underclothes, and she felt
exposed, as though he'd be able to see through the thin
cotton. She slid her feet into her sandals, buckling them at the
ankle. She ran her hands over her smooth calves, taut with
young muscle, and then stood up and straightened her dress.

He'd finished whatever he'd been doing, and was washing his hands in the river. She went over to see what he'd been making. At first she couldn't make it out, and squatted to have a closer look. Then she realised it was a figurine. About six inches high, it was a woman; naked, with huge breasts and thighs and a bulbous, pregnant belly. It was a fertility symbol – a savage's fetish, a neolithic Venus.

She looked over at Michael. He was going to leave it there, on the bank. She wanted to hide it – not out of prudishness, but more out of respect. Like respect for electricity or firearms, or some dangerous and powerful thing: it shouldn't be left lying around for just anyone to come across. Michael was busy tidying up the picnic things, so she plucked handfuls of grass and covered it up.

The return journey involved climbing a ridge of several hundred feet and dropping down into a valley, and as they reached the crest of the rise they paused to look at the land stretched in front of them.

Perhaps it was the light, but to Kate the valley seemed to shimmer and heave with power. Power she could feel through the soles of her feet. It was like walking on the back of some gigantic animal, and she thought that if she was to kneel and press her ear against the ground she would hear its heartbeat.

She looked at Michael and took his hand, and together they walked down into the valley.

SEVENTEEN

'It's time we were going,' he announced one day. They were weeding the vegetable patch, and Kate straightened up to look at him.

'Where?'

'Dublin, of course,' he replied without looking up. Kate stared at the bent figure of the man.

'Today? You mean, now?'

'Of course, now. We'll be late otherwise.'

'Michael, be late for what?'

'Didn't I tell you? We're going to the opera tonight.'

He straightened up with a groan, and she scanned his face. He was serious. The opera? Tonight? She looked at her hands, peaty soil under her fingertips, as if they could supply an answer.

'We'll be marvellous,' he said, ramming the spade into the ground and taking a heroic stance. 'I'll be Rodolpho, and you'll be my darling consumptive Mimi.'

'Michael,' she said. 'Don't do things like that.'

'Like what?'

'Spring surprises on me. It's not fair.'

He ignored her and waltzed into the house, humming.

She followed him through the house, extracting, piece by piece, his plans. *La Bohème*, the opera. Yes, they'd drive. Yes, they'd stay overnight. With friends. He didn't know how long for. Yes, they did know they were coming.

She was amazed that he could have arranged all this behind her back, assuming that she'd go along with it, and at first she thought of refusing to go with him. But actually, she was quite pleased. It'd be a chance to dress up – the first time in God knows how long. She'd had the foresight to bring a couple of evening dresses over from England, but it would be no good dressing up if he was going to be in his collarless shirt and baggy trousers. She asked him what he was wearing, and he said he'd pack a suit; he still had one or two from his younger days.

She folded her evening dress into her overnight bag and put her washbag in as well. Typical of him to make the whole thing so dramatic. She sensed something more to come – he was being too evasive. This wasn't just about a trip to the opera.

Her suspicion was confirmed when, an hour later, after having jammed their luggage in the back seat of the car, he squeezed into the passenger seat beside her with a large wicker basket on his lap.

'Michael? Chickens to the opera? Is this an Irish tradition – to throw chickens instead of flowers?'

'Chickens can't look after themselves, you know. Not like a goat.'

'I'm pleased to hear that – I don't think we could've fitted a goat in here.'

The unhappy fowl were squabbling in their sudden confinement, and she had to raise her voice to be heard.

'So we're going to take them with us?'

He looked blankly at her.

'What are you talking about? I'm giving them to James.'

She noticed a large white spatter of bird-dropping on the windscreen, and considered getting out to scrape it off.

'Exactly how long are we going away for?' she asked.

'You're full of questions today, aren't you?'

'How long?'

'All right, all right, all right,' he muttered. 'Perhaps a month or so.'

'A month! But I've packed enough for only two days! And you can shut up!' she rapped, hitting the side of the basket, precipitating a fresh outburst of squawking.

'Michael, you can't *do* this – make plans without considering others. I mean, people don't behave like that!'

'If you need some extra clothes, you'd better hurry your-self, or we'll be late.'

It was nearly two hundred miles to Dublin, and five o'clock before they reached their destination: an ugly grey building on a crumbling council estate.

To her relief, they *were* expected, though judging by their host's surprised reaction, they weren't expecting some-one in the mould of Kate. As Michael and Mr Ryan, his friend, carried the cases upstairs she heard him remark, sotto voce, to the old man, 'And where, be jeesus, did you find her?'

Mrs Ryan was a small, busy woman with three grown-up sons and an overbearing husband. She was a good Catholic. She smiled a nervous, friendly smile and escaped to the kitchen to make a pot of tea.

Kate glanced around the room. The mantelpiece and tele-vision top were cluttered with framed photographs of the family, a Sacred Heart above the fireplace, a dull red bulb glowing under it. She wondered where Michael and the Ryans could have met – they were both quite a bit younger than him.

The tea arrived and Kate was politely quizzed on who she was, and how she'd come to meet the old man. When Kate explained she'd met him by chance when she'd come over on holiday, five months ago, Mrs Ryan looked sadly and disapprovingly at her, but Mr Ryan burst into laughter.

'The old bugger! He told me you were a nurse sent from London to look after him!'

Three pairs of eyes turned to the door as Michael came in, and three pairs of eyes couldn't believe what they saw. Michael in a dress suit, a scarlet cummerbund round his waist and a matching bow tie.

'Jesus Mary,' Mrs Ryan whispered.

They all stared at him, dumbfounded. It was as if an exotic bird had landed among sparrows, causing, for a moment, confusion and a flutter of feathers while they decided whether it was friend or enemy.

He rapped on a disc he held in his hand with a flourish and a collapsible top hat sprang open. He wiped the brim between forefinger and thumb and put it on.

Kate broke the silence with a laugh. It was as though he'd stepped out of a W.P. Frith painting. All he needed to complete the image was a silver-topped cane. It was daring, probably outrageous, but yes, Kate concluded – a success. His style was undeniable even if his taste was questionable.

Michael lifted his lapel and sniffed at it. 'I don't smell of mothballs, do I? I know it's a while since I've worn this suit, but I don't necessarily want to advertise the fact.'

Kate got up and adjusted his bow tie. 'You smell fine and you look great. Don't you think so, Mrs Ryan?'

'I thought you were going to the opera,' her husband said, 'not a fancy dress hooley!'

'The Grand Opera requires grandeur,' came the unruffled reply.

'That's you all over,' his friend laughed. 'You could never have been a good Socialist. You always had tastes for things beyond the reach of the proletariat.'

'Now, don't rise him, Charles,' his wife suggested.

'Bollocks to the proletariat!' Michael said amiably. 'And excuse my language,' he added, bowing to Mrs Ryan and raising his top hat. 'A revolution'll never get off the ground if you do away with luxury and profligacy. That's the trouble with you bloody revolutionaries. You're too bloody serious!'

Michael was enjoying himself in his old suit, and he wasn't going to sit down for anyone. Kate excused herself and went upstairs to change, and Michael turned to Mrs Ryan.

'Well? Are you tempted to leave this sour-faced husband of yours and elope with his dashing one-time comrade-in-arms?'

'Not when you have such a lovely young companion,' she replied.

'Does that mean you want to but can't, or can do but won't?'

'Who is the gorgeous young thing, Michael?' she asked, pouring him a cup of tea.

'Just a girl,' he said, sitting down.

'But how in Christ's name do you manage it?' her husband asked, jealous and trying not to show it.

Michael turned to him, stiff in his starched shirt. 'It's a sign of greatness when a man in his dotage has the company of a young and beautiful girl.'

'Greatness, you say?' Mr Ryan laughed.

'Yes, greatness,' Michael affirmed, no trace of a smile on his face.

Kate hung on his arm as they negotiated their way through the crowded foyer into the street. The pavement outside the theatre was thronged with the opera audience, mingling in the warm evening air, in no hurry to go home.

Michael was brimming with excitement as he tugged her through the crowd, his bow tie loose, his hat set at the back of his head.

The performance had been wonderful. The music had lifted Kate up and shaken her in a way she'd never felt before. She'd lost herself in the drama; felt every moment of it as though she'd seen the inside of the composer's mind. The musical motifs – echoes and hints like half-formed emotions – had worked their way inside her, exciting her in an almost sexual way until Rodolpho's final, tortured 'Mimi! Mimi!' had gone through her like a blade. The theatre had erupted into applause, Michael on his feet bellowing for more, and she had just sat, her hands limp in her lap, too overcome to applaud.

She didn't care where they were going – she was still in the theatre, in that attic, dying of consumption. She only half-listened to his excited talk about the performance, his hands waving wildly into the night. She caught sight of themselves in a shop window. Actually, from a distance, she thought, they didn't look too bad together. An elegant couple, but progressing at an inelegant pace. She made him slow down, and they paused on the bridge and looked at the winking lights of shops and passing cars in the black mirror of the Liffey. From a distance they could hear the off-key singing of a drunk, sad and comical after the opera.

The statue of James Larkin commanding Lower O'Connell Street seemed to be waiting for them. Alone and magnificent, it loomed over the street. Arms outstretched, fingers spread, head back – an angry and heroic symbol howling at the moon. Michael suddenly dropped her hand and crossed the street and stood under the statue. He was motionless, watching the empty streets, and then she heard the opening phrase of *'Che gelida manina'*. He was singing!

She crossed over to him but he paused as if unsure whether to continue. His eyes were shut, and then his arms rose: a miniature of the statue that stood over him. And then he began to sing again.

At first she thought he was clowning, satirising the melo-drama of the opera, but it was soon obvious that he was serious. His voice was flawed and cracked, but he sang passionately in an effortless baritone, making no attempt to reach the high notes, humming when he forgot the words. A knot of people crossed the road and listened with Kate.

The statue of Jim Larkin towered above the group as though demanding God's blessing on this spectacle. The crowd was spellbound by this man in his old-fashioned suit, his hat on the ground by his feet. The old man with the cracked voice, singing his lifetime of experience. Not pathetic, but exuberant, proud, defiant – two fingers to the gods and up the Republic!

He sang the last phrase in almost a whisper and they could hardly hear him above the sound of passing traffic. And then he was finished. Arms limp at his sides – he had used himself up. The magic had gone, slipped into the night air, and here was a man, an old man in a mothbally suit and tears on his cheeks. Kate looked up at the statue, almost expecting it to have moved, but it was the same. The same stance, the same defiance immortalised in bronze. She saw there was an inscription on the stone pedestal and she read it in the yellow streetlight: *The great appear great because we are on our knees. Let us rise.*

The crowd drifted away, but Michael didn't move until Kate touched his arm. For a moment he couldn't speak, and looked from the woman to the empty street and then up at the statue. He placed an arm around Kate's shoulder and she felt his weight against her.

'Oh Jesus!' he said at last. 'I love this city!'

His skin was sallow under the streetlight; the lines on his face deep furrows. He turned to her suddenly.

'Come on. Let's get ourselves a drink.'

EIGHTEEN

They found a pub. Crowded, smoky and noisy, it was just what Michael was looking for. He was in high spirits and made his entrance as if it was a party and he was the guest of honour. Confidently pushing his way through the drinkers to the bar, he greeted people as if they were personal friends, laying a hand on a shoulder now and then. There was a lull in the conversation as people became aware of the old man in the scarlet bow tie and the attractive young woman who was with him. A few turned to have a better look at the pair, speculating as to who they could be. Someone famous, surely, was the general consensus, though nobody could put a name to the face. Michael was apparently unaware of the stir they were creating, but Kate felt every pair of eyes that were on her, and gratefully accepted the glass from him, glad of something to occupy herself with.

After the dust had settled, and people returned to their drinks, Michael invited himself into a conversation with a group of young men, students from the college. They were more interested in Kate than the old man, and steered the conversation around to her. It was obvious to Kate that they were wondering just what her relationship with the old man was. He wasn't family – she'd said she had no Irish blood. *She* wasn't going to elucidate, and Michael obviously didn't care, so she left them to guess.

Kate was finding the conversation hard going: the students had been drinking for some time, and she had trouble understanding their alcohol-smudged accents above the din, so when Michael took up the reins of the conversation, Kate accepted the proffered bar-stool, and let him get on with it.

He was drinking a lot – whiskey and beer chasers – and talking as though he'd been starved of conversation for a month and was trying to make up for it in one evening. He was on form – witty and outrageous – and within an hour the conversation had turned to a performance and his audience had swollen to include half the pub. He leant against the bar, his undone bow tie hanging halfway down his shirtfront, and told the world the version according to Michael. Stories, jokes, the occasional song – Kate was astonished at his repertoire. He was funny – genuinely funny, even if he *did* borrow a few Flann O'Brien stories as his own. A line of pints was queuing up on the bar for him, bought by a grateful audience. This was the Dublin they hoped for and rarely found: the proud jewel of Erin, mother of genius and eccentrics. The ghost of Brendan Behan – God rest his soul – swirled around their heads as tobacco smoke and whiskey fumes, reached above the bar and switched off the TV. Michael was in his element.

It was nearly one o'clock when the barman hung a towel over the taps and the pub began to clear. Kate took her chance – he was quite drunk by now – and prised him from his stool and propelled him to the door amid a chorus of goodnights.

Kate drove back and they let themselves into the sleeping house. The sofa in the living room had been made up as a bed for Michael – Kate was to have the spare room. She helped him up the stairs to get his bag. He fell on to her bed and kicked off a shoe.

'By God, I'm as tired as a dog,' he groaned. 'And drunk as a goat.'

She watched him for a moment. He'd overdone it; given too much of himself. She rummaged in her case for her washbag.

'Don't fall asleep there. Take your things downstairs, and I'll see you in the morning.'

She went to the bathroom and splashed water over her face. She brushed her teeth, grinning at herself in the mirror. It had been a long day. She noticed she had begun to tan, thanks to the time she'd been spending out of doors lately. Hopefully, with more sun, my hair will lighten more.

He was still lying on the bed when she got back. She sat at the dressing-table and began to brush her hair. 'Come on, Michael. Go to bed.'

He pushed himself up and swung his legs off the bed. His suit was looking scruffy now, and she could see a beer stain on his shirtfront as she looked at him in the mirror.

He spoke to her reflection. 'I want to sleep here tonight.'

'All right. I'll take the sofa bed.' It would be easier than getting him downstairs, and she was tired enough to sleep anywhere.

'With you,' he said.

She stopped brushing her hair. 'What are you saying?'

Their eyes met in the mirror. 'I want to sleep with you.'

She shut her eyes. Why did it always come to this? Why did he have to let her down like everybody else? She looked down at the hairbrush sadly.

'You're drunk, Michael. Go to bed.'

She turned to look at him. He was sitting on the edge of the bed, a hand shading his eyes.

'Look, Michael –' she began. A sound like a squeaky door-hinge made her stop. He lowered his hand and she could see tears squeezing out between his closed eyelids.

'Oh, Michael! I'm sorry!' She stopped herself. No – she wasn't going to feel guilty about this. He was drunk and out of line. She watched him, his body rocking silently with tears, his head in his hands.

'Michael?' she said at last.

His hands dropped. 'I'm sorry. You're right – I'm drunk.' He stood up unsteadily and swayed by the door. 'It's just,' he burped, 'being here in Dublin reminds me of Ann.'

He groped for the doorknob and she got up and opened it for him. Ann? His wife? They looked at each other for a moment, and then she touched his cheek with her fingertips.

'I'm sorry, Michael. I didn't know.'

He smiled crookedly and clattered his way downstairs.

He woke her in the morning – a cup of coffee in one hand, a plate of biscuits in the other. He looked hung over and sat uninvited on the edge of the bed, while she sat up and took the cup from him. She took his silence as an apology for the night before, and reached out an arm to touch him. He smiled painfully, squinting against a headache.

She sipped her coffee. It was going to be a good day, she decided. She heard the swish of car tyres on a wet road and asked him if it was raining. He nodded. She pulled the blankets up to her neck – that was all right. Rain or no rain, it was going to be a good day. She felt so refreshed and so inexplicably pleased, and he looked so miserable, that she had an urge to kiss him. Make him feel better.

'Let's go shopping. I'll buy you some clothes to cheer you up.'

He got up. 'You're on,' he said with a sudden smile.

They drank the city like parched sailors: the clothes shops and vegetable barrows, the bookies and bridges, the wide wet streets. His sad hangover had gone and Michael was as excited as she was: stepping confidently between the traffic, pointing out the historic landmarks with the pride of a native Dubliner.

They spent recklessly. Books, an umbrella, presents for Mr and Mrs Ryan, a road map. She bought a pink summer dress and a pair of green sandals for herself, and a cotton jacket and panama hat for Michael. They celebrated their purchases with a liquid lunch in St Stephen's Green. It was good to be back in the city.

He said she should learn something of the history of Ireland, seeing as how they were in the heart of the country, and suggested that they go to the nearby National Museum. It looked as if the rain had set in for the day, and so she agreed.

It was dim and musty inside the muscum. The lights hadn't been switched on, even though the sky was practically dusk with an approaching storm. They left their shopping by the entrance and went into the first room. Kate peered

uninterestedly into the showcases while Michael told her
about the early struggle for Independence. The same names
kept recurring, names she was already familiar with, had
seen as street names and statues: Gratton, Flood, Parnell,
O'Connell. They moved into another room, lined with glass
cases. Here was the twentieth century and the bloody
campaigns: the Easter Rising, the War of Independence,
the Troubles. Each partisan group was represented by a
wax model: the Irish Volunteers, IRB, IRA, Sinn Fein.
Their uniforms, their home-made flags, the trivia of war:
so-and-so's hat with a bullet hole, a gold watch given by
so-and-so to so-and-so.

Michael would have grown up with this, she realised;
his father one of these forgotten sacrifices on the altar
of ideology.

She read the farewell note of a condemned man, shot the
next day by a British firing squad. Beside it was a brown
and curled photograph of him. No more than twenty, he was
leaning against a wall like a cowboy, a cigarette in his mouth.
There was no fear in his eyes, no doubt. The note wasn't a
letter, as Kate had expected, but little more than a slogan.
He wasn't going to die, and he knew it. They'd take his body
and break it, but looking into his eyes, it was as though he
knew that in sixty years' time it would be *his* letter that
would be read by strangers, *his* photograph that would be
studied. And what the hell for? Kate asked herself.

A part of her envied these ghosts. Envied them their
mission, their awesome sense of right. They had committed themselves to something bigger than their lives,
bigger than law, bigger than morality. They could murder and justify it. It didn't matter which side they were
on – it was war, and they made the rules as they went
along.

Suddenly she wanted to get out. The wax effigies were
crowding round her. It was a mortuary, not a museum: these
were corpses filling the clothes of the dead, being pored
over by necrophiles. She said she'd wait for him outside,
and hurried out.

She sheltered in the porch, grateful for the cool drizzle and the lime-yellow leaves of the overhanging beech trees. He joined her in a few minutes and they watched the rain for a while.

He wanted to go to the National Gallery to see a painting, a favourite of his. Oddly for a picture restorer, she'd never really liked museums, but she said she'd come along with him, and they walked the short distance together.

Once inside he knew exactly where to go, walking up the broad marble staircase, ignoring all the paintings they passed. He sighed with relief when he found the one he was looking for – an El Greco. She gave it a quick glance – the London National Gallery had borrowed it, and she remembered it. She left him and wandered through the rest of the gallery. It was deserted but for some sleepy attendants and a group of American tourists who stopped her to ask where the Rembrandt room was. She hurried through the last few rooms, under the impression she was being followed, even though she knew she was alone.

He was still standing in front of the painting – St Anthony receiving the stigmata – when she got back. It was too blue for Kate, and there was something disturbing and fanatical about the expression on St Anthony's face: a picture of a man who had seen too much. She touched him gently on the sleeve, suggesting they should go.

The drizzle had turned to a downpour and they waited under cover for it to pass, watching puddles forming in the depressions in the gravel courtyard.

A gush of rainwater suddenly spouted from a blocked drainpipe, splashing them both, and they stepped back further into the shelter. She took his arm, slipping her hand into his pocket; finding his hand, warm and strong.

She knew she shouldn't ask it, but the question demanded to be answered. It was stupid and it didn't matter what the answer was, but she asked it.

'Michael. Last night, was that me you really wanted? Or Ann?'

There. It was out now.

Lightning flickered as if in response to her question, and she flinched.

'What answer do you want?'

She knew without asking herself. Me. I wanted him to want me. He is mine.

A cannon roll of thunder unfolded across the sky, and she moved her body closer to his.

NINETEEN

They left Dublin the next day and drove south through the Wicklow Mountains. Kate was glad to be getting out of Dublin: the rain hadn't stopped during the two days they'd been there, and her initial enthusiasm at being in the city had soon given way to a sense of oppression. It was a dank and morose place in the rain. Strange, she'd always thought of herself as a city person, but now she couldn't wait to get out into the open countryside.

She drove quickly through the suburbs and then, suddenly, they were in the country. It was like diving into a pool of green water – cool, almost shocking.

The small side-road she took was untrafficked other than the occasional car, and she slowed down, breathing in the rain-fed lushness of the land. They were soon in the mountains; the grey ribbon of the road meandering through the valley like a river seeking the point of least resistance.

It was good to be moving again. It had always been Kate's escape when things were stagnant, difficult – pack a case, get in the car, on a plane and just travel. She'd covered most of Europe like that, a portion of Asia too. For as long as she was travelling, she hadn't arrived, and that gave her a freedom she craved like a drug.

She didn't know where they were heading, and he didn't ask. She played the car radio loud, her hair catching in the wind while Michael sat, absurdly incongruous in the brash sports car, enjoying the scenery. It was good to be moving. She drummed out the rhythm of the pop tune on the steering wheel, the sunlight that filtered through the branches of the overhanging trees flickering over the windscreen.

Lunch was in a pub, creamy Guinness, a meal in itself, and then back on to the road.

It was about two o'clock when the engine suddenly coughed. Kate frowned, slowing her speed. Another hundred yards, a second cough, and then more frequently until the car began to judder. She freewheeled to a stop.

'Shit!'

They looked at each other. 'It's never done this before.'

She started the car again, but they only got a few feet before it coughed, stalled and stopped.

'Life *is* full of surprises.'

'Very useful, Michael.'

He shrugged. She got out and lifted the bonnet, gazing uncomprehendingly into the guts of the machine, and then slammed it shut. He joined her on the road. 'What about petrol?' he asked.

'Don't be silly – there's something wrong with the engine.'

He half-sat on the bonnet of the car, and took out his pipe. The sky was clearing: the sun coming and going behind fast-moving cumulus clouds, their shadows sliding over the flanks of the mountains.

'We're miles from anywhere – you realise that?'

They listened – silence except for the twittering of a skylark. He lit his pipe, shading the flame from the breeze.

'Doesn't it bother you?' she asked.

He looked into his pipe, checking that it was lit before he answered. 'Not a great deal.'

She tutted and walked down to the bend in the road to gain their bearings. He hadn't moved by the time she returned. 'There's nothing here. Not a house in sight.'

'What will we do then?' he asked.

'You don't know anything about cars, do you?'

He shook his head. She kicked at a pebble in the road, sending it skimming into a clump of furze.

'We seem to have a problem here,' he said, watching her.

'Thank you for your help,' she said with mock politeness. 'You've been a real support.'

He nodded in acknowledgment. She walked down the road in the opposite direction. Nothing – no cars, silence. She came back and they sat side by side on the bonnet.

'All right,' she said at last. 'Tell me.' She recognised it when he had something to say and wasn't saying it.

'*Do* we have a problem here?'

'Of course we do.'

'What is it?'

'The car won't bloody go!'

'The car won't bloody go,' he repeated ironically. 'And what can we do to resolve that?'

'Fix it?' she said sarcastically.

'And if we can't?'

'Get someone else to.'

He pushed himself off the bonnet and stood on tiptoe, looking in all directions. He shook his head, and sat back down. 'Sorry. Out of luck.'

She couldn't help smiling. What the hell – they were stuck here, she might as well enjoy herself.

'Let's call that the sleeves-rolled-up method: the "fix-it" philosophy of mechanics and psychiatrists.'

Ah ha, she thought. Here he comes – what he *really* wants to say. 'And the other method?' she prompted him, the compliant disciple.

He laughed at the game they were playing. 'What I like to call the now-you-see-it-now-you-don't method favoured by shamans and charlatans. You just disappear the problem.'

'Explain.'

'How do you disappear something? There's only one way – and every child knows what it is.' He paused for dramatic effect. 'By using a magic wand. Obviously – there's no other possible way.'

She gave him thirty seconds, and when he still hadn't explained himself, she had to ask. 'And what is a magic wand?'

'It's a white stick about – oh, this long.' He ducked from her pretend swipe. 'No –' he said, suddenly serious. 'A magic wand is your faculty to recontextualise at any moment. I'll explain.'

He stood up and walked round the car, studying it as though he was thinking of buying it. 'This car, this car-won't-bloody-go car, is that really the problem? Would it be a problem if it was in a museum somewhere, not intending to go anywhere?'

She shook her head.

'If that's the case, and we still find we have a problem, that can only mean one thing.'

'We're the problem.'

'Precisely,' he said.

'So how do we solve the problem if our "fix-it" method doesn't work? By recontextualising – by changing the context of the situation.'

'Hold on a sec.' She held up a hand. 'What's this context stuff?'

'*Content*: man,' he said, pointing to himself. 'Woman.' He pointed to Kate. 'Car.' He slapped the bonnet. 'Stuff we can "fix" – or not in our case.

'*Context*,' he continued, 'is all the rest. For instance?' he invited her with an arch of his eyebrows.

She scrunched the gravel by the tyre for a moment, thinking. 'Getting somewhere? And getting there by this car.'

'And how do we change the context?'

'Accept that we're not going to get there?'

'You're not listening – I said *disappear*. I did not say pretend it's not there, or put up with it. When you disappear something, there's nothing to put up with.'

She suddenly understood. 'Choose,' she said suddenly. 'We choose something else.'

'Now, how the hell d'you do that?' he said in a thick Irish accent.

'By using a magic wand – obviously.'

'Ah!' He nodded, feigning dawning realisation.

She was pleased with herself, and said nothing. He stared at his boots, sniffed. 'What are we going to do, then?'

'Do you fancy spending the afternoon sitting on a car bonnet?' she invited him.

They were suddenly bathed in brilliant sunshine and he shut his eyes for a moment. 'Do I have a choice?'

'Of course you do – you could wish you were doing something else.'

He laughed, lesson over. 'Welcome to the club.'

'The club?'

'The Magic Circle.'

She bowed.

'And for my next trick,' she said. She gestured behind Michael, and he turned round. In the distance, a red car, still small, was speeding towards them. 'Ta – ra!'

She stood in the middle of the road, and flagged the car to a halt. 'Excuse me, do you know anything about cars?' she asked the driver when he rolled his window down.

'*Pardon?*'

Ah, she stood up. French. '*Excusez moi, mais –*' she began.

'*Pardon, monsieur,*' Michael interrupted. '*Avez-vous du gasoline?*'

'*L'essence,*' she corrected.

'*Nous sommes . . .* ' he turned to Kate. 'I can't remember – what's "run-out"?'

'But we haven't.'

'Oh yes we have.'

Michael smiled at the French couple as they watched Kate, bewildered, run back to her car. She turned the ignition on. Sure enough – the tank was empty. Then she remembered – the petrol station they were going to use that morning had been closed. And it had slipped her memory to fill up somewhere else.

They offered to pay for the petrol, but the couple wouldn't hear of it. The man siphoned off a couple of pints – enough to get them to the nearest village.

She started the car, relieved when it began to move. 'Why didn't you tell me we'd run out of petrol?'

'What,' he said, pushing his hat on to the back of his head, 'and miss all the fun?'

TWENTY

Towards late afternoon they passed a guest house, and he suggested stopping. Kate turned the car and drove back to the house – a modern Spanish-style bungalow. As soon as they got out of the car, Kate noticed there was something wrong with Michael. Normally he walked with a degree of sprightliness remarkable for a man of his age, but now he was stooped as if he was very tired. Kate asked him if he was all right, but he just asked her to bring the bags to the house. She watched him as he walked unsteadily up the drive, at one point pausing to rest against the fence. She followed him worriedly with the bags.

They were the only guests and they checked into two single rooms. Kate left him talking to the landlady while she carried the bags to their bedrooms.

She was washing her face when there was a soft tap at the door, and the landlady poked her head in and said she'd make some tea.

Michael was in the large sitting room, talking with the landlord when she came in. She greeted them and sat in an armchair. The late afternoon sun streamed through the french windows, and Kate stretched her legs out into a patch of sunlight on the carpet.

The landlady came in with a pot of tea, and the men's conversation was suspended while it was poured out.

Kate watched Michael across the room. There was something odd about him: he looked ill at ease, as if he was in pain. He caught her eye and slowly lowered one eyelid in a wink.

The men picked up their conversation and the landlady turned to Kate.

'Mr Humbert says this is your first time in Ireland.'

'Really,' she replied uncertainly.

Humbert? Kate sipped her tea, looking over the rim of the cup at Michael. Where did she get that idea?

Then she heard him talking. At first she thought he was joking, but it continued for too long. She had a sudden rush of confusion. She couldn't believe what she was hearing. Michael was talking in a preposterous English accent. Not only was his accent different, but his voice too: high and croaky like an old man's. It was as though somebody else's voice was coming out of Michael's mouth.

He was telling the landlord that they'd just come over from England for a holiday, and were touring around. Kate fiddled nervously with her teacup. What was he up to?

The landlady tried to draw Kate into a conversation, but she was listening to the men, and didn't notice the woman.

The landlord asked Michael if they were enjoying their stay in Ireland.

'Oh yes, my daughter here especially.'

Her eyes widened in disbelief. He was serious, even turning to smile at her – no sign at all that it wasn't the truth that he was telling.

She wanted to get up immediately; get out before they realised what was going on, but she couldn't move. It was too outrageous: it couldn't be real.

He told them he'd recently retired from the Church – the ministry, he called it, as though he'd been a civil servant. He was beginning to explain exactly what an Anabaptist footwasher was, when Kate abruptly got to her feet.

'I'm a little tired,' she said grittily. 'I think I'll have a rest before dinner.'

'Good idea, daughter,' Michael said. 'Help me up, will you?'

Tight-lipped, she led him to his room. She turned on him as soon as the door closed behind them.

'All right! What's going on?'

He sat on the bed and began untying his shoelaces. 'Do you mean in a theological sense?' he said in a grotesquely exaggerated English accent.

'Stop talking like that. It gives me the creeps!'

'I rather like it,' he replied in the same voice.

'Why are you pretending to be English? And why did you say I was your daughter?'

He shrugged. 'For the crack,' he said in his everyday voice.

'And what would they think if they knew you were lying?'

'Do I look like a man who cares what people think?' he said, swinging his stockinged feet up on the bed.

She was furious, and he knew it.

'You can be as childish as you like,' she snapped. 'But don't drag me into it. I didn't know where to look when you said I was your daughter.'

'Your birth certificate?'

'It's just a game to you, isn't it?'

'Of course,' he said simply. He got up from the bed with a groan. 'Your poor English pappy,' he said in a high voice. 'On his last holiday before he goes the way of all flesh.'

He walked shakily across the room. His impersonation of an old Englishman was so accurate that she couldn't stop herself from laughing.

'You should've been an actor,' she said.

He stood up straight, his role forgotten. 'I am, I am!' he beamed, his arms outstretched as though addressing an audience.

She shook her head and opened the door. 'I'll see you at dinner. I'm going to have a lie-down.'

'I hear you and my eldest boy have an interest in common,' the landlady began as she cleared the dinner plates. 'It's a pity he's not here – he could've shown you his collection.'

'I'm sorry?' Kate said, unsure who was being addressed.

'Yes, he's got cases and cases of butterflies upstairs.'

Kate looked at Michael, and he shrugged.

'Oh yes?' Kate replied uncertainly.

'Moths, too.' The landlady looked at her expectantly.

'I think your speciality doesn't extend to moths, does it?' Michael asked in his English accent.

Kate looked blankly at him and then at the landlady.

'Now, that must be an interesting job,' she continued, stacking the plates on the trolley. 'Working on a butterfly farm. It's a shame Brian isn't here to talk with you.' She wheeled the trolley out of the room.

'Michael!' Kate hissed as soon as they were alone. 'What have you been telling her?'

'I said you were a butterfly expert.'

'What!'

He nonchalantly picked at a particle of food that had caught in his teeth.

'But why?' She shook her head in disbelief. 'Butterflies?'

The landlady came back with the dessert. 'Why don't you tell Mrs Bryant about that nasty accident you had with that butterfly?'

'An accident, you say?' She put the two bowls on the table.

'What accident?' Kate mouthed silently at Michael.

'The time you were poisoned.'

'You're joking me!' the landlady exclaimed. 'Poisoned by a butterfly!'

'Go on – tell Mrs Bryant about it.'

'I'm sure she wouldn't be interested,' Kate said, flashing an angry glance at Michael.

But it was too late. Mrs Bryant had pulled up a chair and, with a nod, urged Kate to tell her story.

'There's this South American moth – ' she began reluctantly.

'Butterfly,' Michael corrected.

' – that poisons its prey with . . . with a poison. It spits in the eye of its prey, like a snake.'

The landlady glanced at Michael and then at Kate. 'This butterfly eats snakes?'

'No, no. There's a snake – I forget the name – that spits poison in the eye of its prey. The butterfly, the South American –' She hesitated, gesturing in the air as though trying to catch the elusive insect.

'Spitter,' Michael prompted.

'Paralyses its prey in the same way.'

'Never!'

'Yes, it spat in my eye and I was very ill for a time.'

'Yes, she was,' Michael interjected. 'And you'd never know she had a glass eye.'

'Jesus Mary! A glass eye!'

'Michael!' Kate said crossly. They both looked at her in surprise, but she didn't know what to say, and blushed.

The landlady scrutinised Kate's face. 'You poor dear. The left eye, isn't it? But you'd never notice unless you'd been told.'

Michael winked at Kate, and Mrs Bryant left them to finish their dinner.

'Just what is going on?' she asked as soon as the landlady was out of earshot. 'Why all the pretence?'

He glanced at her and took a spoonful of the pudding. '*I* wasn't pretending – *you* may have been.'

'But—'

'A good actor doesn't pretend,' he said with his mouth full. 'He *becomes*. Only second-rate actors pretend.'

'But you're not English! You were pretending.'

'I'm as much a Brit as a Paddy.'

'But I thought you were born in Ireland.'

'What's the past got to do with it?' He poured more cream over his apple crumble, and looked up when she said nothing.

'You're joking, aren't you?' she asked uncertainly.

He leant back in his chair and laughed. 'I'm deadly serious.' His smile faded as suddenly as it had appeared. 'I'm not an Irishman. I'm not any of this.' He patted his body.

'But you said I was your daughter – that's not true.'

'You're my daughter and this is my house if I say it is.'

'You're pulling my leg. Either that or you're crazy.'

'One of us is crazy, to be sure – and it's not the one wearing the skirt.' He looked under the table as if to check which of them it was. 'How can you pass judgment on someone else when you don't even know who you are yourself? You're like a blind man judging a beauty contest. And you expect me to listen to your verdict? *That's* crazy!'

He finished his pudding and eyed Kate's, which she hadn't touched.

'All right. Explain yourself. Why all the games?'

'You know what we're doing, Kate,' he said quietly. 'This is no ordinary trip to the country.'

She looked him straight in the eye. He was right, none of it *was* ordinary. God knows what he was up to, but six months she'd been with him now – and what had it been but games all along? She was fitter and happier than she'd been in years, but something else was going on. Something she didn't understand, didn't *want* to understand.

She pushed her apple crumble across to him. 'I *don't* know what we're doing.'

'Well, perhaps that's not such a bad thing. Before you can know, you have to know you don't know, otherwise there's no space for learning.' He took a mouthful of crumble. 'Are you sure you don't want this? It's tasty.'

She shook her head and watched him eat for a minute. 'I do know some things. I know I'm not your daughter – so why don't you tell me what all this is about?'

'Yes, you know a lot, don't you?' He said it like a doctor confirming a diagnosis of boils. 'That's why there's no room for wonder left.'

He put the spoon down and took her hand. 'We have to unlearn you, Kate. We have to unpeel these fingers off this little nugget of belief you have.' He straightened her fingers out one by one. 'And what better way than by becoming someone else?'

She took her hand back. 'What do you mean, "belief"?'

'You've been believing things about yourself for so long you think they're the facts of life.'

'Such as?'

'Such as you're *this* sort of person – ' he plonked the salt cellar down ' – who couldn't possibly do *that*.' He moved the pepper pot. 'And would die if somebody did the other to you.' He put her spoon between them. 'You know better than me what your beliefs are.'

'And pretending to be someone else will – what did you say?'

'It was *you* talking about pretending, not me.'

'Okay, "becoming".'

'You're in a cage, Kate. You're trapped in a mean little box.'
He indicated the triangle of the salt, pepper and spoon. 'And
you know a lot about that – you've been living in it for the best
part of your life. Or worst part.'

'I'm confused.'

He picked up his spoon. 'It's been said that confusion
and paradox are the guardians of truth.' He hesitated. 'Or
perhaps it's the other way round.' He smiled and returned to
his pudding.

TWENTY-ONE

Midday the next day saw them in Waterford city. It was a close, airless day and they drove with the sunroof down. Michael was in high spirits: cracking jokes about his newly adopted daughter, and shouting greetings to people they passed, his panama hat jammed on his head to stop the wind blowing it off.

He made no mention of the previous night's conversation until they stopped at a pub on the other side of the city. Kate sensed from his playful mood that the game he was playing wasn't over yet. And sure enough, when she was about to get out, he laid a hand on her arm.

'You can only know who you are when you know who you're not,' he said conspiratorially. 'So, who is it you're going to be today?'

'Not again, Michael – please.' She felt uncomfortable and incompetent pretending to be another person. She was sure she'd be found out if she tried it again.

'Don't take it so seriously,' he said. 'It's a game.'

'Well, if it's a game, then count me out.'

He ignored her comment. 'How about husband and wife today?'

'You're joking – nobody would believe us!'

'You choose then.'

The front of the pub was given over to a grocery store: a small room with overflowing shelves and a long wooden counter crowded with dusty sweet jars and a bacon slicer. At the back, through a curtained doorway, was the bar – first apprehended by the senses as an odour of vinegar and stale tobacco smoke. A small window opposite the doorway was the only source of light in the bar, and through the gloom Kate made out two men leaning against the counter. The men turned their heads slowly and inquisitively as cows might do, mooed a greeting and then returned to the contemplation of their beer. There was nobody attending the shop or behind the bar. The silence was total.

She wanted to turn round and leave there and then, but Michael nudged her in the back and she moved forward and sat on a bar-stool. In the car he'd managed to talk her into being his daughter again, and told her to begin a conversation with whoever was in the bar. The men – farmers judging by their clothes – had neither spoken nor moved after their initial scrutiny of the two newcomers. She looked hopelessly at Michael, but he only signalled for her to begin.

'Hello.'

The men nodded in response, no sound issuing from their lips. She looked round for the barman.

'Willie! Customer!' one of the men bellowed. She jumped.

The landlord appeared behind the bar wiping his hands on a towel, and Kate asked Michael what he wanted to drink. She tried to say 'Dad' as she'd intended, but it didn't come out.

The drinks were served, and then the landlord disappeared. The bar declined into silence once more. Even the cat on the settle in the corner was asleep.

She took a deep breath and commented how fine the weather was. Both men sagely agreed with her comment as though it had been one of particular insight, and then fell silent.

She tried again. 'My father and I are just over from England on holiday.'

'Is that so?'

She turned to Michael for help, but he only raised his glass slightly in greeting. A line of beer froth ringed his top lip like a white moustache. She shut her eyes and wished she wasn't there.

Without warning the older of the two men asked her where they lived in England. On hearing that it was London, he informed her that Peter, his nephew, also lived in London. He told her the exact address as though he might expect her to know it, or even its inhabitant, personally. 'I visited him in London once. For Christmas.' He paused to gulp his beer. 'Five years ago.'

'Oh, yes?'

Silence.

'Did you like it?'

'Christmas?'

'No. London.' She cast a beseeching look at Michael and to her relief, he joined in.

'A dorrty bloody place it is, and no mistake.' Kate closed her eyes. His thick Irish brogue seemed to hang in the air.

It wasn't even his own accent – she could forgive him that. It was a grotesque J.M. Synge voice – a music-hall Paddy the Mick.

There was a pause while the two men thought about it. They both began to speak at the same time.

'Is not your father—?'

'Were you being born in—?'

Their confusion gave Kate a second to think. 'Yes, I'm Irish,' she said rather too forcefully, 'but I was brought up in England. My father lives with me in England.'

'No, I don't.'

'Well,' she flushed angrily, 'he does some of the time.'

'That's true – I do that, yes.'

The men looked at each other and fell silent again. As if by some tacit cue, they both finished their drinks and stood to go. 'Enjoy yourselves, now,' one of them said, and they were gone.

'That was a mean bloody trick you played on me,' she said as soon as they were alone.

'I didn't want to make it too easy for you. An ability to improvise is the mark of a good actor.'

'I am not an actor,' she said stiffly.

'Actress, then.'

She picked up an empty glass as though she was going to throw it at him. He flinched, pretending to be afraid of her. 'We're all actors, whether we know it or not.'

She huffed theatrically and looked at herself in the Guinness mirror above the bar. She didn't know whether to be annoyed or not. It was embarrassing, being put in these absurd positions.

'Look, can we stop this? I'm feeling extremely uncomfortable with this play-acting.'

He shrugged. 'It's up to you, but I promise you one thing. Whatever we do I'll make sure you're uncomfortable.'

'Why?'

'Kate darling – I'm your banana skin.'

'You mean you're trying to make a fool out of me?'

'You don't need my help.'

'Thank you very much,' she said sarcastically.

'We're *all* fools – you're no exception. It's just that some of us know it. And when we know it, we've a small chance of being sometimes something other than an eejit.'

' "If a fool were to persist in his folly, he would become wise",' Kate said to her glass of wine, quoting the only piece of Blake she knew.

'He would indeed, as long as he knew he was a fool and didn't think he was a sage. And look at yourself, Kate.' He nodded at the mirror. 'Which are you, fool or sage? Have you really understood just how bloody stupid you can be at times?'

He got up and took a handful of darts from the bar and walked over to the dartboard. 'The fool looks like a sage, the sage looks like a fool,' he said, with his back to her. 'The fool is serious and proud, the sage is humble.'

He threw a dart which skittered crazily through the air and stuck into a calendar hanging beside the dartboard.

'The fool thinks he knows everything, the sage keeps an open mind.'

The second dart bounced off the rubber tyre around the board and landed at his feet.

'A fool is pompous, but a sage has dignity. Dignity, because he's got nothing to lose.'

He took his time with his last dart. 'A sage has got no points to defend, nothing to prove. He knows he's a fool, and doesn't mind if other people know it.'

The last dart hung for a moment in the board and then fell to the floor. He sighed and turned to look at her.

'Which are you, Kate?'

*   *   *

The evening Angelus had just rung when she saw a game of Gaelic football in progress. She stopped the car to watch. The dying sun lighted the playing field with gold, casting long shadows from the players: schoolboys, about twelve years old. They got out of the car and walked to the touchlines.

Kate had never seen Irish football before, and it looked chaotic to her, but Michael seemed to know what was going on – shouting advice to the thin-legged boys, and cheering when one of the team scored. After ten minutes, the whistle blew and the children drifted off to change. Michael took his chance.

'Can you do an Irish accent?' He saw the opposition in her face. 'Humour an old man just once more.'

She sighed. 'I'll be your daughter, but not Irish. I'd be spotted straight away.'

'All right – I'll be English then.'

He took her arm and they strolled towards the sports master who was talking to a knot of boys. 'Now, no more tricks,' she warned him.

Michael introduced themselves and said how interested they were in the game. The three of them chatted for a few minutes, and then Michael said he was going to sit in the car as he was tired.

'But don't hurry back, darling.'

He said goodbye to the teacher and left them alone. Kate watched his retreating figure. Even the way he walked had changed – he'd invented a limp in his left leg, dragging it slightly over the grass.

The sports master was more than happy to have Kate to himself. He watched her as she shook her hair loose from her headscarf, and ran her fingers through its tangles. The evening sun caught it, polishing it into gold and amber. He asked her if they were staying locally, and when she said they weren't, she noticed a flicker of disappointment in his eyes.

He was obviously attracted to her, and as they chatted, a sudden spasm of recognition ran through her. He was like Jacques, her first husband. He was a sports master, and about the same age. The Irishman was perhaps heavier than her husband, and his face was quite different, but they had the same physical self-assuredness, a sort of arrogant health. And just like Jacques, he watched her like a predator: serious and tensed for action.

What was he like? she wondered. Definitely a bird – somewhere between a hawk and a peacock. It was a display he was putting on, no doubt about it. We're all actors, as Michael said.

She wanted to laugh. Now she thought about it, he was uncannily like Jacques – vain and proud and empty. It was absurd, but once she'd been prey to men like this. A consenting if often unwilling quarry.

The man's interest had begun to flag in the face of Kate's preoccupied silence, but just as he was beginning to run dry, she suddenly came to life.

'Yes, Michael and I are really enjoying it here,' she said, as if in answer to a question.

It threw the man a bit. 'Is Michael your father then?'

'No, no – he's my husband.'

He masked his disappointment with politeness and asked her where her husband was.

She feigned surprise. 'You've just met him.'

She could see that her answer had floored him, and changed the subject, but the man had given up. He stuck it out for a few more minutes and then excused himself and returned to the pavilion.

Kate surveyed the deserted sports field. What was she doing, pretending to be Michael's daughter? His *wife*, for God's sake? She wanted to call the man back and tell him the truth, but he was already out of sight. Anyway, what would she say? She was being held captive by a madman?

TWENTY-TWO

The following weeks were as timeless as a childhood summer, stretching into a vague unlooked-at future. In the presence of others they had ceased to be Michael and Kate. They were whoever and whatever he decided: father and daughter, husband and wife, teacher and student, old friends, strangers meeting for the first time.

She finally relinquished the need to understand what was going on. If Michael decided to continue the game, they would. She complied like a child, playing whatever role he gave her with an ease that surprised her.

Every day was unmapped; a discovery. They had left the past behind. There was only the day ahead of them, the sun and the road. And as Kate felt her old self slipping from her grasp, so she felt a new freedom. The freedom of being a human being newborn every day.

They continued their journey, hugging the coast roads, never staying more than one or two nights in the same place. Cork, Bantry Bay, Killarney, Dingle Bay. The summer was hot, and the sea wind tanned their arms and faces. Their hair smelled of the sea; sand found its way between their toes. Landladies of guest houses, bar curates, locals, tourists – they touched and parted from them. They gave some of themselves, took what they wanted, and moved on.

Money was running low. Kate couldn't get her hands on the money from the sale of her flat yet, and Michael's pension allowed them few luxuries. But they enjoyed the challenge of cutting costs: freewheeling down hills to save petrol, talking their way into the occasional free meal, a bed for the night. Once the night was so warm they slept out on the cliffs of

St Finan's Bay, and she curled against his body, only a thin blanket between themselves and the earth below.

The summer seemed as though it could never end. Walking the lengths of sandy beaches, barefoot and hand in hand, it seemed as though the Atlantic was the end of the world. The very frontier of humanness, beyond which was nothing other than an infinity of ocean, and the vast empty firmament.

This was, how long? Little more than two weeks by the calendar. Sixteen days, but time had been left behind. It was summer, and winter would never come.

And then one day they found themselves in Limerick, buying crusty bread and local cheese as orange as a ripe persimmon.

They wandered to the outskirts of the city and found a small park with benches and a pond. It was a school holiday, and children were scattered across the park, playing and squabbling. They sat on a bench and stretched their legs to within a foot of the water's edge, and unpacked their lunch. The ducks, hearing the rustle of paper and sensing food, hauled themselves on to land and waddled hopefully up to them.

Michael ignored the birds and tore off a piece of bread and gave it to Kate with a chunk of cheese. She took the food, but neither looked at it nor ate. Instead she stared at the ducks at her feet, and then at the pond.

'Michael,' she said suddenly. 'I want to go home.'

He took his time in answering, munching thoughtfully on a piece of cheese.

'Home?' he said at last. 'Where's that?'

'I don't know. It's just that I can't stand any more of this.'

Did she want to go? Yes and no. No, it would be impossible to go just like that. She didn't want to go. But what was this thing telling her to run? Telling her that it would be dangerous to stay with him even a moment longer? She felt a swell of almost tangible emotion as though she was standing on the deck of a ship.

'I don't know what's happening to me. I don't know who I am any more.'

'Perhaps you're beginning to find out.'

The untouched bread and cheese lay in her hand, the cheese sweating in the sun. The ducks returned to the coolness of the pond, one or two preening disinterestedly at the water's edge.

'Find out what, though?'

'That you're a machine,' he said simply.

She turned to face him. He glanced at her and then at the pond. 'We're all machines. Like those birds.'

An elderly woman, bundled up in a long coat and headscarf as if it was a winter's day, had come to the edge of the pond and was tossing scraps of bread to the ducks and pigeons. They *did* look mechanical: bobbing and strutting like clockwork toys. If a piece of bread was too large, they'd flick it away from them with a jerk of their head in an attempt to break it up, more often than not losing it to another bird.

'How can you say we're just machines?'

'Push a button and we react. Don't be fooled by the complicated response – human beings are just as mechanical as everything else in the universe.'

'But we can choose,' she protested.

'Can we?' He nodded at the birds around the old woman's feet. 'Can we choose any more than those birds?'

Kate watched the birds with a growing revulsion. There was one pigeon, fatter and sleeker than the others, who seemed to be getting most of the food. Others, older and weaker, went from scrimmage to scrimmage, never getting to the bread in time, like a schoolboy chasing his cap from one bully to another, always too slow to catch it and too stupid to give up the chase.

It reminded her of a scene she'd witnessed in Paris when she'd taken a holiday job in a large department store. It was the winter sales, and people had queued all night for the store to open in the morning. When the doors were finally opened, the people surged in, struggling and elbowing each other aside. A woman was knocked to the floor and nobody had stopped to help her. Kate could still remember their pinched, greedy faces as they swarmed past the woman, heading for the bargain goods. They were mean and stupid. Like these birds.

He saw her watching them. 'That's us, Kate. Except it's not breadcrumbs we're fighting for.'

She wanted to stamp her feet and scatter the birds. But the woman carried on feeding them, and more and more arrived. Two heavy giants of geese waded through the smaller ducks and pigeons, gulping large wodges of bread. Some sparrows, almost hidden in the fray, darted in and out, snatching bits of bread and scampering off to a safe distance. Kate wanted to snatch the bread from her hands and throw it down. Get it over with, not draw it out into this grotesque contest.

Is this all there is? she thought. Just machines? And is this what I've done all my life? Bickered and fought and lied – and for breadcrumbs?

'But what about—?' She turned to him, her hands open.

'Goodness? Love?' He said the words with heavy irony. 'Look around yourself, Kate. How much do you see? Look at this fellow here.' He pointed to a young man wrestling playfully with a huge shaggy dog. 'Giving that dog all the love he can't give to another human being.'

She looked around the park. The sunlight was harsh, like stage lighting: flattening everything into two dimensions; the colours garish and unnatural. Her attention was caught by a group of young boys. They were teasing one small boy, keeping the football away from him, and in their brightly lit faces she could already see the marks of fear and anger taking hold of them; twisting them out of shape.

A young child toddled up to the old woman to watch the ducks. The child, a young boy, watched mesmerised; his mouth open, his hands limp at his sides. The innocence, the uncorruptedness of the child snapped something in Kate, and she found herself crying.

There was an untouched world. The world of this wide-eyed little boy. And she had conspired to destroy it with her own meanness and cynicism. Everything that she touched had been blackened. All the beauty and innocence turned into dross.

It was horribly clear. She saw her past laid out like a criminal charge-sheet. The crime: murder. With callous precision, she'd killed and killed and killed. Killed the life, the beauty, the innocence.

She looked at the bread and cheese she was still holding, and then threw it into the pond, scattering the ducks.

'Let's get out of here.'

They walked back into town, Kate staring down at her feet, morosely silent. She couldn't look at the faces of the people she passed. She was ashamed and disgusted. Ashamed to be part of this gross mistake called humankind. Disgusted at the ugliness, the pettiness, the cruelty.

They stopped by the quay and sat on a patch of grass, watching the boats drifting up the Shannon. It all seemed so pointless, so blindly aimless. An ice-cream van jangled raucously behind them. Here we go round the mulberry bush, cutting out in mid-bar.

Michael hummed the tune, filling his pipe. He started singing to himself.

> This is the way the world ends
> This is the way the world ends
> This is the way the world ends
> Not with a bang but a whimper.

She looked at him. Bastard! What was he doing to her?

'Michael, I'm –' She stopped. She didn't know. It was a hollow feeling, an empty metallic nothing. She couldn't believe it, she *wouldn't* believe it. 'We *aren't* just machines. We *can't* be.'

He lit his pipe and flicked the match out. 'Why not?'

'It would just be so awful. Nothing would mean anything any more.' She plucked handfuls of grass in her agitation.

'Why is meaning so important, tell me that? Animals don't worry about it, but people hang on to it like drowning men on to driftwood.'

'If we let go of the driftwood, then we'll drown.'

He watched an elegant two-mast schooner drift past. 'But we're on dry land.'

He turned to face her. 'We've got ourselves into an awful mess, have we not? We've got ourselves stuck in the way we think we are, the way we think things should be, and then we find ourselves having to defend it. Suddenly survival becomes the most important thing. And you know what they should put on your gravestone? *I survived.*'

She lay back and closed her eyes. 'Stop it, Michael.'

He ignored her. 'It's a tough world, and we very quickly learn to become efficient survival machines. It's debatable if it's worth surviving, given the quality of life we have.'

She sat up on her elbows. 'But love – doesn't that mean anything?'

He shrugged and sucked on his pipe, making it bubble with saliva.

'I can't believe that nothing has any meaning for you. What about your wife? You cared for her, didn't you?'

'I loved Ann, but so what?'

'How can you say that? It's awful!'

'Perhaps it is. But so what?' He unscrewed the stem from his pipe and flicked the spit out of it.

She wanted to grab him and shake him out of his nonchalance. 'But *everything* seems so important to you. Are you just pretending?'

'I'm sincere in everything I do. I was sincere in loving Ann. But I'm only an actor, and I know that as an actor, none of what I do means anything.' He pocketed his pipe and looked at her. 'That sounds like pretending to you, but like I said – a good actor doesn't pretend, he *becomes* his role. He gives everything to his performance, even though he knows it's only play-acting.'

'How can you bear to go on living if you feel like that?'

He shrugged. 'Because I know that some day I'll die.'

'So we might as well kill ourselves, is that it?' There were tears in her eyes and she looked away towards the river.

'That's one way out.'

'You're joking,' she said quietly.

He reached for her wrists and turned them over. He looked at the two thin white scars and then up at her. He shook his head and let her hands drop. The ice-cream van jangled again – on a cold and frosty morning – and she held her wrists to her chest.

'So why do you bother? Why all this explanation? Why take me through this if it doesn't mean anything?'

'Because I'm the sort of person who does things like that. It's in my nature to spend time with you, acting as if everything is so important.'

'So nothing you do has any meaning?' He said nothing. 'But doesn't it–?' She shook her head. He was insane, or joking.

'It doesn't mean anything that it's meaningless.'

A seagull swooped down in front of them, snatching at a paper tissue and then dropping it.

'So is one thing as good as another?' she said after a moment.

He stretched out and laid a handkerchief over his eyes. 'I'm not concerned with good and bad.'

'What the hell *are* you concerned with?'

He didn't answer. She looked at him; his barrel chest and thick neck. The bastard had trapped her – he knew she couldn't leave with things as they stood. He had her at his mercy, hanging on his every word. And his passivity, his amused attitude – she wanted to snatch the handkerchief off his face, slap him, push him into the river – anything just to get a reaction from him.

He spoke without warning. 'If what you do is the result of what you feel or what you want, then it's not an action – it's a reaction. Only if an act is free from all consideration can you talk about free action.'

'But you said we're machines. How can a machine *not* react?'

'What is a machine? A thing that acts mechanically. What is a human being?' He lifted the handkerchief and glanced at her. 'Whatever you choose to be.'

She was getting confused. 'So can we *not* be machines?'

'Do machines fall in love?' He sat up and put the handkerchief in his pocket. 'We're machines if we think we're no more than a collection of things. Our body, our past, our opinions, our job, our mind. Our "higher selves".' He marked the inverted commas in the air with his fingers. 'You're only a machine if you behave like one.'

'So how do you stop behaving like a machine?'

'By seeing what you are. When you see the way the mind works, how most of the time you're just a machine, fighting to stay alive, then you see that there's more to it than this. You realise that you've forgotten something. And it's this –'

He rolled over and rested on his elbows. 'A machine doesn't know it's a machine.' He looked at her. 'If you know you're a machine, then something happens – you discover the difference between the machine and yourself. When you know you're behaving mechanically, you see that "you" and your reactions are separate. You see that you are yourself. You *have* a machine, but that's not what you are.'

She thought about it for a moment, and then pushed herself to her feet. 'I want an ice-cream.'

'Fuel for the motor?'

She walked off, and then paused and turned round. 'My reactions will always be mechanical, right? So just leave me alone.'

He pushed himself to his feet and followed her. 'Your reactions will always be your reactions – mechanical only if you make them.'

She swung round. 'Enough, Michael!'

He shrugged and walked past her to the ice-cream van. It was her turn to catch him up.

'Sorry.'

He squeezed her hand. 'What do you want?'

'I don't know,' she sighed. 'One of those.' She pointed at a picture of a vanilla cornet.

'How about chocolate?'

'I don't like chocolate.'

'I know. So how about it?'

'It's bad for my skin – you know that.'

'I know. So how about it?'

The ice-cream seller was watching them glumly, waiting for them to make up their minds.

She looked at Michael and then up at the ice-cream seller. She started laughing, her body shaking silently. Michael smiled at her.

'Two chocolate ice-creams, please.'

TWENTY-THREE

'It's as democratic a gathering as anything you're going to find in the whole of Ireland,' he said, getting into the car. 'It's the one week of the year when the only breeding of importance is horseflesh.'

It was the first day of the Galway races: the highlight of the cultural year of the west of Ireland, and Michael was determined not to miss it. They drove north from Limerick and were at Ballybrit racecourse by one o'clock. The day was overcast and blustery, but it didn't dampen his good humour. He was full of talk during the two-hour drive, darting from one subject to another, hardly letting Kate get a word in edgeways. She enjoyed listening to him when he was like this. It was a performance put on by a whole troupe of players – jester, minstrel, dramatist, storyteller – each inspiring the other to move the story on: the story of Michael and the rest of the universe.

Kate was surprised at how busy the racecourse was, and they had some trouble finding a place to park. This was the first race meeting she'd been to, and she was also surprised to see that a sprawling fairground had been set up beside the course. They skirted the fairground and joined the crowd milling around the rails. Long queues had already formed at the official betting office – a long concrete building with small windows advertising 50p and £1 stakes. For the more serious punters were the bookies: cloth-capped and raincoated men standing on up-ended tea chests, chalking up the odds for the first race.

Michael breathed in the scene as if it was mountain air. He'd come to the Galway races for the past God knows how long, he told her. It had been one of the sustaining influences in his life, one of the turning points of the year.

He soon got down to business. He bought a race-card and studied the form like a schoolboy cramming for an exam. They emptied their pockets and searched the car for any loose change they could find. Eleven pounds fifty-three pence.

She warned him that they needed to buy petrol if they were ever going to get back to Westport, and he reluctantly gave her five pounds to keep.

He went off to place his bet and she found a place against the railings. They hadn't been able to afford the entrance fee to the stand, but nor had most of the others, and she had to squeeze through the crowd that was waiting impatiently for the race to begin.

The first race was run and finished before she knew it – just an unimpressive gallop past of six horses – but the crowd was excited. They obviously knew something she didn't. Michael lost and tore up his ticket in disgust, casting aspersions on the pedigree of the horse, the trainer and the jockey.

She had to smile at his display of histrionics. It clearly didn't matter to him that he had lost. He wasn't interested in the money, not even in winning. It was enough to behave for a few minutes as if the destiny of the human race and this horse race were one and the same. She could see what he meant by living his life as an actor: it was irrelevant whether he won or lost, but whichever it was to be, he'd do it with passion, as though it was the most important thing in the world.

The next race wasn't for another hour or so, and they wandered through the fairground together. She remembered the St Patrick's Day fair, the way he'd made her go on that Ferris wheel. She'd come a long way since then, but she still didn't know where she was.

The fair was a scruffy, amateurish affair. Most of the stalls were dilapidated, home-made constructions with crudely painted signs. She was surprised to see children betting on a sort of proto-roulette, tossing ten-pence pieces on to the board while the fast-talking stallholder spun the wheel. The children were a miniature version of their parents: serious about their gambling, philosophic about the result.

An old tinker, her face as brown and gnarled as a walnut, stood in Kate's path and offered to tell her fortune. When Kate declined, the old woman swore as if Kate wasn't there at all, and turned upon another passer-by.

Just by the beer tent, two men almost fell into their path. The men boozily and good-naturedly excused themselves and stumbled off into the crowd. Michael noticed her frown.

'Relax, your Honour,' he said. 'You can take the day off.'

He was right. What was she being so serious about? Why not enjoy herself like everybody else?

She watched the passing faces as they wove through the crowd. It was like a moving tableau of the whole of Ireland. Here was old Seamus, sixty untipped and half a gallon of porter a day. His son dressed in shades of brown from his nicotine-stained fingers to his hat to his shoes. Russett-haired Connemara girls as fresh and edible as apples. Mrs Hasset, skin the colour and texture of tripe, showing her gums in a laugh. Kate took it all in: the dog-eared and worn, the stained teeth, freckled faces, patched elbows. Local farmers, red-faced as beef, sharing a glass and a crack.

'As I roved out to Galway town to seek for recreation.' She turned to see Michael grinning at her. He took her arm. 'On the seventeenth of August my mind was elevated.' He started singing. 'There were multitudes assembled with their tickets at the station. My eyes began to dazzle, and they going to see the races.'

He won on the second race, taking their total up to sixteen pounds. As Kate expected, he was no more excited at winning than at losing.

She studied the faces of the punters as they went to collect their winnings, holding up their tickets to the bookies: little gods of chance. Life's a gamble, my friend. Tomorrow is a dark horse and bets are being taken.

The most important race of the day was coming up, and Michael enlisted her help in locating the winner amongst the eighteen runners. Whilst he made pencil marks in the margin, flicking through the pages of the race-card, Kate scanned the list of horses on the display board. 'Why don't you just pick one out with a pin?' she suggested after a few minutes.

He lowered the race-card and raised his eyes to her in astonishment. 'You can't do that!' he said, scandalised. 'There's an exact science to the throwing away of money.'

'Let me choose it.'

He reluctantly gave her the booklet and looked over her shoulder as she scanned the list of runners.

'I suppose you're going to pick one with a fancy name, and pay no mind to whether it's won a race in its life or not.'

She paid no attention to him. It was exactly what she was doing.

'Well, thank God there's not one called Black Beauty,' he said loudly, trying to distract her. 'That would be sure to be a housewife's favourite, even if it was a lame hack ridden by de Valera's mother.'

'Now or Never,' she said suddenly.

'What's that?'

'Now or Never. That's the horse I want.'

He took the race-card back. 'I thought it was a philosophical point you were making,' he grumbled, turning to look at the past form of the horse. Sure enough, it hadn't come close to winning the entire season, and at 12 to 1 there wasn't a hope in hell of it winning today. He marked it with a pencil and put the race-card into his back pocket. 'So how much do we have?' he said to her. 'Sixteen pounds plus five – twenty-one. At twelve to one that would bring in . . . ' He paused to calculate. 'Oh hell,' he said, giving up. 'Let's do it.'

'But that's our petrol money!'

'Now or never, all or nothing, do or be damned.' He held his hand out. 'Five pounds and may the gods smile on a bit of inspiration.'

They placed their bet, and Kate took the slip and kissed it. 'For luck,' she said.

They squeezed through the crowd to the rails and searched for their horse – number six. Kate spotted it first – its rider dressed in flamboyant pink and purple silks. Michael groaned when he saw the horse. It was blinkered and obviously highly strung, and the jockey was fighting to keep it under control. Kate loved it, however, and shouted out a cautious 'Come on, Now or Never,' when it passed them, prancing like a Spanish circus pony.

The starting-line was out of sight and they had to content themselves with the broadcast commentary that faded with the gusting wind. After two furlongs there was still no mention of Now or Never, and they looked worriedly at each other.

The horses had come into view at the bottom of the incline, still an indistinguishable mass apart from one horse, lagging by about five lengths. Kate prayed it wasn't theirs.

There it was! Finally a mention, but impossible to tell in what position. As the horses passed the halfway mark Now or Never was coming more frequently over the loudspeaker. It was in the leading group!

The crowd was beginning to get excited. Individual shouts grew into a sudden roar as the horses entered the home stretch. It was between the first three horses – number six and two others. Kate clung to the rail, bellowing with Michael, both their cries drowned by the roar of the crowd. It was neck and neck between Now or Never and a large black mare. As the two horses passed, Kate felt the heavy thud of their hooves through the earth, and she gave a final screech of encouragement.

And then it was over; the roar cut off as suddenly as a lightswitch, the runners-up ignored by the crowd as it buzzed with excitement. Kate turned and fell into Michael's arms. It had lost! They hugged in consolation, then held each other at arm's length. What a race! Her face was flushed, her nostrils flared like a horse's. They had lost! And it didn't matter.

It was a few minutes before she was calm enough to speak.

'What do we do now?'

'Back to Galway.'

They were in Galway city in twenty minutes. He directed her through the narrow streets until they reached a church, where he told her to stop.

'There's only one thing to do when your purse has run dry. Throw yourself on the bounty of the Lord.' He nodded at the church. 'Let's see if it's open.'

'Michael! What are you planning to do?' The image of him stealing silver candlesticks flashed through her mind.

'Alms, my dear, alms. The Catholic Church is supposed to be the church of the people, and richer than the Bank of Ireland to boot. It's time for a little loan. Off you go and sweet-talk the priest and see if you can't get us some food and a roof over our heads for the night.'

She got out of the car and reluctantly scrunched her way up the gravel path to the church. She paused at the door to look back at the car, and Michael waved her on encouragingly.

It was a long time since she'd been in a church, but the peculiar combination of dust and coolness was instantly familiar. She enjoyed churches, but it never occurred to her to visit them. She paused just inside the door and considered the architecture. Late Gothic arches, now painted a bluey-white; tall plain-glazed windows. The late afternoon light flooded the empty church. So different to English churches, Kate reflected: white walls, bare except for the bas-relief Stations of the Cross.

She walked down the nave to the altar, smiling at her irrational urge to genuflect. She wasn't particularly religious, but alone in a place of worship her agnostic mind was swayed in favour of believing. She stood in front of the altar. It was like a sacrificial stone: a heavy slab of local limestone draped with a crisp white altar cloth. Two intertwined fish were carved into the base of the altar. Ichthys. Beautiful in its own way.

She turned to leave and a movement in the transept caught her eye. She started slightly. There *was* somebody here. Had she been talking to herself? She took a deep breath and walked towards the figure, her heels scraping loudly on the flagstone floor.

The priest looked up when he heard her approach.

'Father,' she began. She paused – that was right, wasn't it? Or was it Padre? How the hell was she going to ask him for food? The old priest waited while Kate found the words.

'Father,' she said again. 'We're hungry and we have no money.' She winced with embarrassment almost before the words left her mouth.

'Well now, I suppose it's all gone into some bookie's pocket. Am I not right?'

She tried not to smile. 'Yes, you're right.'

'And you think it's the place of the Church to bail you out?' came the gently mocking reply.

Kate said nothing. He stepped down and took her by the arm. 'Are you a Catholic, my child?' he asked, leading her to the door.

'Well . . . ' she said, hesitantly.

'Christian of any shape, size or colour?'

There was a twinkle in his eye. He'd found her out. He pulled open the heavy door and they stepped into the porch.

'Some folk think the Church is a supermarket where they can just walk in and take things willy-nilly off the shelves and then walk out without paying or even so much as a "Thank you, Lord". And you know what?' He studied her with his watery eyes. 'They're welcome – every blackened sinner. And of course, I'll see what I can do for you.'

Michael had got out of the car and shuffled up to them, his head bowed, dragging a leg behind him as if he was lame.

'Can ye spare a crust for an old Republican soldier, Father?'

The priest looked in surprise at the new arrival, and then his face lit up. 'Michael O'Brien, is it you!'

Michael looked up, a grin on his face. 'Hello, Thomas.'

'Begod, it is so!' the priest said in amazement. He grasped Michael's hand and shook it in both of his. 'How in the divil's name are you?'

Kate watched the two men as they smiled delightedly at each other, vigorously shaking hands. Damn! He's done it again. Set me up once more!

'Is it true you're broke?' the priest asked.

'As clean as a whistle. We were doing fine until this colleen here chose a horse with three legs and we lost the lot.'

The men turned to smile at Kate. They were about the same age, but the priest was taller and thinner than Michael.

He had the pale, musty look of a cloistered monk, and he blinked his eyes as though he was unused to daylight. His black soutane was stained and shiny with use in places. Kate liked him immediately.

'Listen,' he said. 'I have to prepare for Mass – give succour to the poor fools who've frittered their money away on the horses. You're both welcome –' He caught himself, and laughed. 'Listen to me, invitin' two Pioneers to share a glass of malt with me! But all the same, the door's open and you're welcome to stay.'

'Thank you, Father,' Michael said with mock solemnity. 'But you know how the sight of black takes me – I couldn't guarantee I'd behave myself. And anyway,' he said, scratching his chin and grinning at his friend, 'I have the thirst of two men on me, so if you'll raid the collection box and give us enough for a pint apiece, we'll leave you to do the evening shift.'

The priest reached into his pocket, pulled out a wallet and gave him five pounds. 'Come after Mass and I'll feed the both of you.'

TWENTY-FOUR

They met outside the church at seven o'clock and followed Father Thomas home, crawling behind his bicycle in the car.

He lived on the outskirts of the city, above O'Kearney's the baker. The unlit staircase that led up to his flat from street level was uncarpeted and dusty, a pile of old newspapers nearly blocking their path midway up.

The kitchen betrayed the signs of lifelong bachelorhood: the breakfast things still laid out, a cheesy bottle of milk on the windowsill. Michael looked around the room. 'Still living the life of Riley, I see.'

'I am,' the priest said, lighting the gas and putting a kettle on to boil. 'I'm losing a few hairs on me head, and the stairs get steeper every day, but that's about all that's changed.'

He cleared the dirty plates, piling them into the cracked enamel sink. 'I have a cleaner, Mrs Nolan. She comes in once a week to prevent my final dissolution into household chaos, but I'm afraid she's fighting a losing battle.'

He made tea and they sat round the kitchen table. Michael and Thomas reminded Kate of two schoolboys getting together after a long holiday: excited and bursting with news. It was a few years since they'd last seen each other, and they jokingly compared how old age was taking its toll on them. Thomas had fared worse than Michael: weak and wheezy, but he made light of it.

Kate asked them how long they'd known each other. Michael shook his head, but Thomas knew exactly.

'We met in the spring of 1934. We were two young men studying for the priesthood together, in this very city.'

She turned to Michael, surprised. 'You studied for the priesthood? I never knew that!'

'Studying was as far as I got.' He sipped his tea. 'I'm what's known as a spoiled priest. I left before I took my final vows.' He laughed. 'Praise be to God – I'd have made a bloody awful priest. They were better off shot of me.'

She wanted to know the whole story.

'I had a religious streak,' he said, after thinking for a moment. 'It seemed the only thing to cure it was to get me to a seminary for a year or two.'

'Why did you leave?'

'Every young man of red blood and Catholic breeding was a Republican in those days, and I was no exception. When the Irish Republican Army got out of hand, the word came from Rome – excommunicate the bastards. The choice was between the Church and my country, and I chose the latter. So I left before they kicked me out.'

'Eyes full of fire and a mouthful of Gaelic – that's how I remember you in those days,' the priest said. 'Your heroes were Connolly and Terence MacSwiney when they should have been St Bernadette and the Holy Mother. But Michael, truth be told, it was more than the IRA that took you away from the priesthood. You'd never have been happy as a priest, and you knew it. You wanted more than was on offer, and you did the right thing by leaving.'

He didn't answer for a while. 'And if I had stayed, there would be one more human being walking the face of this earth.'

Thomas looked sadly at his friend. 'You've done a deal of good in your time, Michael.'

Michael frowned and turned to Kate. 'You see, when I left the Church, I joined the bold IRA and began my brief career as murderer. I would've done better to listen to John O'Leary – ' He stared into his teacup. ' "There are things a man might not do, not even to save his country," ' he quoted. 'I was young and stupid, and I took a life for an idea – the freedom of my country.'

He looked straight at Kate, and she could see tears forming in his eyes. 'Some poor British boy died for my ignorance. I never found out his name, but he couldn't have been older than twenty.'

He was lost in thought and then shook his head. 'If I was a priest, I'd perhaps have been a bad one. A rebel and no damn use to anyone. But I wasn't and some mother or sweetheart somewhere cursed the day I was born.'

Thomas and Kate looked at each other. 'Let me cook something for you,' she said suddenly.

The priest turned to her gratefully. 'Now, that would be a rare and marvellous thing. We have the makings of a fry – I have some rashers and eggs and I think there's some potatoes somewhere.'

He stood up and rested a hand on Michael's shoulder. 'I have a bottle hidden. Let's have a sup before we eat.'

They had tea in the kitchen, and then took their glasses and the bottle of whiskey into the study. It was a musty book-filled room; the heavy leather furniture seeming to absorb what little daylight strained through the grimy windows. Thomas switched on a side light and made some attempt to clear his desk, sweeping newspapers and books alike on to the floor in the corner. Kate saw that most of the books were cheap paperback cowboy books.

Michael was browsing through the bookshelf and Thomas went over to him. 'There's a book here you might be interested in seeing.' He pulled out a slim blue volume and handed it to Michael. 'Recognise it?'

'I do, by God!' he said in surprise. 'The Bishop wouldn't be too pleased to see this amongst your cowboy books.'

'Strangely enough, I'm only just after reading it. I was thinking I could use some bits from it for a sermon.'

'And will you do so?' He flicked through the pages and looked up at his friend.

Thomas laughed and lowered himself into his hard-backed chair. 'The only reason it wasn't on the *Index Librorum Prohibitorum* was because there were so few copies, it never reached the Bishop's attention.'

'You flatter me, Thomas! I thought it wasn't banned because it wasn't controversial enough, not because nobody read it!'

'No, a powerful booklet it was for the times. I disagreed with it then, as you know, and still do on certain points, but

I'm afraid it would still be too much for the average Catholic person to take. It's hardly what you might call doctrinal stuff, even in these enlightened times.'

'I'm fascinated,' Kate said. 'What is it?'

'A thing I wrote just after leaving the seminary.' Michael looked at the spine. *'Harmony and Discord.'* He handed it to Kate.

'What's it about?' she asked, turning over its yellowed pages.

'Ask Thomas,' Michael said, nodding at the priest. 'I haven't read it for nearly fifty years.'

'Man is not a creature of sin, but a poor misled fool,' he summed up. 'There is no "good" and "bad" as such, just harmony, which is the will of God, or the law of Nature, and discord, which is the going against of that will. It's an interesting theory, but not exactly orthodox Catholicism. Let me read you some.'

Kate gave him the book. He put on his reading-glasses and looked through the pages for a moment. 'Ah, here we are. "If, as Catholics, we are to be more than frightened children," ' he read, ' "waiting for the dread judgment of our unseen, unheard father, we need to recognise that 'judgment' is on hand *now*; that punishment is, if not immediate, certainly meted out within the lifetime of the individual. Divine judgment *may* follow. That is open to debate. What is beyond debate is the existence of suffering.

' "Is it a leap of faith to suggest that suffering comes, not adventitiously, but as the ineluctable result of an action performed, or a thought entertained? Few would deny that intemperate eating gives rise to indigestion, or that over-drinking leads to a sore head the next day. Can we not also say that guilt is the inevitable consequence of performing actions we know to be wrong; that suffering comes from transgression, or as I have said, discord? If we are to accept that, then where is the need for a divine judge? Isn't the torment of bodily and mental anguish enough reason not to sin, without the added fulmination of a judgmental God? We would be stupid if, as a child, we were to put our hand in the fire whether our parents are going to punish us for it or not. Isn't the pain of being burnt enough reason not to do it? But sin is sweet, I hear you say: we do not burn until later. So I ask you: are you no more than children? Will you continue to gorge yourselves on sweets, even though you know the initial pleasure will soon turn to pain? I speak to you as adults. I say refrain from wrong, not because you fear the divine wrath of God, but because you know, as surely as any scientist, that discord in your life will bring you pain in your life." '

Thomas lowered the book and took off his glasses. 'I speak to you as adults. How old were you when you wrote this? Twenty?'

'About that,' Michael said, pulling his pipe from his pocket. 'But what did you think of it?' he asked Kate.

'What do you mean by harmony?'

'Toss us the book.'

Thomas gave him the book and refilled their glasses.

Michael flicked through the book. 'Let's try this,' he said, clearing his throat and holding the book at arm's length.

' "What is harmony? It is the concord of two aspects into a whole, such as when individual notes combine to create a chord. Concord for humankind takes the form of no individual action working against the larger action of the universe. If we consider the Creation to be a divine symphony with us as individual instruments, then our purpose in living is to play the note intended by the composer, for it is the composer who has brought us together, who indeed validates our very existence. And it is the Creator-Composer's intention that we, as individuals, harmonise with the rest of the orchestra, the rest of God's creatures.

' "Harmony is our purpose and our natural state. Discord is the perversion of our intrinsic nature. Perverted, not in any moral sense, but thwarted from natural expression by an obstacle, as the course of a river is diverted by a boulder. And this obstacle is our own wilfulness: this is what makes us human, and this is what makes us err." '

He put the book down. 'Not bad, a little pompous though.'

'That's all very well, Michael, and nicely put,' Thomas said. 'It's later that we part company. If I can read you the next piece.' He took the book back and read it for a few minutes while Michael filled his pipe.

'Here – listen. "Can we really believe that the baby that lifts our hearts with a smile is anything other than a pure and innocent soul? And yet when we look at ourselves, now adult, we know ourselves to be sinners. And we ask ourselves where that innocence has gone. It has been trampled underfoot by the world and our propensity to err, and in our despair we say this is the way it must always have been. But I propose that Man is not naturally fallen: *no* child is born into a state of sin. It happens in his individual life and is neither irrevocable nor absolute. It is a temporary absence of the light of God rather than the ineradicable birthmark of sin. Every time we transgress the will of God, or shall we say, the law of Nature, we freshly recreate Adam's sin. But because of ignorance, *not* sinfulness. The *absolute* forgiveness of sins, mortal as well as venial, is available to us at every moment of our lives. We carry our sin with us through our lives, but at any moment we can lay our burden down and become as we originally were: as little children. Then the kingdom of God is ours." '

The priest took off his glasses and rubbed his eyes. 'But Michael, leaving aside the matter of mortal sin, can Man save himself? Can he dump the load of his sins and go back home on his own? Don't you admit the need for grace – the helping hand?'

'Of course he can save himself on his own,' Michael replied from behind a cloud of tobacco smoke. 'And of course he needs grace. Grace comes from inside, not outside. Man *is* God – all he needs to do is recognise that and all his sins vanish, because how can God sin?'

'Hmmm . . . ' Thomas said doubtfully. 'We've been over this ground before and I think we'll just have to agree to differ. That's not the Church's view of Man, nor mine either.'

'So what are we?' Michael asked, stretching his legs in front of him and levelling his gaze at his friend. 'Polluted bags of offal blundering around this testing ground of God and damning ourselves to everlasting torment if we don't pass?'

Kate interrupted them. 'Weren't you saying the same thing yesterday? Man is a machine and there's no hope?'

'To a butcher we're bones, flesh and gristle, and most doctors would agree. Just complicated biological machines. But there's one thing Thomas and I would agree upon – there's an aspect of a person a butcher, even a psychologist, can't find. And that, whatever you want to call it, is what we really are. *That*'s our essence.'

Thomas nodded. 'But what exactly is your picture of a human being?'

He puffed on his pipe before answering. 'A human being comes in two parts: the puppet and the puppeteer.'

'And isn't that your bag of offal?' Kate asked.

'The puppet is, to be sure. Just a painted face and a tubful of guts. But the puppeteer *has* no body, has no mind.'

'And is the puppeteer your colourful way of saying the soul?'

'If that's what you want to call it, but I probably don't have the same thing in mind by "soul" as you do. The soul, the puppeteer, the one jerking the strings, *can't* be damned. The puppeteer is pure, unflawed, unflawable, and that's because he's out of the drama. Whatever takes place onstage – arms falling off, strings getting tangled – cannot touch the puppeteer.'

The light was failing and Thomas stood up to switch another lamp on. The blue haze of Michael's pipe gave the room an unreal appearance, as though they were looking at each other underwater.

Kate turned to Michael. 'Does the puppeteer have any will?'

'The puppeteer *is* will. Not the "I want this", or "I should do that" sort of will. *Not* the mind – that belongs to the puppet. But *will*,' he said significantly. 'Energy. Life force. The will to live – call it what you want.'

'So what's discord?'

'It's the thwarting of our natural expression, nothing more. Sin doesn't come into it.'

'And our natural expression – what does that look like?' She put her glass on the side table. She was beginning to feel a little drunk.

'Love,' Michael said simply. 'Unconditional love. And *that* can only be found in harmony – when we're the way we're intended to be.'

'But how do we get there?' she persisted. 'How do we find out who we are?'

The two men sensed the sudden urgency of her question: this was real for her; she needed to know.

'By looking and being honest.' He looked straight at her. 'And then casting out devils.'

She looked at Thomas, but the priest had his eyes on Michael.

'Exorcism?'

He shrugged. 'If you want to call it that, but bell, book and candle have little to do with it.'

'What do you mean then?' she asked.

'What do you think we've been doing all this time?' he said quietly.

Her eyes widened. 'Casting out devils?'

'Life-denying thoughts. Anything that's not love.'

She shook her head and reached for her whiskey. She took a sip and held it in the well of her tongue, savouring its fire. Exorcism?

It was Thomas's turn to ask a question. 'And what's our task when we know who we are?'

'To do whatever's necessary.'

'Necessary for what?'

Michael held his hands like a conductor and gave a long hum. 'The symphony.'

They both looked at Kate, and then at each other. She'd picked up the book and was flicking through its pages. Thomas got up and topped up his glass and Michael's. Kate held her hand over the top of hers.

'And a priest?' he said, sitting down again. 'What job does a priest have?'

'*Not* to be a judge.'

'And when people ask me what to do, what's right and what's wrong?'

'Tell them it's time to grow up. They know full well what's right and what's wrong.'

'But some of them don't.'

'Then knock some sense into them! You should have a large stick in the confessional, and when someone's playing the eejit, you should take them outside and beat hell's delight out of them!'

'Oh, Michael!'

They both laughed at the image.

'The only reason they can't tell right from wrong,' Michael continued, 'is because they're asleep. Harmony and discord sound the same to a sleeping person.'

'But what about the comatose?'

'Are you telling me there are unredeemable sinners? Oh, doubting Thomas! How many years in the ministry and you still think we're not all the same? The comatose are the same. You just have to beat them longer and harder.'

'And the name of the stick I use?'

'Two sticks – one for each hand. One you can call Wisdom, the other you can call Compassion.'

'I beat them with compassion?'

'You do. Ruthless compassion. A love so deep and strong that you'll do anything to save them from their suffering. But – and you know this well enough, don't you, my friend – compassion is only a word as long as you've got something to prove.'

Thomas nodded gently, his eyes fixed on Michael. 'And sin?'

'How can the children of God sin? If they do wrong, it's only because they don't know better.'

Kate began reading unannounced. ' "So what is the sinner, if we wish to call the fallen one that? He is nothing other than a poor fool. Only a fool cheats and lies and steals unless a life depends on it, for only a fool would sell his life for anything less than life itself. But a fool is as much a creature of God as the saints, and we need to love and understand him. (For he is us.) We need to lead the fool compassionately to wisdom, not hound him with morality. If we condemn him for his blindness, he will remain blind. We need to open his eyes so he can see who he really is: a child of the universe in temporary, self-imposed exile. This is Social Science; it is not religion. There is no need for dogma, nor even faith; the evidence is before our eyes: the fool suffers for his foolishness." '

She stopped reading. Thomas had sunk his head, the lamplight shining off his bald patch. He looked up and asked her to read on.

' "How do we deal with evil? Do we meet it head on, vanquishing it with our Christian Army? How do we deal with discord? By trying to drown it out? No. We wait for its reverberations to die out, and then continue on our way. Again and again we will transgress: it is Man's way. When we do so; when the note jars through our very being, have compassion and dignity. Wait for the cacophony to be silenced, and then return to the symphony." '

Michael pulled himself out of his chair. 'Whiskey anyone?'

They shook their heads, so he poured one out for himself. He continued: 'All the talk of morality from the pulpit just adds to the unholy row, can you not see that? Guilt, piety, self-righteousness. What a racket!' He held his hands over his ears in mock horror.

'Morality – the should and shouldn't of things – won't move us one iota closer to harmony. In fact the opposite. The only purpose of morality is to convince us how evil we are. And you know who invented morality?' He swayed a little, pointing at Thomas with his glass. 'The Devil!' he announced triumphantly, 'and a clever bastard he was too! Be careful, he said – Man is a wild animal, and animals need chains. So the Devil chained up Man, and guess how Man behaved? Like a wild animal, of course! And when he's not a wild animal, he's crippled with guilt and frustration.' He sat down heavily in his chair.

'But what's the alternative to morality?' Kate asked. 'Anarchy?'

'If that means people thinking for themselves, then yes. Morality comes down from above – tablets of stone from the mountain.' He lowered his glass on to the arm of the chair to demonstrate. 'And what does that do to us? Keeps us in line –

more or less. But at what cost? The cost of our bigness. The cost of our taking responsibility for ourselves.'

'But can we live without laws?' she asked.

'Can we live *with* laws? We're on the brink of destroying the whole bloody planet with our laws!'

'But wouldn't it be in a worse state without laws?'

'Who can say? It's never been tried, not since the days of Eden. And *that's* a story that's been sadly messed around with,' he said to Thomas. 'We were doing just fine without laws until Adam and Eve decided to be like God, and know good from evil. The spanner in the works was the apple – not the serpent, not Adam, not Eve. The trouble started when Man thought he knew how things should be. Unfortunately the Church has done a good job of convincing us we're basically rotten, and the only thing saving us from ourselves is the commandments. Man is *not* rotten – he's just psychotic – crazy if he thinks he's omniscient.'

He was on a roll, bending forward in his chair, his expression intense, almost fierce. 'Can you understand what I'm saying? Man, like everything else, is energy, and energy is neither good nor bad – it just *is*, and is GOOD. Good in a way a mountain or river is good. Right. Natural. The way it's designed to be. Discord, evil, sin, comes from here –' He tapped his temple.

'When you know who you are, and when you take responsibility for that, then it's not possible to do wrong. And self-knowledge and responsibility come in the same package.' He stopped and fell back into his chair.

Thomas changed his mind about another whiskey, and got up. They listened in silence to the glug as he slopped some carelessly into his glass. 'And what's your solution, then?' he said with his back to the room. 'Disband the churches and the courts?'

He turned to look at Michael. Suddenly Kate saw the doubt in the face of the priest. He was Narciss to Michael's Goldmund. The one who had stayed behind while his friend, the wild-headed Goldmund, had taken on the world. Now they had come almost full circle. They were old men and the experiment of their lives was nearly over. And doubt, the final hurdle, was standing in front of the priest.

'I have no solution, Thomas. All I have is a vision. A vision of a world where people know who they are. A world of people free from suffering. I just raise the question: what is the possibility for life on this planet? How near to God can we get?'

TWENTY-FIVE

'I still miss her, you know.'

He sounded surprised, as though a year was a long time to get over a death. He'd known death: all but one of his family gone, most of his friends too, and yet it never ceased to amaze him, how all that energy could just vanish.

They were standing beside his wife's grave. A year today, she'd died. Just four months before Kate had come into his life.

It was late August and the Atlantic wind flattened the uncut couch grass on the bare hillside. It was a bleak spot for a graveyard: on an exposed slope facing the reek, a triangle of Clew Bay visible in the tuck between two mountains. There was no church or building of any sort, just a drystone wall to keep the sheep out and the incongruous tombstones like granite outcrops. The graveyard had been filled years ago, but now that the last of the remaining families had gone – dead or moved into town – it had been forgotten: a corporation dump, a field of corpses. Ann had wanted to be buried near the cottage and the local authorities had reluctantly bent to Michael's persistent demands that they find a space to squeeze her in. She'd never liked the town, Michael told them, and if they couldn't find a space in the local graveyard, then she'd just stay on the kitchen table until they did so.

Nobody had come here for years. The sheep couldn't scale the walls to graze and so the grass was higher, the weeds more prolific than the surrounding fields.

Kate wandered through the graveyard while Michael tidied up his wife's grave. Brushing aside the weeds and scraping off the moss she read the inscriptions. *Here lies the body of Patrick*

McGuinn; Pray for the soul of Mary Grady. The same names
echoed from one granite headstone to another: O'Down,
Dillon, Finnegan. United in death as in life. Now they lay,
forgotten, beneath the weeds and the lowering August sky.

Michael surveyed his work. The plot had become overgrown during the weeks they'd been away, and almost as
soon as they'd returned to the cottage, he said he wanted
to tidy it up. It was only when Kate had seen the date on the
headstone that she realised it was the anniversary of Ann's
death. They'd cut the grass back and Kate had picked a posy
of wild flowers which she rested on the headstone: celandine,
ragwort and wild orchid.

She bent to clip a final tuft of grass from the edge of the
grave. 'Ann O'Brien', it read simply, with her dates. There
was space on the stone for another inscription. Michael
obviously planned to share this plot with his wife.

He knelt and rested by the stone. Kate half-turned away,
thinking he was going to pray, but he spoke instead.

'It won't be long, Ann. It won't be long.'

Kate touched him on the shoulder. 'Don't talk like that,'
she chided. 'You've got years yet.'

It always depressed her to hear talk of welcoming death,
as if it was a benevolent doctor who was going to make
everything better. Her mother had often talked like that,
frightening Kate and her sister with her glittering black eyes.
When Kate had seen that look in her mother's eyes and
heard her talk of death, she knew somewhere in her childish
understanding that she and her sister meant nothing to her.

She looked down at Michael, still kneeling by the grave.
How many years before he'd be here under the very ground
they were standing on? The plot would be overgrown like
the others. He would be the last to go.

He sat against a gravestone and patted the ground beside
him. 'Sit down out of the wind and rest a while.'

She sat beside him, drawing her knees up and hugging
her shins. Summer had ended suddenly, like a door being
shut. It was autumn now, though the trees didn't show
it.

They sat in silence listening to the dry rustle of the wind through the grass. She plucked the head off a pink clover and drew one of its petals out and chewed on its sweet sap.

'I'm not afraid of dying,' he said suddenly. 'I'm old enough to have made friends with death.'

She wiggled her foot in the long grass. She didn't want to talk about this. 'It comes to us all,' she ventured at last.

He blew a long, obscene raspberry, and she looked at him in astonishment. 'I'm not so old you have to humour me!'

'I meant –'

'I know what you meant. You meant for an old cod like me, death must look like an attractive proposition.'

He put his arm around her and they snuggled closer together. She twirled the head of clover between thumb and forefinger and then dropped it.

'My friendship with death is not a cosy affair,' he said. He tapped the stone in front of them with his foot. 'This is death. It doesn't give a damn about you and me. But death is the man – listen to his advice and he's the best friend you can have. And you know what his advice is?' He leant towards her and pressed his mouth conspiratorially to her ear. '*Live*,' he whispered melodramatically. 'Because it ain't going to last for ever. Death is always here.' He lifted his hand off her shoulder and touched her cheek, making her jump. 'Death can touch you like that: it stares in the face of the old, but it lurks behind the backs of the young.'

'Michael, this is so morbid!'

'Not at all,' he said, surprised. 'It's life I'm talking about. It's only when you know your every moment may be your last that you can *really* live. 'Cos then you realise you don't have time for doubt and hesitation and pettiness. I call the way most people live their lives morbid – they're half dead already. They worry so much about surviving that they forget to live.'

The wind was picking up, rustling the grass like an ebbing tide over a shingle beach. From where she sat, Kate could see the tops of the headstones thrusting through the long grass, like serious headmasters.

'When you see death face-to-face, then you'll be really effective. You'll start living your life as if your life depended on it. You'll do what's needed *now*, not put it off to another day. You'll tell the special person in your life you love them – *now*, not some time in the future. You'll sort out the things you've been meaning to sort out for the past ten years. You'll start to be honest, because you'll see you don't have time for lies. You can't afford to waste time because you don't know how much you have left. All you know is that you've got *now*. Your life is now, and it's here – it always has been and always will be, and the quality of your life rests on your ability to be just that – here and now.'

He fell silent, disengaging his arm from hers. It was true, of course – she'd frittered her life, reckless with her time as if her life, her youth, would never end. And what had she to show for it apart from the storeroom of her memory becoming yearly fuller, and the creeping signs of age appearing in her face? A phrase of her father's came to her, something he always said before he went to bed: another day closer to the grave.

Death had never been real to her. Even when her mother died, she'd never let it in. The reality was too inhuman, too unnatural for the human mind to fathom. She'd told her school friends that her mother was abroad, inventing letters that had arrived from her, and in a way she came to believe her own myth. Anything was easier to believe than that the empty body on the bed was her mother. As she got older it had become a memory like any other: I was born in Paris, I used to live in Oslo, oh, and my mother's dead. Never for a minute did she really believe it. Whatever gave birth to her was still alive. 'Mother' was a brown snapshot, a disembodied memory, a concept of causality. Daughters have mothers, so I must have had one. Once.

How was it possible that this body could cease to breathe and move? It wasn't that she considered herself immortal, it was just that 'death' was outside her vocabulary. It was a foreign word, not a word at all, but a meaningless noise. Like colour to a blind person, death was outside her comprehension.

Michael pulled himself up from the gravestone and helped Kate to her feet. 'Let's go back, they'll probably be finishing now.'

He'd finally given in to Kate's concerned· nagging, and agreed to have electricity put in. Two workmen were there now doing the wiring inside the house.

They waded through the grass and climbed over the wall.

'Do you believe in life after death?' she asked, taking one last look at the graveyard.

He linked her arm. 'I believe in life after birth. The rest can take care of itself.'

They walked arm in arm down the lane, through the tunnel of overgrown hedges. The wind was massive now, collapsing on to the land from the ocean like a tidal wave. It was inescapable, flooding every corner of the landscape. The lane funnelled the wind so that it snatched at their clothes, plucking their sleeves and trouser-legs, catching and swirling Kate's hair. She saw a seagull wheeling backwards and upwards, tossed by gusts like a cork on the sea.

As they stepped from the shelter of the hedge, the full force of the wind struck them. Facing the bay below them, they looked down the slope, leaning into the wind, their eyes watering. Kate's hair flew out behind her, and she laughed, exhilarated at the invisible hands which tried to push her over. She glanced at Michael; but he was unaware of her: his nose and lips tinged blue with the cold, he stared into the face of the wind, his eyes squinting against the blast. For a bizarre moment she thought that Michael had summoned the wind. This is what I mean, his face seemed to say: death is like this wind.

She felt the understanding of his words tugging at her like the wind. The land was an empty vessel being filled from another source. It was a vacuum, inanimate and empty until fractured and filled with the generating power of this. This presence.

Death was like this wind: an indiscriminate force swallowing us, the trees, the birds, the cloud-shrouded mountains.

TWENTY-SIX

The reek, Croagh Patrick, Ireland's holy mountain where Patrick spent his personal forty days in the wilderness and cast the serpents from the top into the sea; it had glowered at her for so long she knew she'd have to climb it sooner or later.

They got up early and hitched the few miles to the base of the mountain. As usual the summit was shrouded in mist: its top cut off as neatly as a topped boiled egg. St Patrick's example had turned into tradition: every year thousands of pilgrims struggled to the top. Michael too, for his own pagan reasons, had climbed it every year. This year, he vowed would be his last – at his age it was time to call a halt to such shenanigans.

Mountains look easy from the bottom. It's easy to imagine yourself striding nimbly up them like a latter-day Finn McCool. A simple three thousand feet – she was surprised when he told her it was a three- or four-hour journey to the top.

From a distance the mountain had always reminded Kate of a breast: smooth and regular, tapering to a nipple at the top. No wonder Patrick had chosen this peak amongst the many. Breast or no breast, there was something significant about the way it rose, symmetrical and perfectly formed, out of the flattened paps of its neighbours. The eye was irresistibly drawn to this almost symbolic sky-pointing rock. Miracles could take place here, and some said they did.

At close quarters it was an angry giant, scarred and glowering. The striations that had looked like streaks of snow she could now see were light-coloured rock showing through the foliage as bare patches. It wasn't anything like the pretty mountain she'd ambled up one day in Wales. That had been verdant and gentle, rising and dipping in a considerate way. The holy mountain on the other hand was all browns and greys – barren except for the furze and scattered hawthorn trees which clung to the rock against the fierce sea wind.

An untidy stream had spread across the scree which marked the beginning of the path, and they had to pick their way carefully over the rust-red stones for a hundred yards or so until they were on dry ground. According to the notice at the base, there were three 'stations' around which the pilgrim was instructed to walk and recite prayers. They reached the first – Leacht Benain, an unremarkable mound of stones – after twenty minutes. Kate was out of breath and collapsed on the side of the path, begging Michael to stop. He reluctantly paused and squatted beside her.

She hugged her hurting chest and looked down to where they'd come from. It seemed only a few hundred yards – the plaster statue of St Patrick at the base was still in sight. Clew Bay was glitteringly laid out; the tiny islets, clumps of green dotting the sea. It looked nicer down there: cars zipping noiselessly along the coast road, thin lines of smoke rising from chimneys.

The climb had annoyed her. At every other step she was either tripped by outcrops of turf or slithered on loose stones beneath her feet. She was hot and she had a stitch and mountains were stupid.

He saw the frustration in her face. 'You can't beat a mountain,' he said, 'so stop fighting it.'

She lay on her back and stretched her arms out.

'Where do you get all your energy?' She directed the question at a patch of blue in the cloudy sky. He'd led the way and she'd barely been capable of keeping up with him.

'The same place as everybody,' he replied. 'It's just I don't squander it swimming upstream like yourself.'

She rolled over to look at him. Twice her age, and he looked as fresh as when they'd started.

'You need to use your energy sparingly, Kate. Stop fighting the mountain and you may just find that it's designed to support you.' He laughed, patting the ground beside him. 'Deftness and not brute force is what's needed in climbing a mountain. It's a matter of finding the right combination, like a thief picking a lock. Watch where I put my feet, and try to follow exactly.'

Head down, she followed his instructions. Keep your attention on the path and off your destination. Concentrate on what you're doing and the journey will take care of itself.

She managed to keep up with him for twenty minutes or so, but as the path got steeper, so her pace slackened and she was left behind.

She'd given up concentrating on what she was doing, and found herself stumbling and cursing as before. The pain in her chest had become a stab with each indrawn breath, and her neck had begun to ache. She was tempted to sit down and rest, but he was almost out of sight.

A group of climbers greeted her as they passed on the way down. Kate forced a smile and turned to watch their easy descent, envying them their stout staffs and sensible shoes. They were already smiling in anticipation of a pot of tea and barm brack in their cosy holiday cottage.

'Come on,' she heard Michael shout down at her.

She craned her neck back to look at him: a stick figure sitting with his back to a rock. Why does he bother? she thought. Why do *I* bother?

She reached him in five minutes. He nodded hello and watched her pull off her boots.

'I'm not enjoying this, Michael,' she said, emptying a small shower of grit from one of her boots.

'I'm sorry about that.'

She glanced over at him, her heart pounding from the climb. Was he being sarcastic?

'I mean it,' he smiled back, adjusting the angle of his beret. 'There's no point in having a miserable time.'

She tugged her boots on and frowned at the panorama. Achill Island was visible as a smudge on the horizon. She was surprised how high they were: the cottages on the waterfront were tiny; the little white blurs at the base of the mountain, sheep.

'What *is* the point?' she asked. 'Why the hell are we climbing this mountain?'

'You tell me, Kate.' He was relaxed, enjoying the view. 'What's the point of a mountain? What's the point of climbing it? In fact, what's the point of any of this?' He pointed with his chin at the steel canopy of the sky, the wind-tugged bracken, the mountain sloping down into the bay.

The wind caught the crepe scarf she pulled from her pocket, flapping it uncontrollably until she tied it in place around her head. 'There isn't a point. Isn't that what you say? Nothing has any meaning?'

He wiggled his feet back and forth in front of him. 'Things have meaning, obviously. The question is: where does meaning come from? Inside or outside? Is significance intrinsic or attributed?'

She thought about it, sucking on her teeth. 'It's attributed – nothing has any meaning unless we say so.'

'Sure?'

'No.'

He followed the erratic flight of a seagull, squinting against the brightness of the sky. 'Try this for size – see if it fits. The world is composed of objects and their functions. We make up all the rest – the significance, the meaning.'

'Functions?'

He pretended to pick up a book and flick through its pages. 'Function – noun; an activity proper to something,' he said, as if reading from a dictionary.

He picked up a small stone and dropped it into his palm. 'The Sermon on the Mount: an object falling through space is a function of mass in a world of gravity. Falling is *not* its purpose. Function is the "how" and "what". Purpose is the "why". And why, why? Because I say so. The purpose of a chair is to be sat on. Why? Because I say so. An ant would want to eat it – that's the purpose for an ant: food. But the functions of a chair are undeniable: to float on water, to burn in fire, to fall through the air. Are you following me?' He shot a questioning look at her.

'Yes. But are you saying a person is the same? There's no purpose in being a human except what you decide?'

'What do you think? Is your purpose the same as Attila the Hun's? Is your major concern rape and pillage?'

She looked round as though considering the proposition. 'But underneath aren't we all the same? Attila the Hun presumably wanted love like anybody else.'

'Precisely! Love is not a purpose. It's a function. Purpose is a matter for the individual to come up with. Function is something we all have in common. We all obey the laws of physics, like chairs and stones do. But we have other functions – activities that are uniquely human. Human beings are designed in such a way that they can experience something that has nothing to do with survival.'

'And what's that?'

'You want a list? Joy,' he began, counting on his fingers. 'A sense of what beauty is, sanctity is. The faculty to worship, to offer devotion, to experience ecstasy. A sense of humour. In one word – love.'

'And hate?' she asked.

His eyebrows went up. 'Hate is survival-oriented.'

She was cold and snuggled into her jacket. Love? He talked about love?

'We're like a sports car, designed just for the crack of going fast. And top speed for us is unconditional love. And there's no point to it.'

They sat in silence, watching the world spread out beneath their feet – the bay, the mountain, the tiny figures of some people beginning to climb.

'But is it worth it, Michael? Is any of this,' she indicated the scene, 'worth a damn?'

He took a deep breath and let it out noisily. 'Who knows? When you see the meaninglessness of your life and the inevitability of your death, then you just have to believe it's worth it. That doesn't mean it *is* worth it, but that you live your life as if it had some meaning. As though you're playing a game.'

He took her hand and squeezed it. 'The situation is hopeless.' He smiled suddenly. 'But not serious.'

She frowned at the bad joke.

'My life is empty of meaning,' he continued. 'I just see the facts: I'm alive now, and what has a beginning has an end. That's all – no great significance in that. But then I say to myself, "You know, Michael, this would be interesting if you played it for all it's worth." So that's what I do.'

He let go of her hand and groped in his pocket, pulling out a pencil stub. He picked up a saucer-sized stone, and scribbled something on it.

'It's another hour or so to the top,' he said, tossing the stone aside and getting to his feet. 'Will you be staying here, or are you coming with me?'

She shook her head. 'I'll wait for you here.'

He turned round without another word and started off up the mountain. 'The top of the mountain isn't necessarily the highest point,' he called without looking back at her.

She watched him zig-zag up the slope, getting smaller and smaller. Without standing up, she crawled to where he'd been sitting and looked for the stone. She found it: curiously smooth as though it had once been underwater. It fitted beautifully into her palm, a miniature discus. She read the pencilled scrawl.

> *If life is a game*
> *we might as well play*
> *with everything we've got*
> *but there's no reason to do so*
> *and neither no reason to not.*

She laughed and lay back, enjoying the unexpected sunshine that suddenly flooded the mountainside.

TWENTY-SEVEN

She tucked the letter in the bib pocket of her dungarees and stretched her legs out on to the front doorstep. London seemed so far away now – another lifetime. It had been, what? She counted the months she'd been away. Nearly five months: a complete summer. She crossed her arms over her chest, wiggling her bottom to settle into a more comfortable position. She was coming up to thirty-five now. Recently she'd noticed that she'd begun to change shape, she could feel it, too: heavier, broader across the hips. Her face was changing as well: it had become fleshier; the crow's-feet lines that fanned out from her eyes, deep and white against her tanned skin. And she didn't mind. Once she would have fretted about it, starved herself until she'd reached her target weight, but now she didn't care. Not from apathy, but something else: it was all right not to be young for ever. She smiled to herself – was she growing up, was that it? Is this what it felt like to be a woman? she thought. This comfort?

London, she mouthed. London. And now here she was, sitting on an Irish doorstep enjoying the evening sun; blue denim dungarees turned up at the ankles, hair sun-bleached and long, tied back off her face. She leant back against the doorjamb, surveying the enclosure in front of her. She didn't miss it, the life she'd left behind. Who was there to miss – Paul? She'd hardly given him a thought, not since the court case. And now? Did this letter make any difference?

Some sort of falcon hung flapping above the copse across from the lane, and she watched it until it swooped down out of sight. She'd come to know this land, its bog acid soil, its sudden tantrums of weather. She knew its smell and feel, had its dirt under her fingernails, its rainwater in her hair. The season – autumn – had turned itself over the horizon as though it was a giant cog, inevitable and irresistible. Kate had watched the trees giving up their leaves, felt the evenings drawing in, felt part of this, this huge unfolding.

She tried to remember how it had first looked to her, all those months ago. Pretty now, as the sun slipped away, a couple of hens scratching in the dust, marsh flowers like stars in the green sky of the turf. But it had been cold and bleak, when she first came here. She remembered the soil, frozen and alien; the levelling of the land under its white blanket. Hard to imagine, the sun-warmed path in front of her, once deep under snow. Things changed: things and how they are seen. That had been another person, the Kate who had struggled and fought her way through winter. And him? Was he different, or was it just her perception of him? He was gentler, more friendly – that was undeniable. He didn't scare Kate so much now: she was beginning to know him, unlock the enigma of who he was. She was as familiar with Michael as she'd ever been with a man: she knew him, and yet she didn't. They were close – he was beginning to let her in, and yet there was something of him she couldn't touch, a portion of his being she had no access to, could have no access to.

So, what was he? Father figure, friend? She didn't know: she tried to grasp their relationship, define it in terms she knew, but it defied her. It was an itch, a fascinating, infuriating itch. They were independent, they kept their distance when distance was needed, and yet she always knew where he was, always had his whereabouts mapped somewhere in her mind. She tested herself: he was out the back, pottering around in the outhouses probably. He was wearing his cream linen trousers with the broken fly, and the black donkey jacket she hated with the plastic cuffs. He hadn't shaved for a couple of days. She'd taken to kissing his cheek in the morning and before she went to bed and he invariably needed a shave, but oddly, she enjoyed the rasp of his bristles against her skin. It was reassuring somehow; manly.

She was suddenly aware of the hen pecking round her ankles, and flapped a foot at it. It clucked and hopped over her leg, making a dash for the doorway. Kate blocked its way with her arm, and it turned and scooted away, rustling its dusty feathers indignantly.

She enjoyed it here: she'd recently become conscious of her enjoyment, surprising herself with it. She was learning to savour moments: the moments of quiet, moments when her past fell away and she was just Kate: a person peeling potatoes in a pan of cold water, scattering grain for the chickens, idly watching the dust motes circle in a shaft of sunlight, flinching from standing barefoot on cold flagstones. It was hers, this oasis, and she wanted nothing to disturb it. No letters from London, no ghosts making claims on her fresh start.

She listened: silence except for the dripping of the tap in the cool interior of the kitchen. She pushed herself to her feet, stretched and yawned, surprised at how sleepy she was.

He was collecting the windfalls from under the two old apple trees in the back garden. There had been a storm the night before, rain lashing against the tiny window-panes of her bedroom. The sky had been swept clean of storm clouds when she woke in the morning, and these apples strewn below the trees.

She watched him wiping each apple carefully with a rag and placing them in a wicker basket. The worm-eaten and damaged ones, he kicked to one side for the goat.

'I thought we could walk over to James's, give him some of these apples,' he said, glancing up at her.

She nodded. 'It was from Mary, like I thought.'

He grunted that he'd heard and carried on wiping the apples. They'd driven into Westport that afternoon to do the week's shopping and pick up the mail from the post office. There was only one letter, from Mary, her sister. She wrote occasionally and once tendered a vague promise to come and stay at the cottage, but nothing had come of it.

'Any news?'

'Paul's got married.'

He straightened up, arching the stiffness out of his back.

'Has he now?'

She pulled the letter out of her pocket, slipping a newspaper cutting from the envelope. Mary had cut it out of the local paper and Kate studied the fuzzy photograph again. It was hard to make Paul out – the photographer had caught him side on, and it could have been a picture of almost anyone, but the bride had been captured full-face by the camera, and not surprisingly: even in a poor-quality snap like this, it was obvious she was a photographer's delight: blonde hair and a dramatic fay-like beauty: she was a young woman at the peak of her powers. Kate handed Michael the cutting, and he wiped his hands on his trousers before taking it.

He held it up to the light. 'Nice-looking couple.'

'Oh come on, Michael! She's a child.'

He held the cutting at arm's length and then shook his head. 'You read it to me. I can't see without my glasses.'

Kate read the brief report aloud. She was twenty-one, the daughter of some Tory MP. Paul was described as a local artist, and a member of the Royal Academy – which was a lie. He'd exhibited once at the Summer Exhibition, and even then he didn't manage to sell the thing. The report didn't mention his age: Kate could just picture Paul turning the indiscreet question aside with a joke – you're only as old as the woman you feel.

Kate stuffed the cutting back into the envelope. 'It looks like he's got his financial security at last. Daddy's obviously not short of a penny or two. Typical of Paul!'

She shoved her hands deep into her pockets, wishing Mary hadn't seen the report. She could do without this clanging intrusion from her past.

'Does it bother you?' he asked.

She wrinkled her nose, her flippancy gone. 'It shouldn't, but it does. A lot.'

'What way should it be?'

'I shouldn't care about him – it's ancient history. It's up to him how he leads his life.'

'But really, you think he should . . . ?'

Her eyes flickered with mischief. 'He should still be in mourning for losing the greatest love of his life – me. And nobody should marry someone so impossibly young and pretty. *And* rich.'

'Do you really want to use that word so much?'

'What word?'

'Should.'

She shrugged.

'Remember the story of Adam and Eve – how they could eat the fruit of any tree except the one in the middle of the garden? Remember the name of the tree?'

'Remind me.'

'The tree of the knowledge of good and evil. Interesting, don't you think? Before – blissful ignorance, but just one bite of that fruit and they'd fallen. They knew right from wrong, how things "should" be.'

He patted the tree-trunk and an apple dislodged itself, falling by his feet. He laughed, surprised, and bent to pick it up. 'If you want to suffer, just keep insisting you know how things should be.'

He tossed the apple to Kate and she caught it.

'Go on, take a bite.'

She instinctively raised it to her mouth, but something made her pause.

'It should be like this.' He mimed taking a bite. 'This shouldn't have happened.' He took another imaginary bite. 'I shouldn't be feeling like this. Go on – have a bite.'

She looked at the apple in her hand and then at Michael.

'Most of us are living on a diet of apples,' he continued. 'A diet of shoulds . . . demands . . . expectations. I should always look good. My parents ought to have loved me more. I've got to be a success. I should get what I want, especially if I behave. God should punish sinners.' He snorted. 'With a diet like that, it's no wonder we get belly-ache.'

She threw the apple back. He made no attempt to catch it, and it bounced off his chest on to the ground.

'The bigger the gap between the way things are, and the way you want them to be – the more you suffer. It's what's called dis-ease.'

She bent and put the apple into the basket.

'And Kate – do you know, truly, how things ought to be? Does anyone?'

She looked up at him, her hand absently grasping the wicker handle. 'But there's good and bad, isn't there?'

'Perhaps there is. But is there a way anything "should" be? I think only God can answer that one.'

She stood up, still holding the basket, and looked back at the house.

'Will you be coming in?' he asked.

'Later.'

He took the basket from her, hooking it in the crook of his arm. She watched him walk back to the house. It was true – she *did* think she knew how things should be – with Paul, with Michael, with everything in her life. And what had it driven her to do? How much had it cost her? But I *do* know, a voice inside her protested. I *do*! Paul should have loved me better. He should have married me.

She frowned. But what if? There was something – a freedom – winking at the corner of her consciousness. What if she gave it all up – thinking she knew what was right, wrong? What would there be? What would she be left with? Things as they were. Her feelings. Her thoughts. No right, no wrong – no should. No effort.

She thought about Michael; his amused attitude, his gentle, persistent mockery. Did she love him? She didn't know. She hadn't dared think about it until now. It was too outrageous: he was far too old. Fifty, even sixty would be acceptable; but he was an old man, for God's sake. She giggled nervously: it was almost obscene. She looked up at the tree, the fruit hanging there – ripe and ready to be picked. Tempting.

'Get behind me, Satan!' she muttered with a laugh, and walked back to the house.

TWENTY-EIGHT

She bought a kite. The idea had come to her as she waited for him, stuck halfway up that mountain, watching the wind catching an empty crisp packet some hiker had dropped. It was years since she'd flown a kite. She and her father used to make their own out of bamboo and varnished paper. Yes, she'd buy a big one, a big two-string affair.

Michael wanted to go home and fly the kite immediately they bought it, but it was too late, so he had to settle for helping her assemble the scarlet and pink contraption in the kitchen. He didn't know the first thing about kite-flying, and was excited as a child. He'd persuaded her to buy the most garish, colourful one in the shop.

The next day was a rare autumn day of startling blue skies and a keen wind. Perfect kite-flying weather. She led him to the rise of the hill above the cottage, facing the moor which dipped away into the hinterland. The furze had lost its summer flowers and the moor was a tangle of brown-green under the unruffled blue of the sky. The breeze agitated the bracken in ripples as though hidden animals were running through it. There was not a cloud in the sky, just a curlew somewhere sounding its mournful cry.

She'd wound her hair behind her head in a swirl like a horse's mane, and as she knelt to untangle the kite strings, it shone in the brilliant light like metal. She didn't see Michael watching her. She'd never looked better – the crimson and emerald scarf against the white of her neck, the hair gleaming and gold. From in front and above, her face was perfect: the prominent nose foreshortened, the lowered eyes giving her face a modesty and allure.

She attached the strings and gave the kite to Michael.

'Now go down there and hold it high above your head.'

He did so. Kate jerked the strings and it rose five feet in the air, flapping like an ungainly bird. Another tug and it was airborne. The wind was good to them and it climbed easily. The long tail snaked into the air behind it, twitching like a live thing.

Suddenly it dipped and looked as if it would crash, but she brought it back up in a series of loops until a gust of wind took it high above them.

From where Michael stood, Kate was silhouetted against the sky, motionless as a tree-stump, two faint lines of nylon joining her and this great soaring phenomenon. It was astonishing and startling: the vivid scarlet against the cerulean. A gaudy and unlikely bird, its tail looping behind it.

Michael was ecstatic: whooping and shouting, his head bent back following the crazy looping path of the kite.

She called him to her and showed him how to keep it in the air, tugging the strings to give it extra height, pulling on one string to have it dip like a darting fish. He took over the spools, and the kite immediately sank. She shouted instructions to him, but he didn't know what to do, and it just arced once and then fell like a shot bird flapping and limp back to earth.

They got it airborne again and she kept her hands on his while he got the hang of it.

'That's it, pull it up again . . . let out more string.'

'Get up, you bugger! No! Up!' Michael shouted, laughing. He had no control over it at all. It was as though it was him at the other end of the string, climbing and dipping in the gusting wind. They stood side by side, his hands guided by hers. When she let go to wind out more string, the kite looped out of control, and she brought her hands back to his once more.

He whooped and jerked the strings, sending the kite soaring higher. He lifted his arm and allowed Kate to stand in the circle of his arms, her back pressed warmly against his front. Together they guided the kite higher and higher, giving it more play, unreeling the string until it was at its fullest extent. The patch of scarlet was small now: high above them as though it was no longer part of them, but an eagle circling over the moor, a life of its own.

'Let's let it go,' he whispered into her neck. He dropped the spools.

The two white nylon hand-grips bounced and trailed along the ground, one of them catching in a clump of furze. Kate darted forward to catch them, but Michael held her back. They saw the kite falter at the far end of the strings.

'But Michael – '

He turned her round till she faced him. She was dizzy from looking up, and steadied herself against him as he completed the circle of his arms around her.

'We were just getting the hang of that,' she chided him, twisting round to try and see the kite. He held her tight in his arms.

'Let it go, Kate.'

She relaxed and slipped her hands into his pockets, looking at him with a question in her eyes. His arms around her were strong, and she was aware of his solidness, the thickness of his trunk. He tightened his grip, bringing their bodies closer. She laid her head in the crook of his neck. He'd grown his hair longer at her request, and she ran her fingers through it, enjoying its silky platinum touch. She brushed her lips against his chin, feeling the roughness of his bristles, and then laid her cheek flat against his, her eyes closed. He raised a hand and traced the line of her jaw, brushing her naked throat with his fingers. Her lips parted and she touched them just below his – two cool, moist petals. She felt the warmth of his breath against her skin, slightly tobaccoey. She brushed her lips against his and he responded, lightly at first and then firmer so she could feel his teeth with her tongue. His hands were on the nape of her neck, holding her face to his.

She was trembling as she pulled him down on to the dry bracken. The fronds cushioned them, warm and sheltered from the wind. She lay, her eyes closed, her hair spilled like honey over the bracken.

Her heart was pounding as his fingers smoothed the silky skin of her belly where her shirt had come out from her trousers. She began easing the buttons open, but he rested his hand on hers and did the task. He slid her shirt open like peeling a grape, exposing the soft unseen interior. She had no bra and she drew his head to her breasts and he inhaled the soft white scent of them, mouthing the hardened nipples, first one then the other. A spring was being coiled inside her – not between her legs, but in the pit of her belly, and she led his hands to her trouser top so he could slip his fingers under the snap of the elastic and massage the tension. She was greedy for his touch. She plucked at his clothes, but made no attempt to undress him. Her hands were occupied in guiding his, slipping her trousers down, easing the damp pants away. He cupped her cunt, sheltering it from the tingling breeze. She pushed against the hand, touching flesh to flesh. She wanted his hand inside her, the whole of him inside her. She tugged at his trousers, and then amazingly she felt the cool length of his penis in her hand. She held his pearl-smooth secret in her palm and then guided him between her legs. He eased himself into her, sinking his final length into her: a dagger into its sheath. She let out a cry and clutched at his back. He stilled her quivering body and then began the gentle pendulum movement; slow and shallow at first, then deeper and deeper. She wanted him inside her womb, she wanted to be filled up with his maleness, flooded with his sperm. She stared with unseeing eyes over his shoulder, lost in the azure of the unmarked sky. She was staring down on a great ocean – this steady thrusting in and out in and out was the ebb and flow of its tide. The sea was inside her and outside her: powerful, elemental. Her orgasm surged forward in contractions and she gasped, holding back her flood until he could fill her. And when he came into her, it was the sea's foam gushing and tumbling into a cove. She groaned, long and animal, thrashing her head from side to side. There was nothing left: no him, no her, no wind, no sky. Just this.

The sky was washed immaculate, the scarlet kite gone, and they lay soldered together, breathing face to face. She watched the sky over his shoulder, stroking the back of his head. She couldn't believe it. His flesh, his seed inside her now. He was hers – her lover. Her final chamber had been breached.

He gently pulled out of her, and they rebuttoned themselves. He wrapped her scarf around her throat and touched her forehead with his.

They found the spools of the kite, and taking one each, wound the string back on. Eventually they came to the kite – a scarlet petal resting on a bush.

Walking back home, arm in arm, he suddenly stopped.

'Listen,' he said, cocking his head.

She did so. There was nothing, not even the wind.

She ran the bath as soon as they got back, piping the hot water from the newly installed immersion heater into the enamel bath.

She wanted to bathe – not to wash, but just to soak in hot water; maintain this peak of voluptuousness. She piled turf into the range, and then without a word to Michael, darted upstairs to fetch her washing things. In her room she caught sight of herself in the blotched mirror she'd recently bought. It was like someone else: some dark-eyed, flushed stranger. She swept her loose hair back, gazing at her reflection. She imagined his sperm inside her like warm medicine; sticky and narcotic as laudanum. It would be reckless, she knew, but suddenly she wanted his seed to fertilise her. She wanted a child. She wanted *his* child. She touched where she thought her womb to be. Neither Jacques nor Paul had succeeded there, perhaps Michael . . . She laughed and blew a kiss at her reflection and ran downstairs.

He was outside, feeding the animals, and she turned off the bath and poured some orange-blossom bath oil into the water. The scent, warm and summery rising with the steam, reminded her of Greece. Hot white walls, silence, dogs sleeping in the sun.

Her limbs felt heavy and rounded as she slid into the bath. The water was hot and she shuddered as it rose up her body. The oil clung to her, exotic and scented, and she ran her hands over her body under the water, smoothing the greasy skin.

Something made her want to pour warmed alcohol, sweet sticky liqueur over her hair, feel it trickle down her face on to her neck, run over her goosefleshed breasts and diffuse into the water. She wanted to soak in sweet intoxicating luxury. Stay like this for ever – her mind blank, her body satisfied.

She lay languidly, inhaling the orangey steam. It was hard to believe it had happened. She could see their two bodies under the vast canopy of the sky; a pocket of warmth in the heath. It was so unexpected, so unplanned. Michael? Making love to her? Her hands strayed to the inside of her thighs. She would not be ashamed, she must not be ashamed.

She heard him by the back door, and it clicked open.

'Can I come in?'

She smiled. 'Of course.'

He was holding Ludo, the cat. 'Look who I've found.' It had been missing nearly five months, and they'd assumed it was dead. It was thin and scruffy, and unsure whether it wanted to be indoors or not. He let it out of the door and shut it.

'Can you top me up, please?' The water was cooling and she didn't want to move. Her hands rested in her crotch, but as the warm serpent of fresh water coiled around her, she allowed them to float away. No – she wouldn't hide from him any more.

She asked him to stay and talk. He pulled up a chair and sat down, his eyes flicking down for a second to look at her body. He filled his pipe while she washed her neck and shoulders. A strand of hair had fallen in the bath, and he leant forward and scooped it out. She caught his wrist and he crouched by the bath, his pipe clamped between his teeth.

'Take your pipe out.'

He did so. She tilted her head, inviting him to kiss her. His lips had a bitter taste from the tobacco.

'Thank you.' She took the pipe from him and puffed on it. 'Let's have a party,' she said suddenly. 'Just you and me.'

She gave him the pipe back and asked for the towel. He held it in front of her so she could get out of the bath without being seen. She patted herself dry in front of the range, and then looked up at him. He was standing by the bath still, his pipe in his hand, watching her. He looked so sad and happy at the same time that she laughed. 'Oh, Michael!'

He strode into her open arms. His woollen sweater was coarse against her naked skin as the towel dropped from her, but she held him tightly. 'Oh, Michael,' she murmured again.

His fingers held her gently on her lower back as he stepped back and looked at her, a twinkle in his eye. 'Do you have a party frock?'

She laughed and kissed him on the cheek and bent to pick up the towel.

'You get dressed,' he continued, 'and I'll go to James's and see if we can't buy ourselves one of his ducks.'

TWENTY-NINE

She took a long time dressing, powdering her slightly oily skin, making up her face carefully. It was ridiculous, she told the face that smiled back at her in the mirror – she was as excited as she'd been on her first date. She remembered it too. A nice middle-class English boy, Eric wasn't it? Sixteen they must have been, both virgins. She'd come a long way since then.

She was pleased with how she looked. She'd been too tall at school; it wasn't till her late teens that she'd begun to fill out. Something had happened to her face in her mid-twenties. Perhaps it was just the fashion catching up with her, but suddenly people were calling her beautiful. The hair helped, she guessed, as she brushed it out. It was long and blonde as a ripe cornfield; streaks of almost white to almost brown.

She'd used her looks too many times, that had been her trouble. She'd happily bought the convention that for a beautiful woman her beauty is all the justification she needs. She can be as empty-headed as a puppet, unhappy, unfulfilled, but if she has the right face, the right body, then what's the problem? Her looks had run her. Her face had been her ticket into the world of the beautiful people. The beautiful people! Paul and all his arty friends, all *my* friends. She thought through all the people she knew in London, hardly one of them English. Were there any she missed? Any she'd exchange an evening with Michael to see?

She ran her hands over her dress, resting them on her stomach for a moment. How much she'd changed since knowing him. What an idiot she'd been when she first met Michael. But she liked the new Kate. She could see the beginnings of how she'd always wanted to be: strong and beautiful. A person and a woman.

And the future? They'd have to talk together, and soon. She'd still got half one foot in London. If she was going to stay any longer it would be as well to withdraw it completely.

She heard the car stopping outside the house and looked out of the window. She watched him get out, a bag of groceries under one arm, the limp form of a duck in the other hand. She felt the touch of his hand on her belly and shivered. Checking herself once more in the mirror, she hurried downstairs.

She felt like a child going to a party – dressed in her best clothes even though it was still mid-afternoon. She'd piled her hair on top of her head, holding it in place with two chopsticks.

'Now, you look grand!' He made her turn round, admiring her dress. 'And perfume too!' He nuzzled her neck. 'Mmm.'

He wouldn't let her do anything, so she sat and watched him prepare the duck. He scalded it and then set to plucking it, stuffing the dun-coloured feathers into a paper bag. She watched, fascinated by his long fingers plucking handfuls of feathers from this strangely beautiful bird. It occurred to her that perhaps it was he who had killed it; perhaps the same hands that had stroked her had wrung the neck of this floppy silken thing.

He had a bath after he'd finished preparing the food, and she put on an apron and lit the fire in the front room. She tidied the room, plumping up the cushions, sweeping the grate. Some curtains – she'd buy some material next time they were in town, and a potted plant would be an idea.

He was wearing the soft cotton shirt she'd bought for him in Cork, a silk cravat, and a new pair of khaki corduroy trousers. She could smell aftershave, and commented on it.

'I got it when I bought the oranges this afternoon. I hope it's all right?'

She'd never seen him like this, so unsure of himself.

'How do I look?'

'Wonderful!'

'You mean, for an old man?' he said, straightening his cravat.

She shook her head. All his jokes about being old – she didn't believe it any more than he did. He wasn't old, and he knew it. Once in pique because of some childish thing he'd done, she'd told him to act his age. He'd turned to her and asked her, laughing, why the hell he should. And he was right. Why the hell should he?

He dug out an antique lace tablecloth from the press in her room, and they laid the table together. She picked some flowers for the table: anemones and a moulting dandelion just for fun.

They sat outside while the meal cooked, watching the sun set like a poached egg over the bay. They hardly spoke, and then only a word or two. There was nothing to be said.

He asked her to stay outside till the meal was on the table, and then ushered her in like a waiter. The curtains were drawn in the kitchen, cutting out the last of the daylight, and two lighted candles were on the table. Ruby splinters of light were cast through the decanter of red wine on to the tablecloth; the wine seeming to glow from inside.

'Michael, this is beautiful!'

He smiled delightedly and sat opposite her. She could see that he wanted to say something, and waited while he found the words.

'Thank you for staying with me,' he said at last. 'I know it's not been too easy.'

She squeezed his hand. No, it hadn't been easy. But that was forgotten now. 'I wouldn't want to be anywhere else.'

He released her hand and reached into his pocket. 'This was my mother's, and then Ann's. Now I'd like you to have it.'

He laid a heavy link bracelet in her palm, the gold almost orange in the candlelight. She murmured surprised thanks, turning it over in her hands.

He poured the wine out, one eye on Kate. 'If I was a younger man . . . well . . . '

He lifted her glass and nodded for her to do the same. He pretended not to notice the single tear glinting like a diamond in the corner of her eye.

'Slante – your health, my dear.'

They touched glasses and drank. She linked the bracelet round her wrist, but she had trouble with the tiny gold clasp and he helped her. She held it up to the light. The gold was still warm from being in his pocket.

'Thank you.'

'Now, what would you say to some food?' he said briskly, getting up and bringing the vegetables to the table. 'You know what Da used to say?' He bent to get the duck out of the oven. 'He used to say the three most nourishing foods in the world are the marrow of a cow, the flesh of a chicken, and—'

There was a clatter, and the duck slid out of the basting tray on to the flags. Michael staggered and nearly fell.

'Michael!' Kate shouted.

He felt behind him for the table, trying to steady himself. She jumped to her feet and helped him into his chair.

'What's wrong?'

He raised a hand to his forehead, a startled expression on his face.

'My God, Michael! What's wrong?'

He struggled to speak, his mouth working, but only inarticulate sounds came out. She didn't know what to do and stood over him, her face white and shocked. He was having a fit of some sort, maybe even a stroke. God no, she prayed. Not now.

He groped for her hand and knocked over a glass of wine, the red liquid spilling across the tablecloth like blood. He was making grotesque noises in an effort to speak, his face contorted.

'Let me get you to bed.'

He nodded, and she helped him to his feet. He could stand easily enough, but when he tried to put his arm around her, it flailed in all directions.

Upstairs, she helped him out of his clothes. 'Don't try to speak. I'll get the doctor.'

She left him in bed and drove recklessly to the O'Neills' and phoned from there. She was back in twenty minutes, and relieved to find him a little better. He still had trouble making himself understood, but whatever his attack was, it was passing. He was more in control, and even managed to smile at his attempts to speak.

By the time the doctor arrived about half an hour later, Michael had just about recovered. Kate saw the doctor up to the bedroom and was about to leave the two men alone, when Michael asked her to stay.

The doctor checked Michael's blood pressure, and looked into his eyes. He asked him a few questions, and nodded reassuringly.

'It's nothing much to worry about,' he said. 'There's no damage been done – just a minor brainstorm. You'll need to take it easy for a day or two, but there's no reason at all why you shouldn't be as fit as you ever were, in a short while.'

He put his glasses in his top pocket and picked up his case. 'I'll be back to see you tomorrow. There's nothing I can give you, but perhaps an aspirin won't do you any harm.'

Kate saw the doctor out. She switched the electric light on in the kitchen and noticed the mess on the table for the first time.

'Are you family?' he asked as he struggled into his coat.

She bent to pick up the duck. It had slid across the floor and was under the meat safe in the corner. 'I'm sorry?' she said, looking up.

'Are you a relative?'

Her hand automatically went to her wrist, twisting the bracelet between her fingers. 'Yes.'

'Well, this is nothing serious – it's what's called a transient ischemic attack. He should be as right as rain tomorrow, but it may be as well to try and keep the old boy in bed for a day. He could have another attack, but in itself that's nothing to worry about. If it happens, just keep him warm and give me a ring. It never lasts more than an hour or so.'

He paused by the door. 'I should tell you that in people of his age, having one of these attacks could indicate a stroke is on its way.'

'Oh no!'

'It's not inevitable,' he added quickly, 'but he *is* getting on in years, and it's a possibility you need to be aware of.'

Kate opened the door for him.

'Were you having a little party?' he asked before he went, indicating the table.

'Just a small celebration.' She looked sadly at their unstarted feast.

The doctor left and she snuffed out the candles and went up to see Michael.

'Perhaps an aspirin won't do you any harm,' he said, mimicking the doctor. 'Jesus, I'm glad I'm not paying for his services.'

There seemed nothing wrong with him now, as though the recent drama was no more than play-acting. He insisted that he was still hungry, so she reheated the vegetables, wiped off the duck, and took him some food on a tray.

She didn't want to eat. The evening had been lost. All she wanted to do was to see that Michael was all right, and then go to bed. Suddenly she felt very tired.

She sat on the edge of the bed, smoking a cigarette, watching Michael eat. This evening she'd glimpsed something in him she'd never seen before: fear. She remembered the mute confusion in his face as she helped him upstairs; his helplessness as he tried to speak. Suddenly he'd been an old man, vulnerable and weak. It had been like a horrible dream.

He noticed her preoccupied silence and put his knife and fork down. 'What is it?'

She shook her head. He slid the tray off his lap and took her hand. 'Tell me.' His eyes were calm and clear again – the Michael she knew back in control.

'I was worried.'

He looked up at the ceiling and gave a short laugh. 'And you're thinking I wasn't? I often thought God would strike me dumb, but I thought the old bastard would give me some warning!'

She laughed in spite of herself.

'So what words did the good doctor have to say to you?' he asked.

'Oh, nothing really.'

He growled and frowned at her in mock disapproval. A sudden mischievous impulse took her.

'He asked if we were married.'

Michael laughed disbelievingly. 'And?'

'Well, I couldn't shock him, could I?'

THIRTY

It was more surprise she felt than anything as she wiped the vomit from the corner of her mouth. She looked at the pool of liquid she'd just spat out into the sink and did some quick calculations. It was about a month ago they'd first made love. She'd missed her period – nothing unusual for her – but this nausea which had swept over her after breakfast; she'd never been sick like this before. Morning sickness? She rinsed the vomit down the sink and splashed cold water over her face.

Could she be pregnant? She'd tried to save her marriage to Jacques by getting pregnant, and thank God she hadn't succeeded. But it had convinced her she was infertile. Hadn't he after all fathered a child before he'd met her? She had only bothered taking the pill with Paul because he was so insistent. She'd been careless so many times, and never with any result; she was sure she could never conceive. But if that was the case, then what was this nausea that had been building up over these last few days?

They'd made love only a few times. She could never remember who made the first move – suddenly she'd just find herself open for him, clutching his muscular back, shuddering under his weight. And every time she carried the warmth in her groin for days afterwards.

Nothing had been said, but she knew he'd rather sleep alone, she stayed in her own room. But they were close during the day, and though he didn't show it, she knew he was happy with her.

But what if she was pregnant? Such a little cause; a few minutes of forgetfulness snowballing into another life. She looked at her blanched face in the shaving mirror above the sink. Did she want a child? How would she manage?

It had been a joke of hers, that they were married, and nothing was ever said again about that. But now, she thought, holding down a spasm of nausea, if this sickness meant she was pregnant, then married or not they'd be bound together. Whatever she did in the future.

Michael commented on her paleness, but she brushed it aside as nothing. But when, the next day, she refused breakfast, and then was sick anyway, he insisted she went to see the doctor. She was glad he didn't ask what she thought was wrong. She'd decided not to say a word until she knew for sure; and then not before she'd had a chance to find out how she felt about it.

They drove into Westport and he asked her to drop him outside the solicitor's office – he had some business to see to. He told her how to get to the doctor's surgery and they arranged to meet in a couple of hours in Ryan's Bar.

Michael's doctor, Dr Furguson, examined her cursorily and took a urine sample. Although he didn't come out and say it, she could see he was wondering who the father could be, if it turned out she was pregnant. He asked how she was getting on at the cottage, hoping to find out if there were just the two of them, but Kate was giving nothing away.

He told her to phone in the afternoon for the results of the test. She got up to go. 'So how is your uncle, then? No more attacks?'

'He's fine – nothing wrong with him at all. Except he's not my uncle.'

'I thought you said he was.'

She smiled at the transparent lie. He was aching to know just what was going on. A bit of scandal hopefully – something to liven up his dull country practice. She thanked him and left.

She had only been twenty minutes, so she walked back to the solicitor's to see if Michael was still there. The office was empty, and she waited by the receptionist's desk, toying with some paperclips. What was he doing here? She hadn't thought to ask. The young receptionist looked flustered when she eventually came back to her desk.

'Mr O'Brien—' Kate began.

'He's in the office. Are you a friend of his? – he's had a turn. He's all right, but—'

Kate didn't give her time to finish. She brushed past the girl and strode through the frosted-glass door into the office.

Michael was sitting in a high-backed leather armchair, and as soon as she saw his face she knew he was having another attack.

'When did it happen?' she asked the solicitor.

'Just a few minutes ago.'

She squatted by the chair, took one of Michael's hands and began rubbing it. He tried to smile at her.

'Do you have somewhere he can lie down?'

The solicitor seemed relieved that someone else was taking control and showed her another office where there was a long couch. When Michael was settled and covered with the receptionist's raincoat, Kate telephoned the doctor's surgery and explained what was happening.

The doctor couldn't come immediately and told her to take Michael home as soon as the attack had passed. He'd visit as soon as he could.

Within half an hour, Michael could speak again, albeit haltingly. He seemed strong enough to make the journey back, so Kate helped him up and they went back into the first office.

The solicitor looked glad to be getting rid of them, but had a few polite words, telling Michael they could finish their business when he felt up to it. Michael's papers were still on the desk, and Kate glanced at the document on the top. The words printed in italic script on the cover leapt out at her: the last Will and Testament of —, and under that his full name: Michael Patrick O'Brien.

Dr Furguson came to the cottage in the late afternoon and saw Michael for a few minutes. Again, he could do nothing, and just recommended that he take it easy for the next few days. Kate saw him out to his car.

'He looks well enough. He's still a healthy fellow – strong as an ox.' He squeezed Kate's arm reassuringly. He'd made the connection between Michael and this young woman. She definitely *was* pregnant – he'd seen the results just before he left, and now there was no doubt who the father was. He just hoped the old boy wasn't going to have a stroke. Two attacks in a month didn't look good.

The doctor gave Kate the news of the test.

'Congratulations,' he suggested, watching her closely to see her reaction. She just exhaled noisily. Relief? Resignation? He got in the car and wound the window down.

'He *will* be all right, won't he, doctor?'

'Ah sure he will, don't you worry yourself.'

The sleek BMW slid away and Kate watched it until it turned the corner of the lane, her arms folded across her chest.

Kate went back upstairs to see Michael, but he was asleep. She sat on the bed, gazing into his face. Pregnant. She was pregnant – another life inside her now. She wanted to wake him up and tell him, but he looked exhausted by the attack. She laid her hand on his, watching him. He looked so old, lying there, his features creased and heavy. Like an old tree: an oak, gnarled and weathered, but – she stroked her hand across her belly – there was this new life from him, like a bud, bursting green and amazing from a dry twig.

Was he going to leave her, now that she had this bond with him? Leave her in sleep, in illness, eventually death? The doctor had said he'd be all right: he was as fit as a fiddle, as strong as an ox, there were years left in him yet. But he *was* old, and he looked it now. She squeezed Michael's hand, but there was no response from his leathery fingers.

She was going to be a mother. She and him: mother and father. She sat in the gathering dusk, listening to the rise and fall of his breath, waiting for him to wake.

THIRTY-ONE

Kate tried to keep Michael in bed the next day, but he insisted on getting up, so she installed him in his armchair by the fire. She was worried about him: he said that he felt better, but there was a drawn look to his face, and when he walked she noticed he was unsteady on his feet. She couldn't tell him the news, not with him like this, so she busied herself preparing his breakfast. He enjoyed the unaccustomed attention, and commented on her cheerfulness when she tucked a blanket round his knees and put the breakfast tray on his lap. She didn't explain the cause and just smiled when Michael called her 'mother'.

There were no visible signs of her pregnancy yet – she'd checked first thing in the morning. She'd examined her belly, her breasts, her face, but nothing had changed. Nothing on the outside, but everything had changed. She was a different person from yesterday. From the moment of knowing she carried this new life, she knew that somehow she would never be alone again. She enjoyed it, cradling this secret bundle of cells inside her.

She surprised herself: pregnant women had always inspired pity in her. She'd thought them the losers in the sexual equation; the hapless incubators of man's seed, ballooning over the months, losing themselves to the voracious lodger inside them. Now, even her nausea was a source of pride. She'd done it, she told herself – she was fully a woman.

She had no doubt that she wanted the baby. *His* baby. It had come as a surprise, a shock, but it sat well. She had wanted the child – she realised it now; been wanting it for some time. It was the next step in her life, but a step that she found had already been taken for her. There was something liberating about the inevitability of the course of the next nine months. She was in the hands of something bigger than herself. It was done now – irrevocably. She could already picture them: the three of them living in the cottage, an unshakeable happy pyramid.

He felt better after lunch, and followed Kate to the kitchen, watching her from a chair as she washed some clothes in the sink. She knew she would have to tell him soon – the pressure of this secret was too much to contain. But perhaps he didn't want a child, she thought. Why hadn't he ever had children? Somewhere inside herself, Kate heard the nagging voice, accusing her. You should have asked permission before getting pregnant. You were only trying to trap him.

'You never told me what the doctor said.'

She stiffened for a second, and then continued scrubbing at the collar of a shirt. 'He said you'd be all right in a day or two – the same as before.'

He sniggered, and she knew she'd been found out. 'You know what I mean. What did he say about yourself?'

She dropped the shirt into the bowl and lifted her gaze to the window. There was nothing for her to focus her attention on and she looked down at her sudsy hands. 'I'm pregnant.'

Kate heard him catch his breath, and she turned to face him. He was staring at her, his face blank.

'Oh my sweet Jesus!'

His features dissolved into a smile, and he was on his feet. They hugged, Kate laughing with relief into his neck.

'Oh you clever girl. You clever, clever girl!' He held her at arm's length, beaming at her. 'But what am I doing? You should be the one putting your feet up. Come on—' He ushered her to the chair and made her sit down. 'Rest yourself now.'

He crouched beside her, and she rested an arm on his shoulder.

'So?' He looked up at her.

'So?' she smiled back, her eyes sparkling. 'I'm so happy!'

He turned his head away, and when she turned it back to face her, there were tears in his eyes.

Kate banked up the smouldering fire with kindling and crouched to blow in the grate.

'Should you be doing things like that?' Michael asked, nodding at the fire.

'I'm pregnant. I'm going to have a baby, not a glass ornament.'

He'd been fussing around Kate all afternoon, assuring her that he felt well enough to do everything. He was looking tired though, and Kate had insisted on making their evening meal.

'It's all new to me – this baby business,' he said.

A finger of flame appeared in the grate and Kate sat back on her haunches. She looked up at him, her face flushed. 'Sit down, Michael. You're making me feel tired.'

He lowered the gas lamp until it was a soft blue glow, and the room contracted into a warm dimness. He'd not once used the newly installed electric lights, and except in her bedroom, Kate had followed his lead. She scooped the cat up and dumped it on his lap when he sat down. 'Now, behave yourself.'

'Getting in training are you for the little girl? Bossy boots.'

She sat in the rocking-chair, stretching her legs out. 'It's going to be a boy.'

'Are you sure?' he said, surprised. 'I thought it was going to be a girl. Girls are much nicer.'

She watched the fire for a moment. 'Why didn't you and Ann ever have children?' she asked him. 'Didn't you want them?'

The cat jumped off his lap on to the floor and on to Kate's lap in one bound.

'We wanted them enough, the both of us, but Ann had something wrong with her woman's department and it wasn't to be.'

Kate's eyes flicked up to the portrait of his wife above the fireplace.

'You never talk about her.'

'She's not an easy woman to talk about. She was like nobody I've ever known.'

Kate waited, stroking the cat on her lap. She recognised it when he wasn't quite ready to speak, and she allowed him time to gather his thoughts. The silence of the room was filled with the cracking and popping of the kindling as it caught.

'I was in a poor state when I came back from Spain in thirty-nine. The war was an ugly affair, and disgusted and bitter I was by the whole thing. I lived here for the best part of three years all on my tod, hardly seeing a soul from one week to the next. Then one day when I was working the plot out the back, this colleen leans over the wall. She watches me for a bit, then she calls out, "What would you want for a cup of milk, mister?" She could see I had goats. Quick as a flash, "Your hand in marriage" I shouted back. God only knows where those words came from. She was pretty enough, and I was lonely enough, but I hadn't the ghost of a notion it would come true.' He smiled at the memory. 'We started courting, and I fell for her with everything I had. I was fascinated by her. She had these eyes that – ' He shook his head with a laugh. 'Am I going on?'

'Not at all.'

'She had a way of being with people that was almost magical. You could see them light up like fairy lights around her. She was good-looking – as pretty a girl as you ever laid two eyes on.'

He gazed up at her painting for a moment. 'But it wasn't her looks that drew people – it was something else. Sharp as a diamond she was, but simple too, almost like a child. A lot of folk didn't understand her.'

Kate tried to see his expression, but he was hidden in shadow, the wings of the armchair shading his face.

'It amazed me at the time what she saw in me – here I was, a jackeen with a head full of nonsense, and a run-down piece of bogland, and she a girl who could have had the best for the asking.'

'I fell in love with her – I would have been hard put not to. So we got wed. June the fifth, 1944 – the day before they invaded Normandy.' He laughed. 'If the Germans thought they had problems on their hands, it was nothing compared to mine. Right from the start she changed – before we even got home from the church. Didn't she just refuse to let any of our wedding guests into the house? Packed them off home, she did. Of course, I put up a fight, and got a tongue-lashing for my efforts. I didn't know what the hell on earth had happened to my black-eyed beauty – suddenly I was married to the barrenest shrew this side of Istanbul. Come that night when I tried to insist on my marriage rights – she flew into a rage and I had to spend the night in the shed. She wouldn't let me in the house – *my* house, remember – for weeks!'

He laughed. 'I reckon I spent more nights in the shed in those first six months than in my own bed. I didn't mind the roughing it – it was the battering my pride was taking that hurt the most. Of course, I couldn't let anyone know I'd married a madwoman. And if they'd known I wasn't let in my own house!'

He shook his head as though he couldn't believe it himself. 'It was a sore time for me those first six months. She worked me like a horse, treating me worse than a dog. A real tyrant she was.'

'But why was she being so difficult?'

'She had to break me. I was a pig-headed young man – brought up by his sisters. I expected the world to give me what I wanted.'

'Break you – what for?'

'She was my teacher, Kate. I didn't realise it for the first couple of years, but that's what she was.'

'So, how long did it carry on like this? Not for ever, surely?'

'She was always my teacher, but the rough stuff only carried on till I cracked.'

'And you put up with it?'

'I ran away – just like you did. And just like you, I came back. It was hell with her, but even worse on my own.'

'What do you mean – just like me?'

'When Ann died, I was on my own again, and then you turned up – my reluctant protégée. I saw the sort of person you were, so I set about laying a trap.'

'What?'

'I trapped you. Just like Ann in her way trapped me.'

'But how?'

'Remember the Giacomettis?'

She nodded.

'You'd never have given me a second thought if it wasn't for them.'

She thought back. 'But I'd forgotten my jewellery, remember? That's why I came back.'

'And why did you stay? I trapped you, Kate. You'd forgotten your jewellery, but I hadn't. I found your things and brought them into Westport that day. If you'd decided not to come back, I'd have given your stuff to you there and then. The jewellery was the hook and the line, the newly discovered Giacometti drawings were the sinker.'

'Meaning?'

'I wanted to make sure you'd stay. You were reluctant, and I thought I was going to lose you, so I invented some sheets of drawings. Yes,' he said when he saw her expression. 'Those weren't genuine. They were mine.'

'But—'

'I was an admirer of his, and being a young and impressionable sort, I produced some poor-quality lookalikes. I'd kept them all these years and when you turned up it was simple enough to forge his signature.'

'And the Brauner?'

'That was genuine. I'd forgotten I had that.'

'But why did you have to trap me?'

'Would you have stayed if I'd told you exactly what was in store for you?'

'But what right did you have?'

'No right.'

She stared at him. She couldn't believe it. 'Why? Why did you do it?'

He leant forward and tossed a briquette into the flames, sending a shower of sparks flying up the chimney. 'What makes people paint paintings, make music?'

'But it's outrageous, Michael! You can't just manipulate people like that.'

He shrugged and sat back in his chair.

She had so many questions that she stuttered her next sentence. 'Why me? Why did you pick me?'

'You chose yourself. It was you who came knocking on my door.'

She was close to tears. In the space of five minutes, everything had turned round. She'd lost Michael – suddenly he was the old man again: distant, game-playing. Toying with her.

He noticed the change in her. 'Tell me about it, Kate.'

She turned her head from him. 'It all sounds so . . . cynical.'

'Which of us is the cynic? Believing the worst of good intentions?'

The tears started flowing now. 'But is this – ' She looked down at her belly. 'Don't you love me?'

'I do. That's why I've been doing this.'

She smeared the tears roughly with the back of her hand. 'But has it just been a game to you?'

She looked up at the portrait of Ann above the fireplace. The pietà-like face, the mysterious suffering the artist had captured made sense now. Kate realised she'd never stood a chance against that face. Ann's presence had subtly coloured their relationship from the first day they met. Even this conversation, she felt, was being watched over by her.

He pushed himself up from his chair and laid a hand on her shoulder, but she shrugged it away. 'Don't!'

Squatting in front of her, he forced her to face him. 'I'm sorry you hurt, but that's why I did it – because you hurt. That's why I trapped you.'

'Were you just playing with me, though?' She sounded like a little girl, and Michael smiled at her.

'If you mean treating you like a toy, then no.'

'And the baby?'

He laid his hand on her belly. 'I love you, Kate.'

A flicker of pain crossed her face, and she leant forward and put her arms around his neck, her hair falling like a burnished copper curtain about their faces. They held each other, gently rocking back and forth, their bodies lit by the flickering firelight.

'Don't leave me, Michael. Don't ever leave me.'

THIRTY-TWO

It had turned into an Indian summer; the mildest autumn Michael could remember. Late October already and the evenings were drawing in, but the days were warm as July, the skies windless and clear. They spent as much time in the garden as they could, Michael overseeing any work that needed doing. More and more he was giving tasks over to Kate, and though his inactivity worried her, she was glad of the work: digging the plot, stacking peat bricks. To her surprise she discovered she enjoyed gardening, getting her hands dirty.

She'd driven into Westport that morning after an early lunch. Michael had stayed behind. He said he had things to do, but Kate wondered: he'd been vague and preoccupied all week, tidying things up round the house, sleeping hardly at all. Something was happening. She daren't think that he was getting ill, but he seemed to have changed after his second attack. He was older.

He was dozing in the garden chair when she returned, his dusty old panama hat slipping over his eyes. He snuffled and sat up when he heard Kate.

'There's your pension book,' she said, putting it on the table. 'And your money.' She kissed him on the forehead. 'I'll make some tea.'

He blinked and looked around, but she'd already turned the corner of the house. He was tired — she could see. He'd overdone it again. She was back in a few minutes, carrying the tea tray, a blanket draped over one arm. She lowered the tray carefully on to the small table beside Michael and spread the blanket over his knees.

'It's not so warm as you think. You'll get a chill sitting out here if you're not careful.'

He smiled vaguely. He'd put on his dark glasses, and with
the cream hat he looked like a Mafia godfather.

'Do you want the paper?' She held the newspaper out to him,
but he shook his head.

'What have you been doing?' she asked.

She'd noticed the smouldering bonfire at the bottom of the
garden.

'Having a bit of a tidy-up.'

She poured their tea out and then walked down to the bonfire.
It had burned down to a ruin of black stumps, but she could
tell from the scorched grass that it had been quite a blaze. She
recognised the remnants of some of Ann's clothes, and by the
edge, blackened and melted by the heat, was a worn-out gumboot.
He'd been clearing out. A box of papers smouldered in the centre,
flakes of ash lifting and floating away when the wind caught it. She
saw what looked like an old curtain, the broken wooden shaft of
a hoe. She looked back at Michael and then over at his studio.
There were piles of clay shards in the ashes of the fire. It wasn't
only the house he was emptying.

She walked over to the studio, skirting the goat which was
tugging against its long chain, trying to reach the potato tops.
Michael had hardly been in his studio since they'd got back, and
she hadn't seen inside it for months.

She pushed open the studio door. As she thought: he'd been
tidying up here, too. Gone the teetering piles of mismatched
pots and bowls, the clay skid marks on the wall. It had been
cleaned out: even the potter's wheel had been scraped free of
clay and washed down. In the corner was what was left: two
neat stacks of bowls and a dozen or so jugs and pots.

When she came back out into the sunshine, he called to her,
'Cut us a couple of those roses, would you? There's some
clippers in the shed.'

She cut him a handful of moulting pink flowers from the
unruly briar that covered the outhouse, snagging her jacket
on the thorns. She brought them back to him, and he took off
his dark glasses.

'Aren't they lovely?' he said, reaching up for them.

'Yes.'

'Smell.' He held them up to her. She dipped her head and inhaled their summery fragrance. 'Mmm.'

She drew her chair up to the table and sat down. She scanned the paper for a few minutes, the only sounds Michael slurping his tea and the chink of the goat's chain as it moved.

'Did you see the solicitor?'

'Yes. He said everything had been worked out, and not to worry.'

She laid the paper on the table and then rummaged in her wicker basket. 'I bought myself a birthday present.'

'Ah!' He closed his eyes. 'I forgot! It's today, isn't it?'

'Don't worry about it. Here – look what I got.'

She handed him a patterned blue tube.

'I'm sorry, my darling. Happy birthday.' He reached out and squeezed her fingers.

He looked at the tube in his hands. 'Now, what have we got here?' It was a few seconds before he recognised what it was. He laughed delightedly. 'A kaleidoscope!'

He squinted into it, twisting the barrel. 'It's years since I've seen one of these things.'

He played with it for a few minutes, pointing it up at the sun and jiggling it around to change the patterns.

'But I've got you nothing.'

She patted her belly. 'You've given me this. A *real* birthday present!'

He put the kaleidoscope on the table and looked at her from under the brim of his hat. 'This place is yours when I'm gone – you know that?'

'Michael,' she chided him gently. 'Don't say things like that.'

'It's not worth much, but it'll see you and the little one all right for a while.'

He turned the paper round and looked at the page it had been folded open to. A photograph of a naked man, covered with blood, another man crouched over his head. The headline: 'Father Alex Reid attempts to revive the dying soldier.'

Michael gazed at the picture and Kate twisted to see it.

'Horrible, isn't it?' she said.

He nodded slowly, his eyes still on the picture. 'None of this has meant anything. None of all this talk of mine. Just one more pattern in your kaleidoscope.'

He leant back in his chair, his face tilted upwards. Kate followed the direction of his gaze. A three-quarters moon, as pale as a piece of cloud, had appeared above the horizon.

'Everything is empty, Kate. Words, actions, thoughts. Saving the world. It's all empty . . . and yet as full as it could ever be.'

He turned to look at her. 'Do you know what the best kept secret of the sages is?'

She shook her head.

'That there *is* no secret. Things are as they are, and all this – ' he flapped a hand vaguely, 'dancing around we do is just a game. A life game.'

She watched him, waiting for him to say more. This was the crux, this whatever he said next, the validation of the life he'd lived. 'And what's your game, Michael?' she prompted.

'My game? Mastery, I suppose you could call it. Mastery of my mind.'

'And is that what you've been teaching me?'

He ignored her question. 'The first step towards mastery is in noticing the rules of the game you're playing – the "shoulds". The next step is when you tell the truth. And the truth is that your opinions are your opinions and no one knows the way it *"should"* be, or is going to be.' He paused and she thought he'd finished, but he continued. 'The third step is in *choosing* what game you're going to play, instead of just finding yourself in one. Because you *can* choose, at any moment, to rewrite the rules of the game. But only if you're willing. Willing to give back the fruit of the knowledge of good and evil.'

He paused to look at the garden. It would be dusk soon, already there was a chill in the air.

'And it's all up to you. It was one of Ann's jokes: there's some good news and some bad news. The bad news is that you got yourself into this mess. They're *your* rules, and no one else is to blame. The good news is that you got yourself into this mess. They're *your* rules, and you can change them whenever you choose.'

He glanced over at Kate as though noticing her for the first time. 'Why *mastery*? you ask. Because this is what it looks like when we're prey to our minds,' he said, nudging the paper towards her. 'This . . . ugliness.'

She looked again at the picture, frowning back unexpected tears. It was a badly taken photograph, a snapshot really, barely in focus. The young soldier was sprawled diagonally across the puddled tarmac, his white body smeared with blood. Only the feet of his killers were visible; even they had backed away to an awed distance. And the priest, kissing air into the hopelessly hurt body.

'Don't forget – it *is* a game,' he said, watching her. 'No matter how dramatic.'

'But the pain and the suffering!' She couldn't take her eyes from the broken body of the soldier.

'Are very real. And they're here to stay. Freedom is wearing that harness lightly.'

He picked his words out of the air, laying them one by one, precious stones on an exquisite path. 'Freedom is choosing the way it is, with all its pain, with all its grief. Saying "yes" instead of "no".'

She saw his face and realised he was no longer talking to her, but addressing the garden, the late afternoon. 'And when that happens, then you can start *really* dancing, because there's no competition left, no goal, nothing to *get*. You just are. And you find you've got all this –' he indicated the garden, the sky, 'to play in.'

His eyes glittered black in the last of the day's sun. He picked one of the roses off the table and held it to his face.

'Leave me now, would you, Kate. I'd like to sit alone for a bit.'

She got up quietly. He looked at her, kind and tired, and lowered his eyes into a smile.

THIRTY-THREE

Kate was surprised to find the kitchen empty. Normally he was up by the time she came downstairs, sitting at the breakfast table with a mug of tea. She felt the range – cold. He wasn't up yet. The turf basket was empty, no kindling either, so she unclicked the back door and went out to the yard. The cat was waiting, hungry, and followed her, mewling round her legs as she chopped the wood for the range. She'd split one log into kindling and was about to start on another when she paused. She tossed the chopper into the basket and hurried back to the house. In the kitchen she listened under his bedroom and then ran upstairs. She knocked at his door. No answer. She pushed the door open and went in. The curtains were still drawn, light filtering through the pattern, dappling the bedclothes.

'Michael?'

She nudged him, but he didn't respond, so she leant over, smiling, to kiss his sleeping face. She hesitated when she saw him. His mouth was partly open, his face unnaturally calm.

'Michael?'

She shook him. No response. She shook him harder, and then panicked and rocked him until the bed creaked and his head flopped from side to side. She stared at him, horrified. He was dead.

She sprang back from the bed, her hand to her mouth, knocking the glass of water from his bedside table. Her back was pressed to the wall, her eyes fixed on the still bulk of his body. But was he still breathing? She edged towards the bed. Yes – she could hear him now.

Her heart was thumping so hard she couldn't feel his pulse, and had to press her ear to his chest to hear his heartbeat. He was still alive. Unconscious. A stroke.

She sobbed in terror as she sped through the lanes to the O'Neills' house, crashing the gears in her rush. James phoned for the hospital, his wife trying to pacify Kate, get some sense out of her. An ambulance would be on its way as soon as possible. She was trembling so much, she couldn't get the keys in the ignition, and then dropped them so they tangled with the clutch pedal. Please God, she prayed, don't let him die with me not there. Ten minutes. Give me ten minutes!

He was as she'd left him: breathing lightly, his face wiped clean of all expression. She snatched the curtains open and began stuffing his razor and some clothes into a bag. She was clumsy in her panic, tearing the cuff of one of his shirts she'd trapped in the drawer.

'Michael. Oh, no!' She couldn't believe it. Why wasn't he awake? He was all right yesterday. He was just tired, that's all. She picked up the glass she'd knocked over, staring at the water-stained floorboard. She scuffed at the wet patch with the sole of her shoes. Don't die. Not now. Please.

He didn't wake up until the next day. It was a stroke, the doctor said, but still too early to tell what damage had been done. He was alive, that was the thing. Kate was weak with relief – she still had him, there would be hope for as long as his heart continued to beat.

They'd taken him to the tiny cottage hospital outside the town and Kate had insisted on staying the night with him. He was in a single room, and when the ward sister saw Kate's determination, she reluctantly supplied her with a camp-bed and some blankets. Kate didn't sleep that night, but at least she was close to him.

He woke up mid-morning, his eyelids springing open without warning. Kate excitedly buzzed for a nurse.

'Michael! Thank God you're awake!'

She touched his cheek, bending over him so their eyes met.

'Michael? It's me. Kate.'

Nothing. No sign of recognition, no flicker of life in those eyes. Normally she wasn't aware of his glass eye – it looked so natural – but now both eyes looked false. Empty. The doctor had warned her that when he came round he'd be confused and probably unable to speak, but they hadn't mentioned this. This blankness. The nurse touched her on the arm, moving her away.

'Mr O'Brien,' she said loudly. 'You've just had a little stroke. Nothing to worry about. Don't try to talk now.'

Talk? How could he? It wasn't Michael. Kate found herself being ushered into the corridor, sat down on a chair.

'The doctor's just going to do some tests. You can go back in when he's finished.'

She cried when she saw him. A drip had been set up beside the bed, the cruel tube taped into his arm. A catheter and bag hung below the bed; a suction pipe slurping saliva from his mouth. The young nurse, uncomfortable at her tears, smiled apologetically and left the room.

She couldn't face eating, and turned down the offer of a meal at lunchtime. She was left alone in the afternoon, waiting miserably by the bed for Michael to wake up, watching the steady drip of the fluid, the bottle emptying.

She'd recently started writing her diary again. It had begun after she knew for certain that she was pregnant – the familiar need to sort her thoughts out on paper. She slipped the red exercise book from her bag, flicked open to the last entry. They'd been happy – *she'd* been happy, profoundly, unshakably – or so she'd thought. And now this: suddenly, without warning, he'd been taken away from her. She'd planned so much for them, the three of them: wintering together, swelling through the spring, readying for the birth, and then the child. There would be no need to work – they could live off her capital, in a year or two she could maybe get a job at Westport House – they'd be bound to have paintings in need of restoration. Michael could do his pottery. The baby would grow strong and healthy, loved by its parents. And now this.

She'd tied herself to people – to men – all her life. Her father, Jacques, Paul, and now, she realised, Michael. She'd bound herself to them out of a fear of being alone. And one by one they had all left.

She watched Michael's face, closed in unnatural sleep. He was so far away – on the edge of his life. From here forward he was alone; she couldn't follow him. He would die, she knew it, and again she'd be left. If not now, then in five years, ten years. It was happening again: the parting.

And this child she was carrying – whose was it? Hers? Almost visually, she saw the image: the child – not the child, the *person* coming through her – a coloured ball through a tube. Through her, not from her. Through her, from another source – *the* source. And when that umbilicus was severed – before – the child would be itself, the child would not be hers; she could not – could *never* possess it, another person. It was its own packet of destiny. As was Michael. As she was.

She glanced at the clock, began writing.

November 11th 1.30 p.m.
My destiny is my *destiny, its fulfilment is mine, no one else's. It cannot be shared. No one can live my life for me, nor I for anyone else. The most another person can be is a companion, someone to walk side by side with me, and then only so far . . .*

He eventually came round, and seemed to recognise her when she leant across and looked at him. She smiled in relief. Perhaps there *was* hope. Perhaps he would pull through.

'You're going to be all right, Michael.'

He blinked acknowledgment. His entire right side was paralysed, that side of his face sagging, his mouth hanging open like a door with a broken hinge. One eye – the false one – was permanently open. She sat by the bed, playing with the plastic identity bracelet around his wrist: Michael Patrick O'Brien, D.O.B. 24.3.-- Kate hadn't known the year he was born.

Kate had phoned Gabrielle, Michael's sister, and she arrived at the hospital at three. Kate rose when she came into the room, and they embraced briefly. They separated and stood by the bedside, both looking down at the still body, the only sound the slurp of the suction pipe. Kate felt the hesitation of the old woman, and then the almost audible sound of wheels in motion as she clicked open her handbag and fished for a tissue. She dabbed at the dribble on his chin. 'I've brought you some oranges, Mícheál. Now, I want to see you eating them in a day or two. This – ' she nodded at the drip ' – is no sort of food for a body.'

She glanced doubtfully at Kate. 'Can he hear me?' She bent close to his ear. 'Can you hear me?' she said loudly.

His eyebrow shot up, giving his face a startled expression. Kate smiled in relief: it was the sort of effect he would have intended. He must be better – his sense of humour was working well enough.

Gabrielle turned to Kate. 'He doesn't look too good, does he?' she whispered. She took off her raincoat and sat down in Kate's chair. Her old face was wrinkled in concern, her fingers doing an agitated dance against the handbag she clutched in her lap.

'And neither do you, my darlin'. Have you been eating properly?'

Kate smiled down at the old woman. She was glad she'd come. Gabrielle hadn't changed – a bit older perhaps, but still the same quirky movements, still as thin as a bird. Kate arranged the oranges in the bowl on top of the bedside locker.

His sister was agitated, still tense from her long journey from Cork, and did most of the talking throughout the afternoon. Michael was dozing, but still, it seemed, a third person in their conversation. In the gaps in their chat, both women would look to the bed, as though waiting for a contribution from him. Kate steered the conversation round to her and Michael, breaking the news of their closeness.

'And –' she took a deep breath '– I'm pregnant.'

'You're not! Pregnant! You mean with Mícheál here?'

Gabrielle came alive for the first time that afternoon. She looked from Kate to her brother and back again. Kate watched her nervously, waiting for the verdict. 'Mícheál, how could you?' Suddenly her voice was full of tears. 'You're forty years too late! Now, at the end of your life, to father a child!'

She didn't see the disappointment in Kate's face, but reached across the bed all the same to take her hand. 'But congratulations, my dear. You *are* pleased, aren't you?'

Kate nodded. She suddenly felt tired.

'When's it due?'

'The beginning of June. A Gemini baby.'

'Does the doctor reckon yerman'll be up and about by then?'

'I don't know.'

'I expect so. June is a fair way off.'

Kate allowed the old woman to prattle on, only half-listening to her, the words reaching her as if from a great distance.

'A baby. A new O'Brien. Well, you're just going to have to get better soon, aren't you, Michéal.'

They both looked at him. He was trying to speak, but only managed an incoherent lisp.

'Are you awake, Michéal?'

His eyebrow went up.

'Well, I hope you look after the girl, that's all.'

Nothing from the old man, and she turned back to Kate to explain. 'We're the last two, me and Michéal. Last of nine children. He's younger than me – you know that? He always has been.'

Kate hid a smile. She hoped Michael was listening.

The daylight was paling and Gabrielle suddenly glanced at her watch. 'It's time I was off.'

She hopped to her feet and leant over the bed to kiss Michael's impassive face. 'You get well now, Michéal, do you hear? You can't get a girl pregnant and then not marry her. I'll be back tomorrow.'

Kate followed her out to the corridor. The afternoon tea trolley was being wheeled into the next ward, and they waited while it passed. Kate realised she was hungry. Suddenly Gabrielle took her hand. 'My heart is scalded, Kate. He looks terrible.'

Kate held her hand in both of hers. 'He's had a stroke, Gabrielle. He's very ill,' she replied gently. The old woman's skin was as fine as wrinkled tissue paper.

'But all the same, he looks awful grey, and not being able to talk like that!' She shook her head worriedly, disengaging her hand. She set off down the corridor, Kate hurrying to keep up with her. 'I'm glad about the baby, though. You'll be getting married, won't you?'

Kate smiled wanly. Gabrielle was tiring her out. 'I don't know.'

'Another O'Brien you'd be. Not the first English one, neither.'

She stopped at the swing-doors. She had her back to Kate, and addressed the next remark to the door. 'But what if he should die?'

Gabrielle turned to the young woman and Kate saw the fear in her eyes. She held the old woman's tiny body until Gabrielle pushed herself away, wet-eyed. 'But I'm being silly – he'll be all right, won't he?'

Kate couldn't meet her eyes. 'Of course he will. You come again tomorrow. I expect he'll be better.'

She opened the swing-door for Gabrielle. A blast of cold air swirled her skirt. 'Now, you're sure you've got somewhere to stay?'

Gabrielle paused in the doorway, tying on her plastic headscarf. 'He's a lucky man to have the likes of you.' She smiled into the face of Kate. 'And such a pretty girl, too.'

Kate watched her to the road, waiting for the old woman to turn and wave, but she didn't. She just continued round the corner until she disappeared from sight.

Back in the room, Kate collapsed in the chair beside the bed. She saw that he was awake.

'Phew! Your sister!'

The eyebrow went up, a formless gurgle from his mouth.

'She's a funny old thing. I think she was really pleased about me being pregnant. She wants us to get married. By the way –' She leant forward to watch his face. 'I've decided. It's going to be a girl.'

A smile twitched at the corner of his mouth.

'After all, they're much nicer.'

He managed a cross between a cough and a laugh. He pushed the suction pipe out of his mouth with his tongue and she stood up.

'How are you, Michael?' She took the pipe off the pillow and let it dangle by the bed. 'I wish you could speak.'

She got up and walked aimlessly around the room, coming to a pause at the drip by his bed. She read the side of the bottle.

'What does this stuff taste like? Sorry, I shouldn't joke.'

She watched the fluid dripping, the bottle inexorably empty-ing: an egg-timer, the sand running, running, running. 'You're going to die, aren't you?'

His face gave no hint, no clue, but she knew she was right. She circuited the bed, her face turned away from him. She made no sound as she cried, her tears slipping silently down her cheeks. Kate stopped at the sink, and ran some cold water into the bowl, splashing her face. A tiny mirror had been tacked above the sink, and she stooped to look at herself.

'I don't want you to die. Not now.' She tried to laugh, but it turned into a sob. 'We just started getting along – you and me.'

She buried her face in the towel, her body shaking with sobs. She would be alone now. Black, cast adrift. Clutching the towel to her mouth, she groped her way to the bed, sitting and then half-lying next to him. She wanted his arms around her, she wanted to hear his voice. Just once more.

'Oh God, I love you,' she whispered.

Dusk was falling and she leant across and switched on the bedside light. It was as though she'd slept, but she'd lain just a few minutes, feeling his warmth, the quiet of the darkening room. She swung her legs off the bed, refreshed, comforted. 'How are you?'

His eyes followed her movements, his left lid lowering itself into a slow wink. He began to groan, and for a moment she thought he was in pain, but no – it was a tune he was trying to hum. She sat on the edge of the bed and listened carefully, and then it came to her. How did it go? She began singing hesitantly.

I knew a man called Michael Finnegan

That was right, wasn't it? He hummed the second line, off-key and fragmented, but recognisable to her now. She took his hand, tapping out the tempo.

He grew whiskers on his chinnegan
He grew fat and he grew thin again
Poor old Michael –

She paused and looked up through the window, at the faint pink ribbons of cloud draped across the evening sky. She turned her eyes to the bed, to his body. This was it, then. This was his life. This death.

She watched him, his eyes gazing wordlessly back into hers. He had loved her, she knew that now. He had loved well, with a greater portion of himself.

Poor old Michael Finnegan, begin again.

She squeezed his limp hand. 'Thank you.'

Thank you? Thank you for caring for me. Thank you for your patience and strength. Thank you for living a life as if it mattered and never giving up.

She glanced at her diary, considered for a moment, and then slipped it off the tabletop. She wrote it on her lap.

4.20 p.m.
The significance of everything will pale in the light of the question: how have I lived my life? How have I spent my time as a human being on the face of this planet? How much have I allowed pettiness and fear to govern my life? How many times have I withheld love, have I given love?

It *was* a game. And this unresponsive body before her was part of it. A game with no point: a dance. A dance of love. And even though he would die, the dance would go on – would go on for ever.

Poor old Michael Finnegan, begin again.

Calmness suffused her body like warm water. Nothing to do with the child inside her, the love for him, his imminent death. It was a calm beyond the touch of anything. A calm which came from nowhere, from nothing.

As she sat in the failing light, his hand in hers, she remembered something he'd said only a few days before: this is just a beginning we've made. And so it was. There was life before her and she stood naked in its face: armed with nothing – no weapons, no knowledge, no hope. And yet the future was not a threat but a promise. Life would continue with all its pain but everything would work out. Not that she would never suffer again, never be lost, confused, lonely, but that this – this whatever it was – underlay everything else. And it was good.

She could be free. She *was* free. She had trapped herself, but the chains were illusory. She *was* free.

Neither of them was asleep. Moonlight lay like spilled milk over the linoleum floor, a shaft bisecting the bed Michael lay in. His eyes were open, and from his mouth came a sound.

Kate rose from her camp-bed and leant over to hear what he was trying to say. It was a word, a monosyllable, again and again. Dance, dance, dance.

A car passed, the light of its headlamps sliding over the ceiling, illuminating her face for a moment. Dance: it was his final request.

She waited for the sound of the car to recede and then raised her arms above her head in an arc. Pausing, she swayed a little: a silver-white statue in the silent moonlight. She brought her arms down. She brushed her feet over the cool floor, trying a few steps, looking for a way into the store of inspiration inside her. And then she began to dance.

Slow and fluid at first, she curved and dipped, her long nightdress hanging in folds about her, obscuring and then revealing the shape of her body.

As though she was trying to carve out some message in the air, her hands began describing movements, and then her head, her neck, her entire being. A current was galvanising her, visibly rippling through her muscles, convulsing her body with its power.

Faster and faster, dancing to silence – she was a dervish, whirling, her hair lashing her face. Something in her broke and she was out of control, spinning crazily like a leaf caught in a vortex, her arms whipping the air. She wasn't dancing any more – she was being danced. Out of control, spinning, being moved by something outside herself.

And then suddenly, the power had gone. She wound down until her body was still and she stood panting by the bed. The old man's mouth twisted into a smile. She heard it clearly now; his final words:

'Now you see me.'

She was dreaming. Dreaming of a field of lime-green grass under a perfect sky. In the distance, silhouetted on the horizon, was Michael. She ran towards him, barefoot through the silky grass, and as she neared him, he turned and began to walk away. He disappeared over the brow of the hill, his body shortening until she could see only his head, and then nothing. She reached the spot where he'd stood and looked about her. He was nowhere to be seen – just the long slope of the hill stretching down into the valley.

He was quiet, his eyes closed. She sat on the edge of the bed and watched his face. He'd gone.

She gazed at him for a moment and then leant forward and took one of the tangerines Gabrielle had left. She touched it against her cheek and closed her eyes. Cool and fresh. She looked at it, almost puzzled, and then dug her thumbnails into its flesh. The room filled with the scent of the orange as she slowly peeled it. She bit into a segment, her mouth filling with its tart juice, and then pressed the buzzer beside the bed and waited for the night nurse to come.

NIGEL WATTS

BILLY BAYSWATER

After losing his job on a London building site, young Billy slips through the social security net. Retarded, disorientated and destitute, he is as vulnerable to deceit and abuse as he is responsive to the girl who shows him temporary kindness, and to the beauty he finds in the parks' trees and flowers. Delightful and devastating by turn, BILLY BAYSWATER draws a poignant, topical portrait of life for the homeless in the big city, at times the loneliest place on earth.

'A tremendous imaginative triumph and should be read by anyone who still thinks that all homeless people are bludgers'
Mary Hope in The Financial Times

'A swelling anger gathers force through the story, made all the more powerful because of an emotional counter to it, a glorious sense of humanity and of the city's beauty'
Judy Cooke in The Guardian

'This fine and careful novel about those who live on the margins of our society is an indictment of that society without saying a word against it'
Andrew Sinclair in The Times

'I believed in Billy. His fine, highly written story worked very well. It's very sad and true'
John Healy, author of THE GRASS ARENA

NIGEL WATTS

WE ALL LIVE IN A HOUSE CALLED INNOCENCE

James is turning thirty, stuck in the dismal routine of a librarian's job, and the doldrums of a long-term relationship with his girlfriend. Then a human hand-grenade explodes into his life, in the person of Tad, a gay wheelchair-bound writer of pornographic stories. Before James knows it, he has an outrageously uninhibited and indefatigably curious new friend who gets him drunk, gets under his skin, and gets him to take a fresh look at his life. It isn't long before Tad's goadings and probings are taking effect, as James attempts to put his sexual fantasies into practice – with totally unexpected results. For James, it's the first dangerous step on a journey into himself that could lead anywhere . . .

Fearlessly honest, painfully funny and wonderfully moving, WE ALL LIVE IN A HOUSE CALLED INNOCENCE confirms Nigel Watts as one of our most daring and original young novelists.

HODDER AND STOUGHTON HARDBACKS